Legacy of a Spy

Legacy of a Spy

by
Henry S. Maxfield

Southwick House
Publishers

LEGACY OF A SPY

Printed in the United States of America

Library of Congress catalog card number:98-96497
Original date of copyright and registration number A
338667 May 14 1958
RE 285 135 Feb 3, 1986

To Betty

Legacy of a Spy

Chapter 1

Decoded, the cables read as follows:

PRIORITY CABLE

TO: OFFICE OF SECURITY
WASHINGTON, D.C.

FROM: GEORGE L. PUTNAM
CONSULATE GENERAL
ZURICH, SWITZERLAND

SUBJECT: BELIEVE LEAK IN CONSULATE HERE. CANNOT PROVE. CANNOT HANDLE ALONE. REQUIRE TOURIST OBSERVE WYMAN. TOURIST MUST BE UNKNOWN IN EUROPE. KNOWLEDGE GERMAN HELPFUL. SUGGEST USE CONTACT PLAN A.

PRIORITY CABLE

EYES ONLY

TO: GEORGE L. PUTNAM
CONSULATE GENERAL
ZURICH, SWITZERLAND

SUBJECT: MONTAGUE ARRIVING 0930, 15 MARCH 1956. USE PLAN A.

The train clattered and swayed, banged and rattled at crazy speed across the Bavarian plains and rolling farm lands on its way to Munich. The occupants of Erste Klasse, Compartment A, in Car 5 surged from side to side in silence. They had been jostled into a resistless indifference all the way from Frankfurt, still strangers as only Europeans can be. The conversation in several hours had consisted of, "Do you mind if I smoke?" or an "Excuse me" when someone had to get up and go to the toilet or go to breakfast on the dining car.

Slater didn't care for European trains, and he wondered if the railroad bed had been laid on elliptical marbles; but the clacking and bumping had jogged him into a relaxed, if somewhat groggy, state. He had long ago given up any curiosity about his fellow passengers, as they doubtless had about him. They all looked so serious and prosperous. Slater believed that no man on earth could manage to look more affluent than a wealthy German businessman. Fat fingers with manicured fingernails, spotless silk shirts, heavy serge suits over expansive frames, smooth bland faces with small pale eyes that could look at you without seeing you.

Slater hadn't needed to travel first class, but the only other possibility had been third class, and he hadn't wanted to endure those thin-ribbed wooden seats. He looked out of the window and marveled at the rolling landscape of snow-covered fields, neat stone houses with tiled roofs, and the scattered, geometric patches of evergreen woods. This was the land of beer, of heavy-limbed peasants, of classical music and Dachau, of big men who loved little children and flowers and war. Slater sighed. He looked at the bland faces around him and again through the window at their beautiful country and shook his head.

The train began to jump some of the myriads of switches. Tracks appeared from nowhere, and Slater realized he was entering the Munich marshaling yards. According to his watch he would be in Munich in ten minutes.

He resisted the impulse to stand up and get his things down from the rack. He sat back and forced himself to relax. What is it this time, he wondered. All the way from Frankfurt he had tried not to think about it. It wasn't the first time he had realized he made his living from man's inhumanity to man, nor was this the first time he questioned his ability to continue. He hadn't even started his new project and already he was having doubts. "They aren't doubts," he said to himself. "Be honest—they're fears. You're afraid."

The train had stopped. Slater stood up and looked around, momentarily perplexed. He reached for his luggage with clammy hands, thinking, "The legendary Montague is afraid. He's a dirty, stinking coward. He searches for fear on Uncle Sam's time. He has no right to prove himself at the possible expense of his country."

Slater dragged his suitcase through the barrier and threaded his way through a maze of knicker-clad, rough-shod men and belt-coated women to the American waiting room. He set his suitcase down by the magazine counter and purchased a paperback novel from the German clerk. She was wearing the same kind of bluish smock they all wore. He thanked her and entered the restaurant of the Bundesbahn Hotel.

He seated himself at an empty table and ordered a beer. He placed his hat on the table by his left hand. He took an unopened package of MacDonald cigarettes and put them within easy grasp of his right hand. He picked up the paperback novel and began to read.

Even a casual glance at George Hollingsworth, seated comfortably in the cocktail lounge of the Hotel Excelsior, would reveal that Hollingsworth was a young man whom nice things were said about. Clear blue eyes, serene forehead, and regular features—combine these with conservative taste in clothes and a well-modulated, cultured voice and here was the perfect picture of what a young American diplomat should be. He sat loose and long-legged on one of the comfortable overstuffed chairs that were grouped along the wall. His expression was alert and serious as he listened carefully to the older man seated opposite across the round, highly polished cocktail table which separated them. The older man looked very much as George Hollingsworth would in later years.

"I trust you have everything straight, Hollingsworth," the older man said.

"Yes, sir, Mr. Preston," said George. "I'm sure I do."

"You're really quite privileged, you know." Preston took another swallow of coffee. He would have preferred a Scotch and soda, but the hotel was under army regulations and the bar wouldn't open until 4 P.M. "Very few of us here ever met Montague. He's one of the best."

"I'm really looking forward," said George, his face lighting up, "to meeting one of those cloak-and-dagger boys. I just hope I don't gum everything up."

"Do as Montague tells you and you won't."

"Tell me, sir," said George, "what do you know about this fellow?"

"Nothing much. That's why he's so good, I guess." Preston looked thoughtfully at Hollingsworth. "I hear he's a bit of a terror. I'd go pretty slowly with him if I were you."

"You don't mean he'd pull a gun on me, do you, sir?" George laughed. "I'm on his side."

"He might from all I hear." Preston's tone was quite serious and Hollingsworth was visibly shaken.

"But that's ridiculous. He sounds melodramatic—a sort of unreliable prima donna."

"On the contrary, Hollingsworth, Montague takes his work very seriously. He absolutely refuses to meet any of us socially, although I understand he's quite acceptable—good background and all that; but he's been in some tight scrapes and he's done some incredible things." Preston took some more coffee. "He doesn't trust anyone. I don't believe he'll trust you."

"But why? Good Lord, I'm trustworthy." Hollingsworth managed to look indignant.

"Montague hates amateurs, and if Webber's suspicions are correct, you are about to enter a world you've never even suspected."

Hollingsworth was silent. It was obvious that the old boy was romanticizing the whole business. He probably wanted to go himself.

Preston finished his coffee. "Time for you to go, Hollingsworth. I'll pay up here."

Hollingsworth stood up. "Thank you, sir. I'd like the privilege of buying you a drink one day."

"Hurry up, man. Get a move on! Being late for this kind of an appointment can be a catastrophe."

"Yes, sir." Hollingsworth looked perplexed. He couldn't decide whether Preston was joking or not. George took another look at the older man and decided he wasn't. He said good-by and left.

Preston watched Hollingsworth's tall figure disappear into the lobby and shook his head. He was unquestionably a nice young man. They had spoken well of him in Zurich. Preston was certain Hollingsworth would go far in the Foreign Service, but, he shook his head, Montague deserved better than that. This wasn't going to be a job for a nice young man.

George hurried across the cobblestoned square, buttoning his coat as he went. He turned up his collar against the cold March wind and, unseeing, dodged bicycles, three-wheeled trucks, tiny automobiles, and American limousines. He looked up at a leaden sky and pushed his way through the glass doors into the American waiting room. He checked his watch and hurried into the restaurant of the Bundesbahn Hotel. He removed his hat and looked for a table.

Fortunately, the place was almost empty, and George had no difficulty spotting an American, in his early thirties, of average build, dark hair, reading a paperback. George hesitated. He checked the position of the hat and cigarettes. He wasn't near enough to make out the brand. George approached the table.

"Excuse me," he said. "Do you mind if I join you?"

Slater looked up at the stranger as though just this moment aware of his presence.

"I beg your pardon, did you say something?" Slater smiled. "I guess I was in a fog."

"I asked if I could join you. It's a pleasure to meet a fellow American who isn't in uniform."

Slater took the young man in from his serene forehead to the cordovan shoes and cursed inwardly. "Sure," he said, his voice calm. "Glad to have your company, but I'm Canadian."

George sat down awkwardly. The little play wasn't over yet, and he didn't want to forget his lines.

"Have a cigarette?" Slater extended the unopened pack.

"Thank you. They look like ours. I've never tried a MacDonald."

George opened the pack and took one. If the pack had been open, he would not have sat down.

"Please don't think me antisocial," said Slater, "if I leave pretty soon, but I only have time for this beer and two cigarettes."

"It would be better the other way around."

"Might at that," Slater smiled. "All right," he said quietly, "where's your car?"

"It's a '53 Plymouth, gray, U.S. Forces Germany plates 2C–15873. Its parked up beyond the Excelsior Hotel—on the same side of the street. It will be facing you as the street is one way. The keys are in the glove compartment. Do you know Munich?"

Slater nodded.

"Drive to the Hofbräu Haus and try and park in the parking place there. You shouldn't have any trouble at this time of day. I'll meet you."

Slater stood up. "Sorry to have to rush off. Nice to have met you."

George stood up. He was surprised to find he was only an inch taller. Montague's appearance was deceiving. George sat down at the table again. He was exhausted. He had felt Montague's antagonism during the entire interview. Old Preston had been right. This fellow Montague was hard. Hollingsworth didn't think he was going to care much for this cloak-and-dagger business.

Slater left the restaurant and entered the station again. He could smell the coal from the engines, but its pungency was whipped away by the wind as soon as he stepped outside. The day was bleak but the visibility was good, and he could see the stubby towers of the cathedral. He stood on the curb and waited for the commanding gestures of the blue-uniformed traffic officer, and then crossed the traffic circle. He still had to dodge bicyclists and vehicles of various types, and he swore because his suitcase kept banging against his shins. He had always expected a people who had lived in a dictatorship to be docile in the face of authority, and automatically queue up as the English did for theater lines and buses. He was still amazed, and invariably irritated, that they did just the opposite, stepping on each other's feet, shoving into line, and shouting at one another.

Slater gained the other side and walked into the wind which funneled down the street by the Excelsior Hotel. Head down, feet wide apart, he pushed his way past the hotel and got into the gray Plymouth. Even the elements seemed to be against this assignment.

Slater sat in the car for a moment and got his bearings. He

started the motor and turned on the heater. His cheeks were red from the wind, and now that he was protected from it, he could feel them burning. He put the car in gear and turned it out into the street, waited again for the proper signal from the policeman and started out into the no man's land. He turned right again toward the Hofbräu Haus.

The young man had been right. There was very little traffic by the Hofbräu Haus and the public parking place was empty. The attendant was not on duty and Slater was not dunned for the customary twenty pfennigs. He left the motor running and waited.

Why, he wondered, did they always assign some amateur who invariably considered this business some sort of ridiculous game, somebody who would undoubtedly blurt out the whole affair at a cocktail party?

A Mercedes with Munich plates pulled up beside him. Hollingsworth got out and came over to the Plymouth.

"Lock it up, please," he said, "and bring the keys and your bag."

Slater complied and got into the Mercedes. He handed Hollingsworth the keys. Hollingsworth took the first left and headed for the autobahn.

Once on the main highway headed for Salzburg, Hollingsworth appeared to relax. "My name's George Hollingsworth. What's yours?"

"Carmichael, Bruce Carmichael," Slater said.

George was aware that Montague was only a code name used for extra security purposes in interoffice and interdepartmental correspondence, and he was naïve enough to suppose that Slater would give a young, untrained Foreign Service officer his right name.

"Well, Mr. Carmichael," George smiled, "this is a real privilege. I realize very few of us know your real name."

"The fewer the better." Slater's voice was very convincing

and George winced. He couldn't seem to say the right thing to this fellow Carmichael. He'd always heard that the Scots were a dour lot.

"Call me Bruce," said Slater. "It's much easier."

Slater smiled. George was amazed. Carmichael had a very warm and disarming smile.

"Well, George, let's have it," said Slater. "What's the bad news?"

George was about to come out flat-footed with what he considered the essential information but hesitated. He was aware that Carmichael knew nothing whatever so far, and as is usually the case with essentials, they had a way of coming out backward, and then sometimes turned out not to be essentials.

"If you don't mind, Bruce," said George, "I'd like to give you the picture chronologically. That way you can better form your own judgment."

Slater looked at Hollingsworth critically for a moment. Hollingsworth could feel the appraisal. "Sure thing. Go right ahead."

Maybe this guy Hollingsworth would turn out all right. Slater began to relax.

"It all started," said George, "when a fellow named Webber, who is assistant to the political attaché, entered the Consulate late one evening and discovered a man named Wyman photographing some reports with the Recordak."

"Who is Wyman?" asked Slater.

"Oh, yes. Excuse me," said George. "Wyman is a young vice-consul like myself." He paused.

"Go ahead," said Slater. "You're doing fine."

"Right," said George. "Well, when Wyman saw he was caught in the act, so to speak, he told Webber he was trying to get a permanent record of certain classified reports for a special project he had been assigned. He said, further, that he did not want to wait to pull these reports until they were old enough to be destroyed, as that might call undue attention to himself and his project.'

"This could be true, couldn't it?" asked Slater. "I mean it's possible that some documents are photographed by Consular officers in order to have a permanent record and, at the same time, avoid pinpointing their interests to those who have no need to know."

"Yes, I suppose so," said George, "but it's news to me. Actually, it sounds like a good idea."

"Did Webber say why he was at the Consulate after hours?"

"Yes," said George, "he said that he had come back to pick up one hundred Swiss francs which he had left in his desk. He told Wyman that and then went to his desk and took out the hundred-franc note."

"Did Wyman accept that as Webber's excuse?"

"I don't know."

Hollingsworth pulled over to let a Volkswagen pass. There was no speed limit on the autobahn, and in spite of the slippery road conditions, car after car, usually German, sped past them. Slater shook his head. He was forced by circumstances to take so many chances he couldn't understand anyone taking risks who didn't need to. The German road department had apparently never heard of rock salt or didn't believe in using it. Although the roads were plowed, only the top layer of snow was off, and the road was covered with a thick, rutty layer of ice and hard-packed snow.

"What did Webber do about all this?" asked Slater as he watched the Volkswagen speed out of sight over the top of the hill.

"He went to Mr. Putnam, the Consul General, but apparently Mr. Putnam chose to ignore it. That," continued George, "should have been the end of it, but Webber was disgruntled, and maybe even somewhat embarrassed. In any event, he decided to conduct his own investigation. Beyond the fact that Webber decided Wyman was definitely living beyond his income and was extremely interested in a redheaded Swiss girl by the name of Trude Kupfer, we have little to go on. Webber made some notes and put them in his personal file. All we really know is contained in a letter from him to Mr. Putnam." Hollingsworth took a letter from his inside coat pocket and handed it to Slater. Slater opened it.

DEAR MR. PUTNAM:

I felt like such a damn fool in your office the other day that I resolved either to nail our subject down with facts or go and hide my head. I realize I have taken liberties, but please believe me, I have done what I have done with the best intentions. I'm writing you this because I'm very much afraid I won't be permitted to give you this information in person, as I have gotten in way over my head; and I don't know how to swim in these waters.

First of all, if I don't return, I want you to know that it will not be because I don't want to, and my disappearance or death—I don't think I'm merely being dramatic—will be because of the subject under discussion.

I followed W to Kitzbühel. He put up at the Winterhof. For reasons of economy, and to avoid suspicion, I stayed at a nearby pension, the Eggerwirt. Here is the evidence so far:

1. W said he was only going to Munich, but he went directly to Kitzbühel.
2. He said he did not like or know how to ski, yet he had ski clothes and he rented skis the first day. I don't remember the name of the rental place, but it is a little red shack across the road from the Talstation, on the right as you face the Hahnenkamm. I believe it's the last one on the way to the practice slope. I observed him go up in the cable car and waited by the ski school in the hope that he would come down that trail. He did—and not very much later. This certainly would indicate some real skiing ability as the Streif is an Olympic run, very tricky and steep in parts.

3. When he left Zurich, both his bank accounts—he has two, one under the name of Martin Hazel—were extremely low. (I have a friend in the Züricher Kantonalbank.) After the second day in Kitzbühel, W was suddenly quite affluent and was observed changing greenbacks to schillings.
4. Although the weather has been perfect for skiing, he has only been once in the three days up to now.
5. He has been chummy with no one. He has tried, unsuccessfully I believe, to get acquainted with a redheaded German woman who calls herself Ilse Wieland.
6. He is staying in room 28. He has eaten dinner at the hotel only once, and that was the first evening. His other lunches and evening meals have been taken at various other places in town.

What has made me most suspicious is that I know I am being followed. I have tried to keep from being observed by W, but I am sure he has seen me, and somehow called out the watchdogs. Furthermore, they have become less subtle.

I cannot describe them too well and I am only sure of two. I don't believe they are local, but I think they are Austrians. One of them, the taller of the two, looks to be in his middle thirties and is over six feet with thin, straight, blond hair, heavy features and small eyes. He seems to be posing as a local resident, as he wears work boots and brown whipcord trousers that resemble riding breeches. The other is dressed like a tourist and recently moved into my pension, room 23. He is about five feet, nine inches, has dark, wavy hair, speaks German and is very clean shaven. His skin seems to have a waxy quality like an artificial apple. He's lean and looks about thirty years old. He watches me like a hawk while I'm in the pension; and the other one takes over when I'm outside. I haven't been able to get the dark-haired one's name as yet, but I wanted to get this in the mail in case my time is running short.

This letter is somewhat cryptic, because I'm having someone else mail it for me, and it might get in the wrong hands. The mailman is a German by the name of Heinz Mahler who says he was a prisoner of war in Russia. I believe he will mail it. He lives in Munich and works at the desk of the Bundesbahn Hotel.

I realize the information is scanty, and you may feel it is my imagination. I hope that I will be able to talk to you in person soon. I intend to leave here tomorrow morning. If I'm not in Zurich by tomorrow evening, you should need no further proof that something is wrong. Needless to say, I hope you don't get that kind of proof.

Sincerely,
C. L. W.

P.S. You can check my personal file in the office for other info obtained in Zurich. The name of my banker friend is there. Please respect the confidence and protect him. He may be useful in the future.

Slater folded up the letter and put it in his pocket.

"That fellow Webber shows real promise. He was at a tremendous disadvantage. I'd like to talk with him."

"I'm afraid you can't," said George. "This letter was received a week ago, and we haven't seen or heard from Webber since."

"Looks like whatever Wyman was up to was important, and his friends really meant business." Slater turned to George. "What about Wyman? Is he back at the old stand?"

"Yes."

"Does he really have two bank accounts?"

"Yes."

"How do you know?" asked Slater.

"I phoned Herr Baumann," said George, "and asked if Martin Hazel had an account there, and Baumann said yes."

"Did you find out how much Hazel had in there?"

"Baumann didn't want to tell me at first, but when I told him I was a member of the American Consulate, he said that Hazel had sent in a postal money order for $835."

"Well, he got quite a piece of change." Slater shook his head. "I'm underpaid."

Hollingsworth looked shocked. George apparently had no sense of humor.

"What about Wyman's Swiss girl friend? Have you checked her?"

"Only enough to find out," said George, "that she's rather promiscuous—for those who can afford her. She showed me some of the expensive presents Wyman gave her. I don't like women like that," George added decisively. "I would suspect her of anything, but," and George looked somewhat crestfallen, "I must admit I don't believe she is involved."

Slater chuckled inwardly at such naïveté, but he was pleased that Hollingsworth had been so thorough.

"Just one more thing, George. I like your thoroughness, but I hope you are not as free with names with other people as you have been with me. From now on don't volunteer a name, unless I ask for it, and please refer to me only as Montague—even when talking with Putnam; he knows me by no other."

"Right!" George tried to cover his embarrassment. "I'll be more careful in the future."

"Does Wyman appear to be suspicious that you are onto him?"

"No," said George, but there was some doubt in his mind. "I don't think so. No one has confronted him with Webber's disappearance. To my knowledge, no one has been assigned to watch him directly. Mr. Putnam apparently received orders from your office to leave him strictly alone."

"Good." Slater nodded. "Do you happen to know if he's planning another excursion?"

"Yes, as a matter of fact, he has asked for permission to take another long weekend. He plans to leave Friday evening and be back on duty Tuesday morning."

"Do you have photographs of Wyman with you?"

"Yes," said George, secretly pleased, because the pictures

had been his idea. "They aren't too good, but I believe they are more or less characteristic."

George handed some snapshots to Slater. Slater looked them over carefully.

"He's a good-looking devil. Looks rather husky."

"He is," said George. "He must weigh 190. His hands and wrists are big. His eyes are blue and his hair, as you can see in that profile, is short, wavy and thick. He has very expensive taste in clothes. He is aggressive and very sure of himself. His one weakness seems to be his desire to keep up with the so-called international set."

Slater was silent. He examined the photographs carefully, weighing the odds, and grimly considering what might have happened to Webber.

"Have you a picture of Webber?"

"Yes," said George frowning. "I had a terrible time finding one." George handed him a small passport-type photograph.

"Is this the best you could get?"

"It's the only one." George was apologetic. "But," he added, "it's a surprisingly good likeness. He's slim, about five ten, and very pleasant looking, as you can see."

Slater looked at his watch. "You better turn around and take me back to Munich."

They were almost at the Rosenheim turnoff, and Hollingsworth made the change-over there.

"We want to know," said Hollingsworth, as he headed the car back to Munich, "what information Wyman is taking out, how it is transmitted, how he is paid, and by whom. We obviously would prefer that you do not disturb the mechanism, if possible, and, of course, we would like to get Webber back."

Slater stared out of the car window. He slumped low in his seat. There were a great many things he wanted to say in response to that last request. He was boiling inside, and he was tempted to take out his anger on Hollingsworth; but he knew

Hollingsworth was only asking what Putnam had instructed him to ask. Slater looked at the snow-covered hills which were higher on this side of Munich—hills, which grew larger and taller as you approached Salzburg, and then, if you turned south, suddenly became Alps.

"That was quite a speech you just made," said Slater finally. "Putnam must think I'm a one-man army." He shrugged. "I should be used to it by now, but I'm not." And then, suddenly, his anger got the better of him. "Tell me why, Hollingsworth! Why does Webber's return rate such a low priority?"

Hollingsworth was mortified. "I'm sorry, Mr. Carmichael, believe me! I know you don't think much of us amateurs. I know now that Putnam was a fool not to have Wyman investigated at once, and probably Charlie Webber was crazy to try it on his own." Hollingsworth took a deep breath and continued, "There was no order to my requests, or Putnam's, I'm sure. Charlie Webber was one of us amateurs; and although he was somewhat aloof, he was greatly admired."

Slater was silent. His outburst was inexcusable. He knew well enough that Webber, and he as well, were expendable. How he hated that word, that word and two others—the "big picture." The Webbers and Slaters, or Carmichaels and Montagues, were all infinitesimal in the "big picture," but he had only himself to blame. This was a voluntary job like all the others. It was simply that now he knew what to look forward to. Find Webber. Who is Wyman's employer? Who's making the pay-off? How? What has Wyman already told? What will be Wyman's next job? To Hollingsworth those requests probably sounded like an exciting challenge—a strenuous little game of cloak and dagger. To Slater they meant fear, naked stinking fear with death at the end, and no recognition should he, by some miracle, be successful. This was the last assignment—win, lose or draw. After that, somebody else could take his place. In the meantime, he was going to stay alive.

~~~~~~~~~~~~~~~~~~~~

Slater looked at George. "Forget it, George," he said. "I guess I'm a little on edge. We haven't much time. I suggest we arrange our future contact procedure."

"Yes," said George uncertainly. He took his eyes off the slippery road for a minute to have a look at Carmichael.

For the first time, George noted the lines of worry. Carmichael couldn't be more than thirty-five, and he looked hard-muscled and very fit, possibly too much so, like an overtrained athlete. Hollingsworth suddenly realized Carmichael was like a watch that has been wound too tight. Someone or something would open the back, and the tight mainspring would snap out of its case and strew the works all over the place. George felt apprehensive, but not for himself. He didn't want to see this man, whose exploits were legend, suddenly come apart at the seams. It was George's turn to get angry, angry at the people who continued to put the pressure on a man who had already done so much. Why couldn't they give him a rest? Montague, or Carmichael, was battle-happy.

Slater knew he was being assessed and he didn't like it. He wanted no judgments from a young, smooth-faced diplomat.

"Give me your phone number in Zurich," said Slater, "and always leave a number there where you can be reached at any time of the day or night. I don't want you to call me under any circumstances, at least for the present. I will arrange for some method of two-way communication, when I get located. When I call you, I will call myself Karl. Don't be alarmed if you don't recognize my voice. I will know yours, and I will always ask you the time before I give you any instructions. Do
~~~~~~~~~~~~~~~~~~~~

you speak German well enough to understand a phone conversation?"

"Yes. I also speak the Zurich dialect." George was proud of his linguistic accomplishments. Much to his surprise, Carmichael immediately switched to Zurich Deutsch. George was glad he hadn't been bluffing.

Slater was pleased. There weren't half a million people in Europe who could speak or understand Swiss German. The Swiss Air Force had spoken it on their intercom during World War II and had driven the Germans crazy trying to understand it.

"All right," said Slater, "now let's set up our meeting places. If I suggest on the phone that we have a drink in Munich at the Bundesbahn Hotel at ten hundred, that means I'll meet you on the southwest corner of the Staatsbrücke in Salzburg at eleven hundred. That goes for all meeting times: they will always be one hour later than either of us indicates on the phone.

"If I suggest the Winkler Café in Salzburg, we shall meet where we met by the Hofbräu Haus. If you say no, I will expect you to be there. If you say yes, but mention another time, I will add one hour to your suggestion and be waiting for you at the new time. Should either of us give an unqualified yes, that will mean the meeting is out of the question.

"If, for reasons of emergency, either of us wishes to break into clear conversation, he must ask, 'How is Horst?' and if the reply is, 'He has been ill lately,' we can go ahead. If, on the other hand, the reply is, 'He's fine and wants to be remembered to you,' that will mean we can't now, and the one who has given the answer will try to call back from somewhere else later or will give another number where he can be reached in an hour." Slater paused and then asked, "Do you think you have all this straight?"

George frowned. "I think so. Let's see, all meeting times

will be one hour later than stated. The Winkler Café in Salzburg means the Hofbräu Haus in Munich, and the Hofbräu Haus means the southwest corner of the Staatsbrücke in Salzburg. A negative answer means everything is understood and will be complied with. A qualified yes with another hour means okay, same place, but at the new time, again plus one hour. An unqualified yes means the meeting can't be held. I'm not to call you yet. You will identify yourself as Karl, and we will speak Swiss German. You will identify yourself by asking immediately for the correct time. Should either of us wish to break into clear conversation, we should ask how Horst is. If the answer is that he's ill, it's okay to go ahead. But if the person says that he is fine, then that person will call back as soon as he deems it safe to do so or will give another number where he can be reached in an hour."

"Good," said Slater. "This may all seem like hogwash to you, but I assure you it's of the utmost importance. Don't forget it.

"Now," he continued, "the next thing to arrange are the danger signals." George looked puzzled. "I've got to know," said Slater, "if you think someone is following you. That's for my protection. For your protection, you need the same information."

The word "protection" and the idea of being followed caused a responsive twinge in Hollingsworth, but his admiration for the man he knew as Carmichael was rapidly increasing.

"In Munich, I will be standing by the blue-and-white parking sign nearest the Hofbräu, and I will be looking for this Mercedes. Remember, George, you must always use the same car. If my hat is on, keep right on going and wait for me at the Bundesbahn Hotel restaurant, where we first met. If I don't show within two hours, forget me and go home. I'll try to phone. If I take my hat off, everything is all right as far as I know. If the meeting is to be in Salzburg, follow the same procedure, but wait for me at the Hotel Horn in the Getreide Gasse. Better get a city plan, so you will know where it is. In both cases take at least fifteen to twenty minutes to get to the second meeting place."

"Sure," said George, "but why?"

"Because," said Slater evenly, "if I get there first, I can watch you go in and satisfy myself that you aren't being tailed."

"I see." Putnam had been right; Carmichael was not going to trust him entirely. "What do I do to indicate that I'm being followed?"

"In the case of Salzburg, you will be turning right to cross the Staatsbrücke. Turn on your right directional signal and move past me. I'll know. In Munich you will be turning left. Use your left signal and keep on going. My arrival, before you, at the second meeting place will allow me to tell whether you are clean. If I don't meet you, you'll know you're still under surveillance." Slater looked carefully at George. "If you think you have all that, repeat it. If not, let's go over it again."

The two men went over and over the entire procedure. George was finally convinced he had never learned any lesson so thoroughly. By the time Slater was satisfied that George had the signals straight, they had reached the outskirts of Munich.

"I have one more request to make, George, before you drop me at the Hofbräu. I want you to have Wyman at the bar of the Baur-au-Lac Hotel in Zurich at 10:30 tomorrow morning. You can invite him for coffee."

"I'll try, but Wyman and I aren't on very good terms."

"Then get someone else to invite him, Putnam himself, if necessary, but get him there. I would like to look Wyman over in the flesh."

"Right." It was obvious that Carmichael really knew his business. "I don't suppose I could drive you to Zurich?" George smiled.

"I'm afraid not." Slater returned the smile.

The Mercedes maneuvered nicely through the narrow streets and George pulled into the parking place by the Hofbräu Haus. Slater got out and grabbed his suitcase. He set the suitcase on the sidewalk and, keeping the door open, poked his head inside.

"Hollingsworth," he said, "sorry to have been quite so ornery. I think you can see this is no business for amateurs, but I think you'll do." George was obviously pleased. "And one more thing, don't worry about me. I'll admit I'm honed down pretty fine at the moment, but I'm not going to bust apart." George flushed scarlet. "If Webber's still alive, I'll get him out."

Before George could say anything, Slater had shut the door, picked up his bag and was walking across the street toward the main entrance to the Hofbräu Haus. The wind had picked up the bottom flap of his coat, and he was forced to hold onto his hat with his free hand. To George, he looked a lonely figure, tall and slim and straight, despite the wind. Slater disappeared into the beer hall, and George put the car in gear and drove off.

Carmichael—Montague—was a strange man, also positively clairvoyant. George's face flushed again at the thought that he had been caught in judgment. As George turned the corner, he realized that, in spite of their long conversation, all he could distinctly remember of Carmichael was a strong face, dark hair, green eyes and a surprisingly gentle smile. If, as he had said, Webber was alive, Carmichael would find him.

Chapter 2

Slater entered one of the many dining rooms on the first floor of the Hofbräu Haus and sat down at a table which was covered by a checked cloth. He remembered the Hofbräu Haus was not only for beer drinkers, who wanted to see true Bavarian entertainment, but also for those who really enjoyed plain German food. It was the noon hour, and a glance at the rough hands and coarse clothing of the clientele was enough to reveal that here was a place where the working men and women ate. Slater was fascinated by one giant of a man at the next table. His face was gaunted by years of hard, manual labor, but his body looked hard and well muscled. He had a prodigious appetite, and washed his food down with great gulps of beer, occasionally taking time to wipe the foam from his upper lip with his sleeve. "If that bruiser ever quits working," thought Slater, "he'll blow up like a balloon."

Slater ordered a Filetschnitte "Meyerbeer," feine Erbsen, pommes frites, a liter stein of beer and set to with a will. He had a difficult job in front of him; but past experience had taught him to enjoy the free moments while he had them, and that a full stomach will carry a man a lot further than an empty one. He quaffed his beer and marveled at its wonderful taste. As far as he was concerned, there was no beer like the draft beer at the Hofbräu; and here a man could eat as a man should, with both feet if he wanted to. Slater couldn't match the giant at the next table for his pure "go to hell" style of eating, but he did put his body and soul into it. He was surprised when it was all over, and he had nothing left to do but light a cigarette and pay the bill.

Slater found a small hotel nearby and checked in. The room was just large enough for a dark-paneled wardrobe with two drawers at the bottom, a piece of furniture common to every hotel in Europe, and a tremendous four-poster. The window looked out on a dark alley. Slater was glad he didn't have to spend the night there. He had paid for the room in advance and intended to slip out unnoticed a few hours later. He had signed for the room in the name of Bruce Carmichael, but had shown his passport only briefly.

Slater locked the door and returned to the washstand, where he opened his heavy suitcase. He took out a tweed sport coat, a pair of oxford-gray flannels, a white button-down shirt, a pair of argyle socks and a pair of rubber-soled cordovan shoes and laid them on the bed. He turned to face the mirror and looked at himself closely. He believed he looked natural enough, as long as he could keep some sort of a tan. He removed his hat. He moistened one of the hand towels and dampened the top of his forehead and his temples. Deftly, he removed the toupee and laid it carefully on a piece of tissue paper which he took from the suitcase. He turned back to the mirror and scrubbed his eyebrows. A good deal of the black came off. Next, he bent over and untied his shoes, When he stepped out of them, he was three inches shorter or about five feet, ten inches in his stockinged feet. With regular shoes on he was about five feet eleven.

Slater went back to the mirror and smiled. Everybody couldn't be six feet one with his shoes on. Who wanted a widow's peak anyway? Slater's own hair, now very short, was brown and coarse and his natural hairline was higher than the wig. The first touches of gray were noticeable at the temples.

Slater took a very small half-moon piece of foam rubber from inside each cheek. His face now had a flatter, longer look; his cheek bones were a little more prominent, and he looked more Teutonic.

Slater dressed himself and checked his appearance once again. He could have been a young executive on a holiday. There would always be the impression that, whatever else he did, he managed to spend time out of doors. Preston would have said that Slater was "quite acceptable—good background and all that."

There was one more important detail. He had to put Carmichael's American passport carefully away and take out his own. Since he had entered Germany as Slater, he would have no trouble leaving as Slater. At some future date, if he thought it advisable, he would have to copy the entrance and exit stamps into Carmichael's passport. He wasn't going to do it now, as he might need an alibi for his whereabouts someday, and a Carmichael who hadn't left Germany, or possibly hadn't even entered, might come in handy. There were some things it didn't pay to do immediately. Papers were a problem to Slater, particularly in Europe, but, fortunately, an American didn't require visas in most of Europe; and there were times when the travel regulations could be extremely useful.

Slater carefully put everything back in his suitcase, including his hat. He put on his overcoat, picked up his suitcase and, leaving the key in the door, walked down the two flights of stairs, past the small lobby and into the street. Luckily, there had been no one in the lobby.

Slater hailed a taxi and drove through the late afternoon crowds to the station. He never could sleep on trains, particularly European trains, which screeched through the night like banshees and continually threatened to jump the corrugated roadbeds. He preferred to take the next train, instead of the later sleeper, and check into a hotel in Zurich. He wouldn't get to bed until late but he could sleep until nine the next morning.

On the train, Slater sat by the window and watched the countryside flash by. There was a timelessness about the European scene. An observer had the feeling he was witnessing a vast pastoral setting which hadn't changed for hundreds of years and wouldn't change for many, many years in the future. Horses and oxen still pulled the wagons. The farmers milked by hand. Everything was done today as it had been over a century ago. Only the main roads were modern.

Even the people were the same. Wars didn't seem to have any lasting effect. The farmers went right on planting and harvesting their crops, getting ready for winter; and now that winter was almost over, they were patching and mending, preparing to begin the cycle all over again.

Slater continued to watch until darkness enveloped the scene, and he could no longer look anywhere but inward. He hadn't wanted to but before he knew it, he was remembering.

The Office of Security, or whatever it had called itself in 1948, had first approached Slater in Zurich. He had been doing graduate work at the University, simply marking time, wondering what to do with his life. Government service had seemed to be the answer. They would pay him enough to live on, send him all over the world, and he could be of real service in the protection of his country's security.

He had done that first job successfully, in spite of the government organization. He had been appalled at the department's slipshod methods and cavalier approach to international security; and when they had asked him to take on another project, he had refused unless he could work his own way—and alone. He had been told that if he didn't become integrated into the organization, he couldn't advance his career. Slater had said he didn't care, that he had no intention of making this a career. Slater smiled ruefully.

He had had a great many ideas of his own. He had believed in training, for one thing, and the government had paid for it. Slater had sought out professionals to give him, individually, the skills he believed his job required. He had learned judo the hard way from a professional wrestler in Japan. A German mercenary in the French Foreign Legion had taught him the use of firearms and knives. Slater had gone into the prisons to learn forgery and illegal entry. He had learned how to make an effective bomb with several timing devices from things anyone could purchase at a drugstore.

His superiors had laughed at him when he had requested permission to study the art of make-up from a well-known Broadway authority. That was cloak and dagger Hollywood style; he would never use it. But Slater had stuck to his guns, and, little by little, the wheels had finally become convinced by his successful performances that, for him at least, this training was worthwhile.

The idea that had been gnawing at Slater for eight years was the increasing realization that his primary reason for all the special training he had received was his own fear. He had to be good, or he would be killed. This thought kept running through his mind and had, to a large degree, spoiled any feeling of accomplishment. Each new mission, every close call, and there had been many, left him more and more fearful. He had deliberately isolated himself from contact with people in his own organization. This had been done out of fear for his own security, but lately it had boomeranged. He needed desperately to confide in someone, and there wasn't anyone.

Slater knew he had built up a legend about himself. He was considered the best counterespionage agent his country had, and now they counted on him for too much. They told him too much. He knew almost every important Allied counterespionage operator in Europe. The Communists would give a great deal to nail the man called Montague, and Slater knew this for a fact. He had seen a copy of one of their dossiers on him. They had given him credit for some things he hadn't done and had missed a few he had been in on, but they were still too close. That dossier was now two years old.

Over the years, Slater had used so many identities he had no concrete idea which were compromised. He was pretty certain that the only one he could be sure of was his own, William A. Slater. In any event, it was a pleasure to be himself for a change. He had already made up his mind that this was to be his last mission.

At the Swiss border, the passport inspector took Slater's passport and looked him over carefully.

"You are a tourist, Mr. Slater?" he asked.

"Yes," said Slater cheerfully, "that's right."

"What is your business in the United States?"

"Well, I'm about to open up a ski resort in New Hampshire." Slater smiled. "I'm sort of on a busman's holiday. Thought I might get a few good ideas from your country."

"This is your first visit to Switzerland?"

"Oh no," said Slater. "I was a graduate student at the University of Zurich, but, unfortunately, that was a long time ago."

"I knew it." The inspector looked pleased with himself. "I thought I had seen you before. You Americans," he shook his head, "you never grow old."

"What do you mean? Look at that gray in my temples." Slater put his head to one side and invited closer inspection.

"Ach! Your hair is too light for it to show. No one would ever know."

Slater laughed. "Tell me, where did we meet?"

"Oh, we didn't meet, Mr. Slater! I only checked your passport in Basel." He chuckled. "I pride myself on remembering faces. I remember you because you tried to speak German with me. My English wasn't so good then, and I was pleased that an American had taken the trouble to learn our language. Well, I must go. I will see you again, I hope. Auf Wiedersehen."

"Auf Wiedersehen!" Slater was amazed. You never knew. If he had lied about himself, the officer might have sent in his name to the Swiss authorities; and he would have been watched. By telling the truth he avoided suspicion. After all, he mused, he really was William A. Slater, and Slater had nothing to hide. Anyway, he hoped not. How outgoing he must have been then—in spite of a war. Well, he thought, I'll never be that way again.

Slater got off the train and jostled his way through a crowd of skiers who were waiting for the Thursday-night trains to Davos and St. Moritz. Some would go north to the Schwarzwald, to Garmisch in Bavaria and to the Austrian Tirol. Prices were lower there. Slater loved to ski and had been to all of these places. He hadn't had time for skiing in the last two years.

He stood by the currency exchange booth and watched the skiers laughing and shoving, their bright costumes forming a contrast to the gray concrete of the station. He wished he could go along as one of them. The girls all looked beautiful in their tight-fitting ski pants. He turned away from the crowd and changed some greenbacks for Swiss francs. As he left the station, one of the girls winked at him, and her friends shouted for him to come along. Slater waved and smiled and headed for the street. He crossed over to the Schweizerhof and checked in. He went straight to his room, took a bath and went to bed.

He awoke at eight, refreshed but terribly hungry. He

pushed off the great white feather quilt and dressed. The only thing he added to his wardrobe of yesterday was a pair of horn-rimmed glasses. He didn't like to wear them. He didn't need them, and he had a very high-bridged nose which the frame irritated. He remembered that his oxygen mask during the war had nearly driven him crazy. He had wanted to rip it off, even at 24,000 feet. The only time he hadn't been aware of it was during actual combat.

Slater was an eater. It was one of the few pleasures he permitted himself. He ordered croissants with Swiss butter and jam, milchkaffee, and roesti with ham and eggs. Breakfast took over an hour, and the waiter marveled in silence at the still trim figure of a man who could eat like that. When Slater had left, the pale-faced waiter shrugged his shoulders. "That one can eat, because he is rich and has nothing on his mind."

He turned to a fellow waiter. "Glück und Geld sind nur für Amerikaner." Fortune and money are only for Americans.

Slater bought the *Neue Züricher Zeitung* and walked along the Bahnhofstrasse. He stopped at a fashionable men's store and purchased a green Tyrolean hat, complete with a Gemsbock ornament. All he needed now was a camera slung over his shoulder, and the perfect picture of an American tourist would be completed. He decided to forego the camera.

He sauntered along the main streets of the town he knew so well, trying to recall his student days when his irrepressibility had gotten him into one minor scrape after another. Zurich was a beautiful city, the modern blended with the medieval, the old city with its narrow, winding streets clinging to the side of a hill, the new city in the valley split by the Limmat River, a mountain on either side, and the Lake of Zurich for its southern border.

Slater walked to the stoned embankment at the water's edge and looked across the lake and, far beyond, to the snowcovered Swiss Alps. He remained standing there for a minute. Finally he turned slowly, almost sadly, and crossed the street to the Baur-au-Lac Hotel.

He entered through the main door, went past the desk, through the main public rooms and into the bar and coffee shop in the back. He sat at the bar and ordered a pilsner.

It wasn't quite 10:30 yet, and he opened the newspaper. The Zurich paper was one of the best in the world for unbiased, honest reporting, particularly when it dealt with international affairs. Most of the news people were allowed to read was hopelessly biased and often incorrect. Even the publishers didn't know the facts, nor did many government officials know what frequently lay behind treaties, their sub rosa agreements and ulterior motives. Slater knew why and how some of them had started; he no longer believed the rest. A nation's stated intentions were often so far from the truth.

One article caught his attention, and he read it through from beginning to end. According to the writer, the European satellite nations, particularly Poland and Hungary, might be planning an organized break with Russia. Slater doubted that, without American military interference, any revolution would succeed unless it was just another puppet state whose leaders were working with the Communists. Tito wouldn't be any help. He was sitting pretty, getting aid from both sides.

At that moment, three men entered the bar from the street entrance. Slater turned enough to see Hollingsworth and two others. He knew Wyman immediately from the pictures. Wyman was handsome in a flashy sort of way. He reminded Slater of an Ivy League fullback he had once known, whose background with a capital B had been obscure, but whose football ability had given him access to the best clubs. He remembered that the club boys had considered themselves quite democratic in accepting him. He had ended up becoming the worst snob of all.

Wyman certainly was big. Slater guessed he was outweighed

by at least twenty-five pounds. Slater would have disliked Wyman even if the man hadn't been under suspicion. He was convinced Wyman was an arrogant free-loader, whose only ambition was to get enough money and power to push people around. Why did Uncle Sam hire men like that? They were perfect bait for Communists.

Slater asked the bartender to bring another bottle of pilsner beer to a booth and walked over to the booth next to Wyman's. The paneled sides were just higher than a man's head. Slater could listen without being observed. He put the paper in front of him and pretended to read.

"What's in Munich that isn't available right here, Wyman?" That couldn't be George talking. Slater smiled inwardly.

"Or have the local girls seen through you already?" That was George!

"This town is dead, and you know it. A man can really live it up in Munich. Besides," said Wyman, "I've got contacts up there. You should see their place. It's like a castle. I don't believe the owner's family have worked for five generations."

"Really!" George's tone was sarcastic. "What are their names?"

"You're too young."

Slater was sure George must be blushing. He was surprised that Wyman hadn't appeared to take offense at Hollingsworth's attitude.

"Are you driving up?" the other man asked.

"No, I'm taking the four-thirty train this afternoon."

That was all Slater needed to know. It was too bad George couldn't have gotten Wyman to mention the names of his Munich friends. Slater called the waiter over, paid the bill and left.

The three men were still talking. Only George looked up at Slater, as he went past their table. George believed there was something familiar about the man. He considered asking one of his companions but, for some strange reason, decided not to. There was something about the man and the way he moved.

George was disappointed that Carmichael hadn't shown up. He hoped nothing had gone wrong at this early stage of the game.

Chapter 3

Slater turned into the Bahnhofstrasse and walked the length of it back to the Schweizerhof Hotel. He purchased a couple of American magazines and went up to his room. He left a request with the switchboard to call him at 4 P.M.

There were some letters he would have liked to write, but the postmark would place him in Zurich, and he wasn't sure at this point whether that would be advisable. There were very few people with whom Slater still kept in touch. His father was no longer living, and his mother had remarried many years ago. She had her own life, and his job had prevented him from much personal contact with her. Even his letters were necessarily few and inadequate. There was so much he had to leave out and so much he had to invent.

He went into the bathroom and turned on the tap. He took the glass tumbler and allowed the cold water to cover the bottom, and then passed the glass under the faucet, quickly, so that there was just the least bit more water. He turned off the tap and took a tablet from an aspirin box in his pocket and dropped it into the water.

He re-entered the room and set the glass on the small writing table. He took a ball-point pen from his inside jacket pocket and, seating himself, dipped the pen in the water and began to write. As the pen worked across the paper, there was nothing visible. The only way Slater could be certain he wasn't writing over the same space twice was the heavy, black-lined paper beneath the sheet he was writing on. He had to keep pen to paper and write continually. When he was forced to dip again, he would carefully mark his place with his left forefinger. Looking at the apparently empty page, Slater reflected that this secret writing was symbolic of these last ten years of his life. He had moved forward continuously and had left nothing visible behind.

After the message had been completed, he wrote a regular letter over it and addressed it to a man named Fred Stanton at the Hotel de Ville, in Paris. The visible letter was innocuous, and Slater signed it, "As always, Ben."

He tried to read to while away the time, but the magazines bored him. At lunchtime he went downstairs and ordered another big meal. This time he wasn't hungry, but he forced himself to eat.

He returned to his room and slept for two hours, waking himself just as the phone rang. It was the girl at the switchboard. He liked her voice and was tempted to talk to her. He thanked her instead and hung up.

At 4:05 Slater checked out of the hotel and crossed the street to the station. He mailed the letter and loitered around the ticket windows, leaning against the concrete wall, apparently reading his paper.

At 4:20 Wyman arrived, and Slater joined the ticket line, two places behind him. He heard Wyman ask for a round-trip ticket to Munich. Slater bought a one-way ticket to the same destination and followed Wyman to the train. He watched with satisfaction as Wyman boarded a first-class car. Slater entered two cars forward of Wyman and found himself a seat in the second-class coach.

After Slater's passport had been checked for the second time at Bregenz, he pulled his suitcase down from the rack and took it with him along the corridor to the men's room. The train was going full speed now and rocking from side to side. It was cramped quarters in the men's room, but he managed to get into Carmichael's clothes. His biggest difficulty was the toupee. He should have gotten a haircut. His own hair was getting a little too long.

Slater stepped out of the men's room as Carmichael and headed back to Wyman's car to claim the seat in Wyman's first-class compartment to which his first-class ticket entitled him. Slater was prepared to strike up a conversation. What he had heard in Zurich was enough to know the proper approach to Wyman. A little name-dropping of international socialites, and he would be in.

Slater checked his ticket and opened the sliding door to the corresponding compartment. Slater looked from face to face, appeared bewildered, muttered an "excuse me" in German and backed out into the corridor. Wyman was gone.

Chapter 4

Slater went from compartment to compartment. He even went to the dining car, but he knew he had been tricked, and by the oldest one in the book. Wyman had undoubtedly left the train at Feldkirch and would pick up the Arlberg Express. He was probably already on his way to Kitzbühel.

By the time Slater had exhausted all other possibilities, the train was well on the way to Kempten. He stood on the platform between cars, and his cursing blended with the clackety-clacking of the pounding wheels. He lighted a cigarette, returned to the first-class compartment and promptly fell asleep. He didn't wake up until the train pulled into Munich.

He got a room in a small hotel near the station and started working on Carmichael's passport. Maybe Slater's identity was compromised, as far as Wyman was concerned. Probably Wyman was just being cautious. In any case, Slater decided to enter Austria as Carmichael. He took a rubber stamp and ink pad from his suitcase and stamped an Einreise stamp in the back of his passport. It was done carelessly, and the letters were blurred, but it definitely looked like the entry in Slater's passport. He then compared the numbers and date inside Carmichael's stamp and stippled them in by dotting the page repeatedly with a fine-pointed pencil, which he had first rolled on the ink pad. The result he smudged lightly with his finger. He again compared the forgery with the original and was satisfied.

It was too late to do anything more, and Slater realized it, but he felt frustrated. He had acted like an amateur, and this was only the first round. If Wyman wasn't in Kitzbühel, there would be hell to pay. He went down to the lobby and got some change. It was late, but he called several car-rental agencies, until he found one that answered, because it also dispensed gas. He reserved a Volkswagen for 6 o'clock the next morning. There were some protests, but an offer of a few extra marks, and a larger than customary deposit, and the arrangements were completed.

Slater awoke at 5:30 and picked up the car at 6. He drove through a false dawn, all the way to the Rosenheim turn-off, and turned south. The day was cold and still, and deep clouds clung to the mountaintops. He crossed the Austrian border at Kiefersfelden and entered the mountain village of Kufstein.

From there, he began the climb up into the Alps. It was a lonely ride. At night, Slater thought, it must be the loneliest drive in the world. The road was a winding white ditch edged into the mountainsides. The embankments of ice and snow were twice as high as a man's head, and the icy roadway was narrow and full of ruts. Slater was glad he didn't have an American car. The Volkswagen bumped and slid, but maintained its headway up the steepest grades. At various places, great sidings had been dug out of the banks, presumably so that one car could pull over, and another, coming in the opposite direction, might get by. Slater was glad that he hadn't been forced to use one. If he had had to stop, he doubted that he could have gotten enough traction to start again. If two cars met head-on, where there was no siding, he didn't know what they would do.

He drove for miles, high up in the mountains, in and out of the mist, without seeing anything but the narrow track in front of him. He knew that steep-roofed houses must be above and below him, but they didn't exist for him. He thought of the spring thaw that couldn't be more than a month away, and he no longer doubted the danger of avalanches was very real. The high sides of the road were not a great deal higher than the snow-covered fields. He got the feeling that they acted, nevertheless, as dikes against the tons of sliding snow.

And finally, just as he was about to believe he would go on driving around and around and up and down, aimlessly and forever, into eternity, he started down out of the mist and into the clear bright sunshine. Below him lay Kitzbühel with pastel-colored, steep-roofed houses, a church tower, a winding stream choked with ice and snow but beginning to move with the warmth of the new day. An electric train was droning its way through the valley from Wörgl to Kitzbühel. This was a ski resort in a picture-book setting. Slater was spellbound.

The main street was almost bare. In another week the slush would be gone. He drove the car slowly past the bright shops, through a medieval archway, and was stopped by the colorful, morning crowd of skiers on their way to the cable car. Slater nudged the car to a parking place in front of the Winterhof Hotel. A porter opened the door for him and took his suitcase.

The small, dark-paneled lobby was crowded, and Slater doubted that he would be able to get a room.

"Yes, sir?" The clerk at the desk was tall and thin. He was wearing the traditional black suit. His shirt front and cuffs were frosty white, but Slater noticed that the sleeves of his jacket were beginning to shine. The man looked worn and tired.

"I would like a room," said Slater.

"Do you have a reservation, sir?"

"No." Slater smiled slowly. "It was foolish of me, but I forgot. I hope you can help me."

"I am afraid, sir, that all—"

Slater looked down at his right hand, resting on the counter. When the clerk followed the glance, Slater lifted his hand and revealed an American ten-dollar bill. The clerk looked directly at Slater. Slater was still smiling. The clerk bowed slightly. He didn't appear quite so tired.

"I don't care if it's a large room," Slater said. "Anything will do."

"Yes, of course, Mr.—?"

"Carmichael."

"Yes, Mr. Carmichael, I can give you room twenty-three." The clerk was very businesslike again.

Slater handed over his passport, and the clerk wrote down the number and Carmichael's home address, then carefully palmed the ten-dollar bill and, without a further look in Slater's direction, tapped the bell for the porter.

Room 23 was on the second floor and overlooked the main street. There were a double bed, the ever-present wardrobe, a wash basin, a bureau and a night stand. Slater checked his watch. It was exactly nine o'clock. He left his room and headed downstairs for the dining room. He stood in the entryway for a moment and looked around at the diners. He was in luck. Wyman was seated in a corner by himself. Slater had the waiter conduct him to the next table. Wyman looked up as Slater approached. Wyman's eyes rested on his for a second, looked vague and then passed on elsewhere. Apparently, he had been there for some time. When the waiter came to take his order, Wyman appeared angry.

"Where is Rüdi? I want to tell him about this fast service!"

The waiter was a little old man, and obviously upset. "Rüdi will not be on duty until this evening, sir. I assure you I am very sorry for the delay."

Wyman gave his order as disagreeably as he could. Slater gritted his teeth. People who shouted at waiters and called for the managers inevitably irritated him.

The breakfast was excellent, as much of it as Slater permitted himself. He had noted that Wyman had ordered a large one, a breakfast that would take some time to finish. Slater had a cup of hot chocolate, a roll, some jam, and left.

Back in his room he changed from Carmichael to Slater as fast as possible, only this time he put on ski clothes. They were his own. He hadn't had them on in two years, and they felt very comfortable. He put on his ski boots but tied the laces very loosely. He didn't care to walk in the boots because he believed it ruined them for skiing.

Slater was back in the dining room in fifteen minutes, just in time to follow Wyman out the door and into the street. Wyman crossed the street and turned left toward the cable car which carried the skiers up the Hahnenkamm. There was still quite a crowd going in the same direction, and Slater took a chance and got ahead of Wyman. The candy-striped railroad-crossing barrier was down, but Slater stepped over it and gained the other side without calling too much attention to himself. He looked for the red ski-rental shack Webber had mentioned in his letter to Putnam. Webber's memory had been good. There was such a shack and it was the last one on the way to what obviously was the practice slope. Slater asked the woman attendant for a pair of skis. She told him to take his choice.

While Slater was inspecting the various skis, Wyman entered. He asked the woman for Mr. Schlessinger's skis. The woman went over to a special section in the corner and took out a pair. They were a little short for Wyman, but they were in good condition. They were Erbacher skis. Apparently, Mr. Schlessinger preferred German craftmanship. Fortunately, several more customers entered and Slater didn't think Wyman had noticed him.

As soon as Slater saw Wyman leave, he picked out a pair of skis and poles for himself, had the harnesses fitted to his boots and went outside. The sunshine was dazzling, and it took a moment for Slater to adjust to the brightness. He looked for Wyman's green and white sweater, but couldn't find it. There were so many colors that they all blended into a moving, shapeless crazy quilt.

He went over the base of the cable station and looked at the long ticket line. Wyman was in the middle. Slater spotted a girl three places ahead of Wyman and then joined the line at the end.

After he had bought his ticket, he looked for the girl and found her leaning against the wooden railing, sunning herself on the wide veranda just below the cable car entrance. He had picked her out of the ticket line because her hair was the color of copper, and he thought she wouldn't be hard to find again. As he approached her now, he saw she was unusually attractive. Subconsciously he thought, I must have spotted her for much more obvious reasons.

"Excuse me," he said in German, "but I have a favor to ask."

Her green eyes looked him over with mild, but not unfriendly, interest.

"Your German is excellent, but you must be American," she said. "No German would cut off so much of his hair." She smiled, and her smile was charming. "You may ask your favor in English if you wish."

"Well," Slater hesitated. Her eyes made him feel strangely self-conscious. "I wondered if you would be good enough to trade tickets with me. I have discovered an old friend," he went on hurriedly, "who is riding up in your car, and I would like to go up with him."

"What number do you have?" she asked.

"Thirty-one."

"I would have to wait another half hour." She was indignant.

"I would be glad to pay you."

"No," she looked away from him, "if he is your friend, he will wait for you at the top, or he will trade his ticket with someone in your car." She turned her eyes back to him. "Now, please, go away. You are standing between me and the sun."

"I'm sorry, Fräulein." Slater turned away.

He felt like a fool. He stepped down from the veranda and walked over to his skis. He wanted to look back at the copper-haired girl with the cat-green eyes. It took him several minutes of fumbling with his skis to get over his embarrassment. Finally, he turned to have a look. She was walking across the veranda to pick up her skis. Her car number was about to be called. Slater liked the way she walked. It was both supple and graceful. Her shoulders were broad. She was saved from having an hourglass figure because of her long slim legs. Wyman was right behind her. Slater was bitter. Wyman would not pass that up—no man would.

It was a perfect day for skiing. The sun was warm on his back and the snow would have at least a three-inch powder cover up on the mountain. He had never skied in Kitzbühel before. There were other things he should do with the morning now that he had lost Wyman, but Slater kept working around the problem, until he had almost rationalized himself into thinking that a morning's skiing would be an excellent conditioner for whatever he might run into; and that, after all, he should know the lay of the land up there—which ski trails went where, etc.

Slater waited for his car number to be called, handed his skis to the attendant to put on the rack outside on the front of the car, and got in.

A ride in a cable car to the top of a mountain is a unique sensation. It's not like flying, and it isn't like being on top of a high building. Slater always had an insecure feeling. The ground was a long way down; and when the occupants or the wind caused the car to sway and he looked up at the cable, he inevitably had the eerie sensation of hanging by a thread in the middle of space. The scenery was what made him forget to be concerned. The great expanse of white that opened up, the ever increasing vista of mile after mile of snow-covered peaks, the air so clear that it appeared to turn, suddenly, into a clean blue, all made the journey seem too brief. The cable car seemed a floating tower of Babel with its passengers describing their reactions in five different languages. Slater thought that the German name for this swaying gondola was more descriptive. The Schwebebahn approached its steel and cement harbor and slowed perceptibly, until at the entrance it almost stopped and nudged its way in, bumping slightly against the concrete piers. Slater took his skis from the rack and stepped out into the snow. He watched a pony-driven cart with two passengers moving slowly along the shoulder to a hotel just below the top of the adjacent peak. He walked along the shoulder, looking down into the next valley and across to the mountain beyond. According to the map, it was approximately six thousand feet, and he could barely make out the posts of a chair lift which would carry a skier from the valley floor to the top. He could see from his map that there was another chair lift opposite which would take him back up to the hotel on his side of the valley.

The first trail dropped off to the right and came out by the practice slope. This was the Streif and, according to Webber's letter, must be the Olympic run. Slater decided against trying it until he had had a little practice. He changed his mind abruptly when he saw two skiers coming down from the hotel. He saw the green and white sweater and the coppery red hair.

Apparently, they had just had coffee at the hotel and were about to ski the Streif. He bent over to put on his skis, pretending to be unaware of the newcomers. They came to a stop about five yards away from him. The girl was asking Wyman if he had tried the Streif before. She was speaking English.

"It's an Olympic run, you know. I believe it's rather fast," she said. "If this is your first day, Mr. Wyman, I suggest you try another one first." Sensible girl, thought Slater. "I have a luncheon engagement," she added, "or I would take the Kaseralm to the village of Kirchberg and come back by train."

"I've been down the Streif before," said Wyman. "There's nothing to it." He turned to her. "Europeans aren't the only skiers in the world, Fräulein Wieland."

"I see," she shrugged. "If that's the case, Mr. Wyman, after you."

Wyman pushed off and went straight down. Slater watched him hit the first turn at least fifty yards below. Wyman took it wide open and gracefully and surely, his weight well forward and on the downhill side. Slater shook his head. There was no doubt about it, Wyman could ski.

Fräulein Wieland went next. She rode her skis easily, checking her speed occasionally, keeping them well under control. She was beautiful to watch. Slater was mesmerized by the long fluid motion of her body, as she maneuvered her skis in several long turns and disappeared below.

Slater pushed off. He turned repeatedly, trying to get the feel of the deep powder snow, hoping to regain his ski legs and make up in one run for two years of no practice. As he rounded the turn, he saw Fräulein Wieland below. She had stopped, and Wyman was nowhere in sight. He was probably halfway down by now. Slater skied up to her. When she saw who it was, she started to move off.

"Wait," said Slater. "Don't go away." She hesitated. "I want to apologize for being so stupid."

Fräulein Wieland regarded him frankly and critically for a moment. "All right," she smiled slowly. "I accept. Anyway," she added, "apparently my escort has left me behind, and I don't think anyone should ski the Streif alone."

"I agree," said Slater, "but you're a beautiful skier. You certainly won't have any trouble."

"I have skied since I was a child," she said simply. "Anyone can have an accident on skis."

Slater was flattered that she spoke to him in German.

"I could use some instruction," he said. "I'm a little out of practice."

"I thought you were doing very well," she said. "Go ahead and I will watch you."

Slater left her, feeling very self-conscious. He resisted the crazy impulse to take the trail straight. He would have liked to impress her. Instead, he tried to control his speed and practice his turns. It was very steep, and he continued his run until he was below the timberline. He christied to a stop and turned to look for Fräulein Wieland. She pulled up neatly beside him just as he turned.

"You do very well," she said. "Apparently, your legs are in good condition. Perhaps you are not getting your weight quite far enough forward. Otherwise, I would say you are very good."

"Thank you. I did better than I thought I would. What's your name?"

"Ilse Wieland. What's yours?"

"Bill Slater."

"It is nice to meet you, Bill Slater."

Slater felt like a schoolboy again. He thought that was the nicest sentence he'd ever heard, and he couldn't think of anything to say. He looked down and realized for the first time that he had stopped on a knoll, that immediately below, the trail was very narrow and looked as steep as the inside of a cup. It was a plunge of at least a hundred yards with no turn-off except at the end of a short level stretch that curved away, out of sight, into the woods. Once he started over the lip, he would be committed to going straight the whole distance. It was probably icy, way down there in the trees.

Ilse looked down with him. "It is quite steep," she said, "but you will do all right." Slater flushed. "Oh, please," she was immediately upset, "don't be embarrassed. I meant nothing."

"That's all right," Slater said hastily. "I am a little afraid. I didn't mean to show it."

Much to his surprise, he found himself smiling at her, ruefully perhaps, but smiling. It was the first time in ten years he had ever admitted to anyone but himself that he was afraid of anything. It felt surprisingly good.

"I think I'll do all right, Ilse, but you better go first. I don't want to clutter up the trail and force you to crash into a tree or something."

"I trust you, Bill. You can go first."

"Please go ahead." His smile was quite gentle. "I won't be offended."

Slater knew German well. He spoke it with ease. He was well aware of the important difference between the polite and "du" form of address. Germans who had known one another for years rarely used anything but the formal "Sie," yet Bill found himself calling Ilse by her first name and referring to her as "du." It wasn't until she had started over the lip that he realized she had responded in the same way.

He watched her anxiously, as she rapidly picked up speed. By the time she hit bottom, she looked like a little bug. He estimated that she must have been going at least fifty miles an hour. She hit the flat track between the trees, her little black figure standing upright and as sure as if the skis were glued to the snow, and disappeared around the corner.

Slater muttered a "here goes nothing" to himself and began the crazy plunge down the side of the mountain. The wind tore at his clothes. His ski pants, flapping against his legs, sounded like a partridge taking off in the brush. His eyes stung as he crouched lower and lower and felt the trees go whipping past. He zoomed into the flat, going at least a mile a minute. He straightened up slowly, took the turn at the far end still standing and managed to stop himself in a snow-spraying turn about fifty yards beyond. He rubbed his smarting eyes and looked for Ilse. She was pulling herself out of the snow about twenty yards above him.

"Are you all right, Ilse?" he yelled.

"Yes, but I could use some help."

The snow on the sides of the trail was very deep and soft, and he could see that she was having difficulty getting herself out.

"What happened?" asked Bill as he walked up to her and offered his arm so she could pull herself up on her feet.

He had removed his skis and stacked them in the snow. Ilse's right ski was buried in the snow, and he waded in, thigh deep and managed to unfasten her harness.

"What a relief! Thank you."

She stood up and brushed off the snow. Her face was wet, and snow clung to her eyebrows and copper hair. Her cheeks were flushed, and her eyes looked greener than ever.

"I made the turn all right, and then I started thinking about you." She looked at him and smiled. "The next thing I knew, I was neck deep in snow."

"Every copper-haired, green-eyed Fräulein should be covered with snow," said Slater. "It's very becoming."

"Dankeschoen!" Ilse looked up at him expectantly.

"Bitte schoen!" Bill was about to take her in his arms when

they were both startled by someone shouting, "Track!" They got off the trail just as a skier rushed past them and stopped in a violent christy about twenty yards beyond. Bill immediately recognized the green and white sweater. It was Wyman.

Bill got back on the trail and walked down to his skis, wondering how the devil he and Ilse had passed him. There were no turnoffs. Either Wyman had something special to do, someone to meet, or that conversation at the top of the trail between him and Ilse was deliberately staged and Ilse had been left behind to find out more about the brown-haired American who had tried to get her ticket.

Bill was angry with himself. He had no business flirting with some Fräulein, even if she was beautiful—especially if she was beautiful. He put on his skis and started off without a word, letting himself go wide open the rest of the way down through the timber, out onto the steep open slopes, past a wooden goatherder's hut and down again over the practice slope. He turned in his skis at the red rental shack and walked to the hotel. There were things he had to do. He couldn't fritter away his time, skiing all over Kitzbühel.

Chapter 5

Back at the hotel, he changed into Carmichael's clothes again and found his way through the back streets to the Eggerwirt, the pension at which Webber had stayed.

The little back streets were slushy, and Bill had to share them with horse-drawn carts and hand-drawn sleds with wooden runners. The boardinghouse was just beyond a sawmill. The Eggerwirt was typical of the hundred or so pensions in Kitzbühel: a steep roof with a foot of white frosting on top, scrollwork edging the roof and a wooden balcony on the second floor. Bill entered the main door, framed with stacked skis, and went along a corridor to a door with a small sign which read "Büro!" He knocked on the office door, and a gaunt young man with steel-rimmed spectacles told him there were no vacancies.

"I'm not looking for a room," said Bill. "I'm looking for a friend by the name of Heinz Mahler. I had a letter from him a week ago. I wondered if he was still here."

"One moment." The young man was old before his time. He shambled, stoop-shouldered, to a wooden file in the corner and took out a folder. Bill wondered how a young man who lived in a place like Kitzbühel could be so pale and unhealthy looking.

"Yes," he said, looking up from the folder, "just as I thought. Herr Mahler is here, but he intends to check out at noon today. He should be here at any—ah," he looked over Slater's shoulder, "here comes your friend now. Good afternoon, Herr Mahler. I have a pleasant surprise for you."

Slater turned around and broke in quickly, his back to the proprietor. "Hello, Heinz! A good friend of ours told me I would find you here. I hope we have time for a drink before you leave." Mahler looked perplexed. "We have a lot to talk over," Slater added.

"Yes, we have," Mahler said slowly. He knew this tall man must have some connection with Charlie Webber, but he'd expected an American, not a German. Mahler looked at Carmichael's clothing. Nothing visible appeared typically German, but, on the other hand, his clothes didn't look particularly American. Mahler was on his guard.

"May I have another hour before check-out time, Herr Nadler?" Mahler asked.

"Yes, yes, of course. Perhaps your friend will convince you to stay with us a little longer?" Nadler added.

Bill expected to see Nadler rubbing his hands.

"Come, Heinz," said Bill. "I will show you a little café I have already discovered."

"I see you haven't changed a bit," said Mahler, and the two men left the pension and walked back past the sawmill toward the main street.

Neither man said anything until they had gone a couple of hundred yards from the house. In ski clothes, Mahler looked at the moment much more like an American than Slater. Mahler was well under six feet, had black, short, curly hair above a wide forehead, and regular, smallish features. His build was athletic and wiry. Slater thought he was probably in his early thirties.

"Well, Herr—"

"Carmichael," said Bill.

"What do you want from me?"

"Can you speak English, Herr Mahler?"

"Only a little. I am still learning." Mahler frowned. "You are an American then?"

"Yes. I am a friend of Charlie Webber's," said Bill.

"A friend," Mahler smiled, "or an enemy?"

Slater looked thoughtfully at Mahler, trying to make up his mind how far he could trust him. In ten years of counterespionage, Slater had not found any sure way to eliminate all the guesswork. There were times when you had to operate by intuition alone. If you didn't show trust in a man when you should, you couldn't win his confidence later, and you couldn't tell him enough of the truth to make him sufficiently useful. If your impulse was wrong, and you exposed yourself to an enemy, well, that was that.

"Look here, Mahler," said Slater, "I don't know anything about you, beyond what Webber said in his letter to Putnam. Webber apparently liked and trusted you."

"He had good reason to trust me."

"Where is Webber now?" Slater asked.

"I don't know." Mahler appeared surprised at the question.

"What do you know, Mahler?"

"I know only that I have never seen you before, that you talk exactly like a German. Webber is an American. As far as I know, Herr Carmichael, I was the only German friend he had."

"You also know now," said Slater, "that I have read Webber's letter; otherwise I couldn't have known about you."

"I didn't read the letter!" Mahler was indignant. "I only mailed it. You could have intercepted—or stolen it."

"True, Mahler," said Slater, his mind made up, "I could have, but I didn't, and I am an American." Slater produced Carmichael's passport. "You've seen enough of these at the Bundesbahn Hotel to know the genuine article."

Mahler looked it over carefully. "You still could be working against Webber." Mahler's glance was shrewd. "Another American was."

"Do you know his name?" Slater asked quickly.

"No. And I don't know his reasons for disliking Webber."

"Did Webber tell you where he was going?"

Mahler hesitated, and then said, "Yes. He said he was going back to the American Consulate in Zurich."

"Did you know that he never got there?"

"I assumed that he did not."

"Why?" asked Bill. "How could you have assumed that?"

"He promised to send me a card, if he had made it." Mahler paused. "I never received that card."

Slater tried to think of a way to establish himself with Mahler. Europeans were much less gullible than Americans, and Mahler wasn't going to be easy to convince. Slater tried again.

"Why, if you know that Webber is missing, do you suspect me? The fact that I am trying to find him should be proof that I mean him no harm."

"Because I know," said Mahler, "you are not his personal friend."

"True," said Slater, "but I'm not his enemy and I must find him."

"Then why don't you produce some official papers and tell me you're from the American police or something? After all," Mahler continued, "Webber is an official in your Foreign Office."

Mahler might look American, Slater reflected, but his respect for official papers was German to the core.

"Look, Mahler," said Slater, shaking his head, "you've got

to trust me! You're the only direct contact with Webber I know. As for the lack of papers, let us say that my government prefers, for the moment anyway, not to do anything in an official way."

"Why?"

Slater looked at Mahler's serious, stubborn face, looked desperately at the sky, and suddenly began to laugh.

"Dammit to hell, Mahler. You are the most stubborn man I've ever met. To use a favorite expression of mine, you are a pistol!"

"I am a—revolver?" Mahler looked perplexed. "What kind of an expression is that?"

"Never mind." Slater laughed harder than ever. "Look," he said finally, "Webber's enemy is a man named Wyman who also works in the Zurich Consulate. Charlie Webber had reason to believe that Wyman was working for another government, and followed him down here to make sure. Wyman must have gotten suspicious and had Webber tailed. Now Webber has disappeared. I have been assigned by my government to find out what happened and why."

"Wyman was working with Communists?" asked Mahler.

"Presumably, but so far there is no positive proof that he's doing anything wrong. The United States wouldn't exactly care to announce to the world that one of the members of its Foreign Service has been kidnaped by another member who is a Communist agent."

"Yes," Mahler nodded slowly, "I can see that." He looked up at Slater. "You were afraid I might be a Communist."

"We have them in our country," said Slater.

"Did Charlie say in his letter that I was a—"

"—a prisoner of war in Russia," Slater finished the question. "Yes, he did. POW's have been brain-washed."

"Not this one." Heinz Mahler smiled for the first time. The smile made him look very boyish. "I will do anything I can to help, Herr Carmichael, but I don't see what I can do. I have to go back to my job."

"Can you possibly extend your vacation?"

"Perhaps," said Mahler, "but I have no money."

"Don't worry about money. I'll take care of that."

"I don't want your money," Mahler said quickly. "Charlie Webber is my friend, and," he smiled again, "I'm not very impressed with Communism."

"Neither am I, Heinz," said Slater, "but I get paid. People still have to live."

"What do you want me to do?" asked Mahler.

"Well," Slater smiled, "you might start off by answering some of my questions for a change." They both laughed at that.

"I have no idea where Charlie is now," Mahler began, "but I do know the name of one of the men who was following him."

"The one who lived at the Eggerwirt?"

"Yes. He is called Stadler, Fritz Stadler. He has a German passport."

"Webber described him," said Slater, "as having a face like a waxed apple."

"Is that another American expression?"

"No," Slater chuckled.

"I like your American expressions. I don't understand them, but they're very comical," said Mahler.

"They gain something in translation." Slater smiled. "Is Stadler still at the inn?"

"Yes. He seems to be staying indefinitely."

"Would you say that he is keeping an eye on you?"

"I don't think so, but I don't know. I've seen him talking with the other man Charlie suspected. I don't know his name, but he is also here."

Slater tried to assess what little information he now had.

One thing was certain, he and Heinz Mahler had to organize their meeting times and places. Fortunately, on this occasion, the weather was beautiful, and a noontime stroll through the small back streets of the town was as good a way to get acquainted as any. Stadler and his rustic friend must be at least aware of Mahler, so there wouldn't be much use in his trying to follow them; but Mahler could call him and let him know when Stadler was in or had just left. Slater debated telling Mahler of his dual existence, but decided to wait.

Finally, Slater said, "I will be at the Winterhof Hotel this evening. I expect to enter the dining room with Wyman, if possible. If I'm not with him, I will arrange to sit near him. I will find some way to point him out to you. To cover all possible times, I want you to be there, preferably at the center table, from six P.M. on until, let's say, nine o'clock. If I haven't shown up by then, forget about me.

"Tomorrow, if things go as scheduled, I will phone you and tell you what time I plan to go skiing. That will mean that Wyman has just left in his ski clothes. Incidentally, he wears black ski pants and a green and white ski sweater. I want you to go, as quickly as possible, to the red ski-rental shack near the practice slope and pick him up there. I want you to follow him and try and remember everyone he talks to, and what trails he takes."

Heinz Mahler repeated the instructions carefully.

"One more thing, Mahler," said Slater. "If you have a girl friend, it would be better if you could bring her along tonight —and tomorrow as well, if she's a good skier. On second thought," Slater continued, "you'd better bring a different one tomorrow, if you can arrange it." He grinned.

"There are plenty," Mahler smiled. "Anyhow, those who are good skiers eat too much."

"I'm happy to know," said Slater, "that I didn't exhaust your supply of girl friends."

"That's not easy to do with a Rhinelander." Mahler made a low graceful bow.

Slater found himself returning it.

"Here's some money," said Slater. "I'll see you this evening."

Mahler took the money reluctantly.

"Don't you want a receipt?" he asked.

"No," Bill smiled. "This is tax free."

Mahler grinned and turned back down the narrow street. He waved and disappeared around the corner.

Slater stared after him for a few moments. Receipts were sometimes valuable. They were proof that a man had worked for you and could constitute a hold for the continuation of his services. Slater believed that, for the present at least, Mahler was acting out of sympathy for a friend and possibly ideologically against Communism, but that could change should some more important motivation or pressure come along. Suppose the German government had its own ax to grind and requested Mahler to act for his country in some way counter to United States' interests? Suppose money was offered by any other government? Money was the greatest temptation of all. A man in Mahler's position, as desk clerk at a crossroads hotel, could be very useful to a lot of people. He should have asked for a receipt. The threat of giving it to the appropriate German authorities, as proof that Mahler was working for a foreign power, might deter him from acting contrary to Slater's wishes, and it might secure Mahler's services in the future.

Slater shook his head and turned back toward his hotel. This was a dirty business, and he must be getting soft, but he had always believed that it was much better to motivate a man positively than negatively with potential threats. He differed in this aspect of his profession with some of the best operators in the business.

Chapter 6

At seven o'clock that evening, Wyman entered the dining room alone and was conducted to an empty table. Slater entered less than a minute later and looked for Mahler. He was seated at the center table talking to a very busty blonde German girl with a peaches-and-cream complexion. Slater stood in the entryway until he caught Mahler's attention and then asked the waiter to show him to Wyman's table. The dining room was almost full and there was nothing unusual in Slater's request, since the custom in Europe was to fill up every available seat.

"Excuse me," said Slater, as Wyman looked up, "I hope you don't mind my joining you." Slater appeared to hesitate. "You are an American, aren't you?"

"Yes." Wyman looked annoyed. Slater didn't seem to notice.

"My name's Carmichael, Bruce Carmichael. I'm over here on a buying trip—leather business. What's your business?"

"My own," said Wyman dryly.

"Nothing like being your own man, I always say." Slater looked cautiously around the room. "Confidentially, I'm really here on a pleasure trip. My father owns the department stores—at least he will be the owner. He runs them for my grandfather. They think I'm an idiot, and they just wanted to get me out of the way, but," Slater's smile was positively ingenuous, "I'm not so dumb." He looked very smug.

Wyman inspected Slater. The "department stores" hadn't landed on deaf ears.

"My name is Ronald Wyman. I'm vice-consul at the American Consulate in Zurich."

"A diplomat! Well, this is an honor, Mr. Wyman."

"Thank you, Mr. Carmichael, but I'd much rather own some department stores." Wyman's smile was charming.

"Why, for heaven's sake? It's terribly dull."

"There's more money in it."

"Money isnt everything, you know," said Slater cheerfully. He could tell that Wyman was growling inwardly at his fatuous remark.

The headwaiter was nearby, and Wyman signaled him.

"Rüdi," said Wyman, "I want you to take my order personally. I want to make certain I get better service than I did this morning."

"Yes, sir. I'll be happy to take your order." Rüdi appeared very uncomfortable.

Slater noticed that he seemed to bulge all over. His collar was too tight, and his body strained at every button. He had a face like a great chunk of dough.

"I want whatever you recommend, Rüdi," Wyman smiled. "I'll leave everything in your hands."

"Yes, sir. A chateaubriand, perhaps, medium rare, and a bottle of dry red wine, Beaujolais."

"Sounds excellent, Rüdi," said Wyman, "except for the wine. I would prefer a bottle of Tuborg beer."

"Ah—yes, sir—," Rüdi hesitated.

Slater had been watching him carefully. Something had happened between Rüdi and Wyman that had suddenly changed their relationship. For the moment, whatever it was escaped Slater.

"And what would you like to order, sir?" Rüdi turned to Slater.

"Steak sounds fine, but I would prefer that dry red wine you were talking about."

"Yes, sir." Rüdi appeared relieved. It was difficult to tell exactly, but Slater thought that Wyman also appeared relieved.

Slater leaned across the table after Rüdi had left and said to Wyman in a stage whisper, "These Kraut waiters are an obsequious bunch. No wonder we beat them in a war."

Several heads turned in their direction. Slater was pleased to note that Wyman actually looked embarrased.

"Do you ski, Mr. Carmichael?" Wyman asked stiffly.

"No. Who wants to ski?" said Carmichael. "I came here to find something young and tender. I like some of those English girls I've noticed around here."

"What's the matter with the German girls?" asked Wyman.

"They're too fat. They look too much like peasants–thick ankles, big feet, heavy arms. I wouldn't mind having one for a maid—if you get what I mean?" Slater practically cackled.

Wyman winced, and Slater decided he'd better not overdo this rich moron, but he was beginning to get a kick out of making Wyman uncomfortable in public.

Wyman looked across the dining room and, suddenly, stood up. "Excuse me, Carmichael, but I see someone I know. I want to see if she'll join us."

"Sure thing," said Slater.

He turned and watched Wyman intercept Ilse Wieland as she entered the dining room. The two of them stood near the entrance. From where Slater was sitting, it looked as though Wyman was pleading his cause and not doing very well. Finally, she appeared to accept reluctantly, and Wyman guided her over to their table. Slater stood up.

"This is Mr. Carmichael," said Wyman. "We just met this evening. May I present Miss Wieland. Miss Wieland," Wyman added pointedly, "is from Munich."

"How do you do, Miss Wieland," Slater said.

She was wearing a smartly tailored, dark wool dress that clung to her. In ski clothes, Ilse had looked a vibrant and healthily mature young woman, but now she looked very chic and smart, cool and self-assured.

"Mr. Carmichael was just telling me," said Wyman, "that he preferred English girls."

"Really, Mr. Carmichael?" Ilse turned her green eyes on Slater. "The English girls are very lovely." She turned back to Wyman. "I don't blame Mr. Carmichael."

Slater did. He was mentally kicking Carmichael all over the dining room. Carmichael could have been anybody. Why had he chosen to make him a fool? It was all right in front of Wyman, but not with Ilse Wieland looking on.

"Tell me, Miss Wieland," said Wyman, "what do you do in Munich?"

"I have a small dress shop," she said.

"Business must be good," said Slater, hating himself for the remark, but deciding that he must say something.

"Why?" Ilse looked at Slater questioningly.

"You can afford to take a vacation," said Slater.

"Austria is not expensive," she said.

"Not for an American," said Bill doggedly.

"Or a German." Ilse's tone was icily sweet.

Slater wondered if Wyman's apparent ignorance of Fräulein Wieland's history was just for his benefit. Certainly the implication was that they did not really know one another. Anyway, Slater was determined to play out his role.

"Switzerland," said Wyman, apparently trying to smooth

things over, "is very expensive for everyone, and it isn't as much fun as Austria."

"Have you ever been to Switzerland, Miss Wieland?" asked Slater.

"No, Mr. Carmichael, I'm afraid I haven't, but not," she added, "because business is poor."

"You Germans have made quite a comeback since the war," said Slater.

"The Germans," said Wyman hastily, "are a very industrious people."

"I wish I were industrious," said Slater, "but I simply can't make myself. No incentive, I guess."

"Incentive, Mr. Carmichael?" said Ilse very sweetly. "Or something else?"

"Most people," said Slater, "work for money. Since I have plenty of money, Miss Wieland, there is no point in my working, so," he added smugly, "I don't."

There was a lull in the conversation, and Slater could see that Wyman was definitely disgruntled. But he had proved his judgment of Wyman. Wyman, obviously, couldn't decide what to do. Ilse Wieland was a very desirable woman. On the other hand, a man with more money than brains was a contact he didn't want to lose. Slater was beginning to enjoy himself. He looked in the direction of the center table. Heinz Mahler and the busty blonde with the peaches-and-cream complexion were gone, and an older couple were being seated. The man was built like a barrel. Slater noticed his hands as he reached for the napkin. They were enormous, and the fingers were fat and without any apparent joints. They curved like sausages when he grasped the napkin. His bright blue eyes were almost concealed in the flesh of his face. His mouth was ultra sensual, and Slater noticed that the man was continually licking his thick lips. The woman was considerably younger and quite thin.

"That," said Wyman, "is the Baron von Burgdorf." Wyman smiled in his direction and received a friendly nod.

"Who is the Baron von Burgdorf?" asked Ilse. Slater was very interested himself.

"Yes," he said, "I've always wanted to meet a real baron."

"This one is real all right," said Wyman. "His family haven't worked for generations. They made their money from beer."

"He's a good advertisement for his product," said Slater.

Ilse glanced at Slater. The comment was out of character for Carmichael, and she seemed to notice it. Slater determined to be more careful. "He's built like a beer barrel," he added.

"You should see his place outside of Munich," said Wyman, ignoring the reference to von Burgdorf's shape. "It's like a castle."

So this, thought Slater, must be the contact in Munich that Wyman had mentioned at the bar of the Baur-au-Lac Hotel.

"The Baron," Wyman continued, "has been spending the last two months here. He throws a good many parties."

"Who is the woman with him?" asked Ilse.

"I've never seen her before," said Wyman. "The Baron isn't married, and none of his women last very long."

If he picked on such little ones, thought Slater, it was no wonder. The beer baron must have weighed all of three hundred pounds.

Wyman had signaled for Rüdi, and the waiter arrived with the check and set it beside Wyman. Slater started to reach for it, but Wyman beat him to it.

"Allow me," he said and smiled. Slater shrugged his shoulders. This was out of character. He would have bet a month's salary that Wyman would have juggled the check back to him, but he would have lost.

Wyman signed the bill and put down his room number.

Rüdi looked at the signature, thanked Wyman very much and left.

"Are you ready, Miss Wieland," asked Wyman, "to let me show you around Kitzbühel?"

"Thank you, Mr. Wyman," she said. "The dinner was delightful, but I want to get to bed as I plan to get up early for the skiing tomorrow."

Ilse stood up and so did the two men. She turned to Slater.

"It's been a pleasure, Mr. Carmichael." She looked up at him and smiled. "You are deceptively tall." She offered her hand, and Slater shook it. Her grip was strong. There was something about her smile that made him feel uncomfortable. She thanked Wyman for the dinner, and the two men watched her move off between the tables.

"Do you still prefer English women?" Wyman asked.

It was a question that didn't require an answer, and Slater didn't give one. Wyman grinned.

"There's something about European women, particularly German women, that is irresistible," said Wyman. "They're feminine, of course, but they don't really flirt. There's an intensity about them. They seem to take your measure. If they like what they see, they let you know it unmistakably; and you're hooked."

Slater thought that was a remarkably sage observation. It came very close to paralleling his own feelings. An American woman endangered a man's independence, because she was so demanding and independent. The European was a threat for opposite reasons. Anyway, he thought, there was no room in his life for Ilse Wieland, no matter how irresistible she might be.

He wondered what she meant by his being deceptively tall. Slater knew that it was more difficult to maintain a disguise when there was a woman involved. A woman noticed so many things like the color of a man's eyes, the shape of his hands.

The voice was the toughest problem. Fortunately, Slater had spoken to Ilse mostly in German, and that helped to change his inflection as well as the sound of his voice. But he could change his voice when necessary.

"Would you care to meet the Baron, Mr. Carmichael?" asked Wyman.

"Very much," said Slater. "Maybe he can give me some advice."

"Advice?" Wyman frowned. "On what?'

"In America a man who doesn't work for a living is generally looked down on," said Slater. "Here a man in the same position is apparently looked up to."

Wyman laughed. "Just jealousy in the States," he said.

The Baron von Burgdorf didn't stand up when the two men approached, but he was very gracious and invited them to sit down, which Wyman did immediately. Frau Waldecker was a sour young woman and was obviously displeased at the interruption. Slater noticed that the entire dining room seemed interested in their conversation.

"I am having a party Monday night, Mr. Carmichael. I would be honored if you would attend."

"Thank you, Baron," said Slater. "I would be delighted."

"I am giving the party at the Hotel Ehrenbachhöhe."

"That's on top of the mountain to the right of the cable-car station," said Wyman. "Better be prepared to stay all night."

"Sounds like quite a party," said Slater.

"All of the Barons parties are unusual." Wyman's tone was proprietary. He spoke smugly, as though the Baron's party were his party.

"Well, good night, Frau Waldecker, Baron. It's been a pleasure." Slater turned to Wyman. "Thank you for the dinner."

Slater went into the bar. He ordered a brandy and asked the waiter to find Rüdi. He sipped his brandy and wondered if what he was about to do would produce any results. Procedure was very important in espionage activities, and Slater was extremely sensitive to any exchange that sounded rehearsed.

Rüdi came up to him, and Slater took him to one side.

"Yes, sir," said Rüdi. "May I help you?"

"Rüdi," Slater began seriously, "I meant to ask for you earlier tonight and put myself entirely in your hands."

Rüdi frowned and looked puzzled.

Slater began to doubt his approach, but he continued, "I would have asked for Tuborg beer instead of wine." Slater paused and looked carefully at Rüdi. Rüdi was silent. "I would have signed for the check with my name and room number, Rüdi."

"Why didn't you—sir?" Rüdi had almost forgotten his position.

"Apparently," said Slater slowly, "there were two of us."

"I see," he said. "Excuse me, sir, but," Rüdi hesitated. His dough-white face looked strained. "This is highly unusual."

"Coincidences are rare, Rüdi," said Slater smoothly, "but they do happen."

"Yes, sir." Rüdi wiped his forehead. The handkerchief came away moist. "What is your room number, sir?"

"Twenty-three."

"Thank you," Rüdi said, and he left.

Slater turned back to the bar and ordered another brandy. "I plugged in something, all right," he thought. "The trouble is, I don't have the faintest idea what it was!" He shook his head.

"Excuse me."

Slater turned to the voice.

"Please forgive me, but aren't you an American?" The man who had addressed him was terribly British and abnormally thin. Slater thought the man was built like a pencil.

"That's what it says on my passport." Slater looked bored.

"Oh, really, that's awfully good." The pencil laughed. Slater winced at the sound. The man actually giggled. His clothes were very expensive. There wasn't a wrinkle anywhere. They reminded Slater of a freshly pressed suit that was still on a wire hanger. Nothing seemed to fill them out.

"You Americans are really the limit! May I buy you a drink? I rarely have the opportunity to chat with an American."

"You mean you want to practice your English," said Slater dryly.

The pencil looked blank for a moment and then started to giggle again. Slater began to feel the contagion of the man's laughter. "Practice my English! If you keep on at this rate, you won't have to buy another drink all night. My name is Hormsby, Phillip Hormsby. What's yours?"

"Scotch and soda," said Slater. This was a bit wearing. If he was going to keep it up, he would need a Scotch. Besides, he thought, I've got to hear him laugh again.

"Scotch and soda?" Hormsby looked puzzled.

"You want one also," said Slater. "Make it two then."

Hormsby had finally connected, and his inane giggle made everyone at the bar look at them. That giggle was too much for Slater. He couldn't hold himself in any longer, and the tears rolled down his cheeks as he rocked with laughter. Their duet began to take its toll of the bystanders, and, eventually, the whole place was in an uproar.

"I think," yelled Slater over the laughter, "that we are a lethal combination. If you'll excuse me, I'll go to bed so I can survive until tomorrow. Good night, Mr. Hormsby." And Slater fled.

Chapter 7

Slater had several things to attend to before changing his clothes and starting his investigation of Kitzbühel's night life. He had already decided to go as himself.

He wrote a letter to Paris requesting information on Heinz Mahler, Erich Nadler of the Eggerwirt, Rüdi Petsch, Anton Reisch, the desk clerk, Baron von Burgdorf, Frau Waldecker, Ilse Wieland, Fritz Stadler, one of the men who had been watching Webber, and Phillip Hormsby. The last name was added almost as an afterthought, but so many important things stemmed from simple coincidences in his business that Slater no longer overlooked any possibility. When he had finished his cover letter and signed it, "as ever, Ben," and written Heinz Mahler's name and pension as the return address, he put down his pen and frowned.

Slater realized he didn't have an adequate support set up; but the more people he rang in on this problem, the more people there would be who might compromise him. The big trouble with the mail was that it was too slow. By the time he got what he needed, it might be too late. Moreover, there wasn't enough room in an average letter for him either to ask or receive enough information. He sealed the letter in an envelope with another return address and a fictitious name and put it in his sport jacket. He got into his own clothes and carefully packed up all traces of Carmichael in his aluminum suitcase. The suitcase had a false bottom that probably would not fool anyone in his profession but getting into the bag in the first place should take quite a while. He had had an additional combination lock of his own design installed on the suitcase some years ago by a locksmith in New York. The man had been a real craftsman and had installed three tiny dials edgewise and almost flush with the cover. These he had concealed with a well-known brass trade-mark, which looked to the casual observer as though it had been riveted onto the suitcase. The conventional snap lock had been left in place; and any intruder would have a difficult problem with that one, as it had a pin-tumbler lock and was consequently difficult to pick. Slater had selected an aluminum suitcase because of its fire resistance. He closed up the suitcase, turned the key in the conventional lock and then moved the dials and screwed on the trade-mark plate.

He went downstairs past the desk with his room key in his pocket. He had very nearly turned in the key. If Anton had taken it without connecting the face with the room number, he would still have had a hell of a time getting back into his room. In spite of all the years of dual, and sometimes triple existences, it was still so easy to forget. Slater began to sweat at the thought of what he had almost done. "You're Slater, you idiot," he said to himself. "That's Carmichael's key you were about to give away."

There was an advantage in keeping your room key. No one could be certain that you were out. Slater went into the street. The night was cold and dry. The slush had frozen into ridges along the narrow sidewalks. He inhaled deeply and could feel the air's icy fingers probing deep into his chest. He breathed in heavily several times. He turned to go toward the cafés he had seen advertised in the hotel when he noticed the menu behind a lighted glass on the outside wall. Tomorrow's menu already, he thought. Such efficiency! However, Slater liked the European idea of posting the menu outside a restaurant or a hotel. You knew not only what they served, before you went in, but the prices. Slater started down the sidewalk and suddenly turned back. Rüdi had asked for his room number, not his name. Whatever the exchange between Wyman and Rüdi had meant, the number of the room was obviously vital. Slater had to let the desk clerk know somehow that Carmichael was not in his room. He re-entered the lobby and went to the desk. Anton was not there. I'm getting some luck, he thought, in spite of all my blunders.

"I was looking for Mr. Carmichael," said Slater to the clerk on duty.

The clerk was a young man. He hadn't had time, as yet, to acquire Anton's tired look. He turned to the register and then looked at the rack.

"Room twenty-three," he said. "His key is not in the rack, sir. He must be in his room. I will ring him for you." The clerk picked up the house phone, but got no results. "I'm very sorry, sir," he said, shaking his head. "He must have gone out and forgotten to leave his key. A lot of people forget. Can I take a message?"

"No," said Slater slowly. "I'll probably run into him at one of the cafés. He told me to meet him at the Café des Engels, if I didn't find him in. Thank you."

"Quite all right, sir."

Slater went out into the street again. He had picked out the Café des Engels from a poster on the wall. The Café des Engels it shall be, he thought, and headed in the direction of the Hinterststrasse. He liked these small Alpine villages with their narrow, complicated, cobblestoned streets. The sidewalks, except on the main street, were too narrow to walk on and everyone walked in the street. The side of the town behind the Winterhof had no sidewalks. Slater passed several couples and groups of six and eight people. Almost none of the men wore overcoats, and everyone was obviously having such a good time that Slater felt quite alone. The languages, mixed so by the number of nationalities, sounded to Slater like a potpourri of unintelligible gaiety.

The Café des Engels was packed. Slater felt he could have blown smoke rings from the inhaled atmosphere. The lighting was dim, and the couples on the dance floor seemed to be standing still. The music was supplied by a three-piece orchestra. He could hear the zither above the piano and the drums. The ubiquitous zither. Ever since the movie *The Third Man,* the European café owners must have decided that tourists from across the Atlantic expected to hear a zither, so a zither was what they heard—all over Europe.

Slater managed to squeeze himself into a place near the bar and order a cognac. He leaned his back against the stool and turned to examine the crowd. It was difficult to see in the smoke-blued gloom, but there was no mistaking the copper-red hair. Slater was immediately aware of a feeling of excitement within him. His pulse quickened. What's the matter with you, Slater, he muttered to himself. She's just a woman. Odd, she had told Wyman she was going to bed.

Slater watched her talking with some man. His back was toward Slater, so he couldn't tell what the man looked like; but he had Wyman's build. He turned, and for a moment Slater caught a glimpse of the man's face. It wasn't Wyman. The man was definitely European, somewhere in his late forties, Slater thought.

Slater left the bar, still carrying his glass, and started through the crowd toward Ilse. He noticed that she didn't seem to be getting along too well with her partner. He appeared to be one of those creeping conversationalists. He kept moving toward her as he talked, and she, in turn, kept backing up. She backed into Slater just as he was circling two people to get to her. His glass tipped and spilled cognac on her shoulder.

"Excuse me!" said Slater. "I was trying to get to you, but you zigged when I zagged."

Ilse turned and looked up at Slater. "Oh," she said, "it's you. I wondered where you were. It's too crowded here after all. Let's go somewhere else, Liebchen."

"All right," said Slater. "It really is terribly crowded." He turned to have a better look at the man she was either trying to get away from or, for some reason, didn't want him to meet. "I don't believe," said Slater, "that I have had the honor."

"Oh, excuse me, Liebchen." Ilse's eyes glinted at Slater's like those of an angry cat. "Herr Slater, I would like you to meet—Herr Krüpl."

Slater nodded and shook hands. Herr Krüpl had an indentation the size of a golf ball in the left side of his forehead. The result, thought Slater, of a very bad head wound. It gave his face a decidedly lopsided look, and his left eye didn't appear to have any eyelashes and looked abnormally large. Herr Krüpl muttered the formalities and left. Slater looked after him thinking that there was a face in a million—a face that no one could ever forget. He turned back to Ilse.

"Sorry to spill my drink on you," he said. "do you want me to take you someplace? I don't think it's necessary now," Slater added. "Herr—whatever his name was—won't bother you any more."

"Thank you, Herr Slater," she said, "for coming to my rescue. He is a terrible man."

"He's no oil painting," Slater shook his head, "I'll say that."

Ilse laughed. "It's not his looks that I don't like. It's the way he acts."

"Who is he?"

"I don't know. I've seen him here and there a few times. He's always so crude. The way he looks at me makes me feel like some animal."

"Well," said Slater, "I guess I'd better leave you to your own plans." He started to leave.

"Wait!" Ilse put her hand on his arm. Slater turned and looked at her. "You have the habit of always running away," she said. "I don't understand. Don't you like me, Herr Slater?"

Ilse was frowning and looking anxiously at Slater. He wasn't sure what to say. Surely she must know of her feminine power. She had to know. Power like hers couldn't possibly be a secret.

"Fräulein Wieland," his tone was unintentionally stern, "since I'm not made of stone, of course I like you."

"Well," she started, but his eyes stopped her and she was momentarily confused. "You don't have to look so angry about it."

She tried to go on and say something else, but he just kept staring at her.

"Look," she said finally, "I can hardly breathe in here, it's so close and crowded. Please, take me outside anyway—and then we can decide where to go."

Ilse took Slater's hand and pulled him to the checkroom and got her coat.

"Do you have a coat?" she asked. Slater shook his head.

"Well," she said, "let's go."

"Now," she said, when they were outside breathing in the sweet clean air, "if you want to run away from me again, you may."

Run away, Slater thought. That was it. For ten years he'd been running away. Ilse might be an agent. She was keeping bad company. Every instinct that it had taken years of hard work to develop told him to leave this woman alone.

"I don't want to run away." Slater heard himself as he said

it. It didn't take long for the accompanying smile to be really his. "I like you very much, Ilse Wieland."

Ilse took his hand.

"You should smile more often, William Slater. It becomes you."

She slipped her arm through Slater's, and they walked through the quiet streets to the outskirts of the village. Here, the darkness of the night descended to the snow, unimpeded by any lights. Ilse was only a shadow beside him. He should have felt more relaxed, now that he could no longer see her face; but even her shadow was vibrant.

"Aren't you cold without an overcoat?" she asked. Her voice seemed awfully close.

"No," he said. "The air is so dry that it doesn't seem very cold. What about you, Ilse? Are you warm enough?"

"Oh, yes. I could walk like this forever. Please, tell me about yourself."

Slater was immediately on guard. He'd been waiting for the question.

"I'd rather hear about you," he said.

"There isn't much to say about me." He could feel her shrug. "I have a small dress shop in Munich. My father was a professor of philosophy at the University before the war. Both he and my mother were killed in an air raid. My brother was a Nazi SS officer and was killed on the Russian front. After the war I had a difficult time because I was suspected of having been a member of the Nazi party."

"Were you?" Bill asked.

"Yes," she said.

Slater was pleased, not to discover that she had been a Nazi, but that she at least admitted it. If he were to believe all the Germans he had met, there wasn't a Nazi among them. They all denied any previous affiliation.

"Are you a Nazi still?"

"No. It was pretty exciting in the beginning. To be told that you were of the generation and race that would inherit the earth, that your only crime would be to deny your heritage and your country, to be encouraged to develop your body in all the wonderful sports, to walk beside your men to victory all over the world."

Slater was interested. He had never heard what National Socialism had appealed to in the German youth expressed by one of them.

"I watched Germany grow," she continued. "I mean before the invasions. I saw my country become prosperous and expand the highways. I listened to the young soldiers singing as they marched in the streets."

"What changed your mind?"

"Many things," she said. "My father was against Hitler from the beginning. He tried to explain the inconsistencies, lies and inhumanity of Nazi philosophy, but he did it on such an intellectual plane I didn't really understand him at first. He and my brother had terrible arguments. And then I went with my brother to several parties. He deliberately tried to pair me off with his superior officer. The man was a beast. He made me feel that I was there only to satisfy his lusts. That, he said, was the function of all German women. He struck me; and when I tried to strike back, my brother slapped my face. And there were others." Ilse paused and then said quietly, "The final blow was the death of my parents."

"I think," said Slater, "we'd better turn back now."

"Yes," she said. "You must be cold."

They turned around and looked down at the twinkling lights of Kitzbühel. They had been going gradually uphill and had not realized it. "On the outside, looking in," said Ilse. "That's the way it has been for me most of my life. It's not so bad when you're with someone." She hugged Slater's arm.

"I've been feeling that way for some years," he said.

Slater looked down at the village. It was a place where people belonged—no matter how temporarily. They were together, laughing, arguing, loving, hating perhaps, but they were on the inside. He and Ilse were on the outside.

"Why haven't you married?" said Bill, "or do you detest all men because of your brother's friends?"

"I don't detest men," Ilse laughed. "I want to get married, but as you Americans say, I guess I have just not found the right one.'

"You will." It wasn't what he wanted to say, and he suddenly got the impression that it wasn't what Ilse wanted to hear.

The two trudged in silence along the black road between the high banks of snow. Ilse had removed her arm from his and was carefully skirting the patches of ice, but her high heels caused her to slip on one of the rutty places. Slater grabbed her, and they were together, arm in arm, again. When they walked between the first street lights and Ilse tried gently to disengage her arm, Slater held it. She gave up any further attempt to free herself.

They entered the hotel and walked to the desk. The young clerk was still on duty. He handed Ilse her key and turned to Slater.

"Did you find Mr. Carmichael, sir?"

Slater could have shot him.

"No."

"I don't believe he's come in yet, sir. At least I haven't seen him."

Ilse was standing, key in hand, regarding Slater with interest. "Do you know Mr. Carmichael? I met him this evening."

"I only met him recently."

Ilse turned and started up the stairs. She paused on the first stair and looked back. "Your friend Mr. Carmichael doesn't care for German women." She smiled. "I think, perhaps, you have something in common."

She laughed and disappeared upstairs.

Chapter 8

Slater turned and went back out into the night.

Did Ilse suspect that he and Carmichael were one and the same? It was difficult to fool a woman, especially one like Ilse. He would have liked to choke that clerk.

It was midnight, and he still had things to do. He found a telephone station and called Zurich.

"Hello, George?"

"Yes."

"Karl here. What time is it?"

"Midnight."

"Sorry to call so late, but I thought you'd like to know that I've checked in and our friend is here, but I've found no trace of Charlie. Any news at your end?"

"Yes, Karl. I think I've an idea about our friend's next job. When could we get together in Munich?"

Slater didn't answer right away. He didn't want to leave Kitzbühel for the time being. He decided he'd better try to break into clear conversation.

"I don't think I can get away just now. By the way, how is Horst?"

"He's been ill lately," said George.

"That's too bad," said Slater, "but I can't leave right now. I'd like to know what our boy's next assignment is going to be."

There was another lull while George tried to think of some way to state what he wanted to say.

"His employers," George began, "want him to meet someone, in his official capacity, whom we should be meeting."

"Is this person a man who would like to avoid our boy's employers?" Slater always felt foolish during these necessarily cryptic conversations. He was pleased, however, that George's Swiss German was so fluent.

"Definitely. He's a Hungarian colonel with the wrong ideology," said George.

"Contrary to our friend's employers'?"

"Yes. He flew the coop recently. They're looking for him and so are we. Your office has asked me to tell you that your Saxon friends are also trying to contact him."

"Are they working with or against us?"

"With. They knew he was going to make a break and sent a man to meet him where you are, but that man has disappeared. I believe they have someone else down there now."

"Can you find out who?" asked Slater.

"I tried to, but they wouldn't say. They're afraid to tell anyone."

"Try again," said Slater. "I've got to know."

"Right."

"Why is this man so important to everyone?"

"I don't know exactly," said George. "He has some special information which he will trade for our protection and asylum. Your office said it was extremely important."

"I see." Slater paused. "It's bad form, but you better tell me his name."

"Imré Dinar," said George.

"Never heard of him. Have you a description?"

"Six feet tall, heavy set, bushy eyebrows, gray hair, in his fifties, has a mustache. As far as anyone knows, he's traveling alone," said George.

"Where would our friend fit in?" asked Slater.

"Your office thinks he may be used to convince the Colonel that his employers are our employers."

It was a definite possibility, thought Slater, provided the Communists didn't know whatever it was that Dinar knew. If they could convince Dinar, through Wyman, that they were American Intelligence officers, he would give them his information; and they could dispose of him afterward. This assignment was shaping up into something a lot bigger than Slater had anticipated.

"Anything else you want to tell me?" asked Slater.

"No," said George, "but do you want me to come down there? I've got a feeling you'll need help."

"Thank you, but you'd better stay put. I'll mail you my address. Find out at exactly what time your mail is delivered, and be there in person to collect it. If I need you, don't worry, I'll let you know."

"Good luck, Karl," said George.

"One more thing." Slater paused. "If you have to call me here at the address I will send you, please use a telephone station either in Germany or Austria."

"Right. Auf wiederhören, Karl."

"Auf wiederhören."

Slater hung up. He remained in the slim warmth of the sidewalk telephone station. He didn't believe anyone could have monitored the conversation at his end, and there was, as yet, no concrete reason he should be connected with Zurich. A phone call from Munich or Salzburg should appear innocent enough. The Swiss German would narrow down their listening audience.

He opened the glass door and walked to the corner. He took

the letter out of his pocket and mailed it. He would write another requesting any information on Herr Krüpl.

Slater entered the hotel by the back entrance. He waited out of sight of the desk clerk until his back was turned and went up the only stairs and entered his room—Carmichael's room, he reminded himself sourly.

He was more tired than he had thought, and he fell asleep the moment his head hit the pillow. He had first bolted his room from the inside. He didn't want to be taken by surprise as Slater in Carmichael's bed.

When he awoke it was after eight o'clock. He put on his heavy socks and slipped on his ski pants. He tried to put his right foot into his ski boot, but he couldn't get it in. There was something in the boot. He turned it upside down. An object fell out and rolled bumpily across the floor.

Slater bent over and picked it up, not believing that he held a roll of American ten-dollar bills. He counted seventeen—one hundred and seventy dollars. If this was what Wyman was selling out for, he was even less of a man than Slater thought. Slater took off his ski pants and heavy socks and put on Carmichael's clothes. He put the money he had found in his wallet and went downstairs to breakfast.

Wyman was at the same table he'd been at the morning before, and he motioned Slater to join him. Creature of habit, thought Slater, bad habit. He went over and sat down.

"Coming to the party tomorrow night?" Wyman asked. "You'll meet a lot of interesting people. I thought," he added smugly, "if I introduced you to the Baron, you would get an invitation."

"I'm looking forward to it." Slater added to himself, You pompous ass. He had said, "You'll meet a lot of interesting people," in the same way that a woman would have said, "My dear, everyone who is anyone will be there."

"Do people usually have parties on Monday nights in Europe?" asked Slater.

"No." Wyman laughed. "But when you have a large party on a Monday, you eliminate some of the riffraff—the weekend skiers. Besides," he added, "the Ehrenbachhöhe Hotel will not have to turn down so many reservations."

"You mean," said Slater, impressed in spite of himself, "that the Baron is taking over the entire hotel for this party!"

"Exactly."

"Aren't you going skiing today, Wyman?" Slater was surprised to see that Wyman didn't have his ski clothes on.

"Never go on Sunday. Much too crowded," said Wyman.

"I see."

"There'll be a line a mile long for the cable car."

Slater turned his head just in time to see Heinz Mahler enter the dining room. Slater was annoyed. Heinz had deliberately disobeyed orders. Mahler came closer to looking jaunty than any other German he had ever seen. There was something about his walk that indicated a happy-go-lucky vitality. The Rhinelanders had the reputation of being much more carefree than the rest of their countrymen. Slater hoped that Mahler wasn't too carefree.

Wyman had finished his breakfast and was obviously becoming restless.

"Don't wait for me, Wyman," said Slater. "I'm a slow eater, and I'm planning to write some letters this morning. Thought I might send my father some of those 'wish you were here' postcards."

"If you're sure you don't mind." Wyman stood up. "The Baron has invited me for some mid-morning refreshment."

"Not at all," said Slater. "Go right ahead."

Wyman left the dining room, and Slater fully expected Mahler to follow him. Instead, Heinz looked over at Slater and indicated that he wanted to come to the table. Slater shook his head, got up and headed for the men's room. Heinz took the hint and followed him.

The men's room was empty.

"Why didn't you follow Wyman?" asked Slater.

"I received a letter this morning I think you should see immediately." Heinz handed the letter to Slater. It was postmarked from Kitzbühel and was written in German on plain cheap stationery.

LIEBER HEINZ,

I hope this letter reaches you, as you are the only person I can trust. By now the Consulate must have received the letter you mailed for me and sent someone down here to find me.

I hate to admit it, but I'm afraid to expose myself to anyone, unless he can offer me some protection; but I am going crazy cooped up here, and I have very little money left. The man with whom I am staying will keep me hidden only so long as I pay him.

If you have been contacted by someone from my government, get in touch with him. Tell him to come any evening at 10 P.M. to the place indicated on the map.

Slater looked up from the letter. "Was there a map in this letter?" Heinz handed him a piece of a local map.

"This place is on the way up the Kitzbüheler Horn," he said. "I think you can drive a car up there all right, but the road is steep."

Slater returned to the letter.

Tell him to come in the front door; it will be open. He's to walk into the room on the right. I will be there. Have him come by car and be prepared to drive me to Zurich. Do not fail me, Heinz. I must be gotten away from here soon.

dein Freund,

CHARLIE

P.S.—Do not come yourself. You might be under surveillance.

Slater kept the map and returned the letter. He took out Webber's letter to Putnam and compared the handwriting. He showed them both to Heinz.

"What do you think, Heinz?"

"I think that's Charlie's handwriting," he said.

"So do I." Slater frowned. "But this letter poses a lot of interesting questions."

"Yes," Mahler said slowly. "For example, why did Charlie wait until now to contact me?"

"And why," Slater added, "did he think you might still be here?"

"I don't believe I told him when I was leaving," said Mahler.

"Why didn't he write to Putnam or some friend in the Consulate?"

"Maybe he was afraid that Wyman had some co-workers in Zurich."

Slater looked at Mahler carefully. "Smile when you say that, partner."

"Partner?" Heinz looked confused.

"Another American idiom," Slater smiled. "Does sound kind of silly in German."

Mahler shrugged. "Smile—partner," he muttered.

"What I meant," Slater said patiently, "was that one traitor per embassy is enough. Casting aspersions on the loyalty of our Foreign Service employees in general is neither fair nor accurate."

"Oh," said Heinz, "I meant no offense. Anyway," he added, "why didn't you say so in the first place?"

"I will in the future, Heinz, believe me," Slater laughed.

"Are you going?" asked Heinz.

"I have no choice." Slater shook his head.

"I will come with you," said Heinz.

"No. I'd like to have you, but Webber may be right. You might be under surveillance."

"I don't think so."

"I hope you're right, Heinz, but I want you to stay here and keep an eye on Wyman. Before we break this up," he continued, "if you get a letter from Paris, I want you to keep it for me—unopened."

"Yes, of course."

"Don't put it in another envelope and leave it for me at the desk. Either deliver it to me personally—or destroy it." Mahler nodded. "If I don't contact you by eighteen hundred tomorrow," Slater went on, "I want you to call this number."

Slater wrote Hollingsworth's home phone on a piece of the envelope and handed it to Heinz. "Ask for George and tell him that Carmichael has disappeared. And then," Slater added quietly, "you better get out of town—fast."

"Why?"

"Our Communist friends have a way of getting all the information a man has. They'll undoubtedly want you out of the way in any case."

"It would have been safer for me if I had ignored this letter," said Heinz matter-of-factly.

"Much," Slater nodded.

"I'm not sorry," he said slowly.

"You're a good man, McGee," said Slater.

"McGee?" said Heinz frowning. "What is McGee?"

"Oh, no!" said Slater. "I've done it again."

"Another American expression?" asked Mahler.

"Yes."

"Explain then—please. What is McGee?"

"McGee is a who, not a what. It's a man's name—a good man," said Slater desperately.

"Someone in the Bible, perhaps?"

"Not that good."

"Who, then?" Mahler was determined.

"An Irishman."

"What?"

"Look, please!" Slater was about to become hysterical. "Let's drop it, what do you say, please. McGee was just a great guy, that's all. It was just my way of saying how much I admire your courage."

"I see," said Heinz.

Slater couldn't be absolutely certain, but he thought he detected just the trace of a twinkle in Mahler's eye. He'd been had. The wiry little rascal had been joshing him along.

"Had you ever seen Wyman before last night?" asked Slater finally.

"No," said Heinz. "I don't think so."

"Good. Then the chances are he probably hasn't seen you, but you'd better be careful. Do you need some more money?"

"No, but I am traveling in more expensive circles since I met you, Herr Carmichael." Heinz smiled.

"Well," said Slater, "I'm going to give you some more money, anyhow. I want you to take all your meals at the hotel, and I want you to observe, carefully, all of the people whom Rüdi, the headwaiter, takes care of personally."

"Is there anything specially that I should be looking for?" asked Heinz.

"Listening for would be more accurate," said Slater. "I want you to listen, if you can, to any conversation between Rüdi and his customers. Let me know if you detect any similarities in their dialogue."

Slater wanted to say more, but decided against it. It didn't pay to condition a man's mind in advance, so that he would hear only what you expected him to hear.

The men's-room door opened, and Slater turned to the sink and started washing his hands. Mahler passed the man who had entered, and left immediately. Slater turned off the tap and wiped his hands while the man, whom he had never seen before, went into one of the stalls and shut the door. Slater waited patiently for the sounds that would indicate the stranger's sincerity and left a moment later, muttering to himself that the stranger was indeed sincere.

Slater returned to his table, signed for the check and went up to his room. The chambermaid was just finishing up. She was a great deal younger and prettier than most; and when she saw Slater, she looked flustered and swished and fidgeted around the room until he was forced to ask her to leave.

He bolted the door and got into his ski clothes. Regarding himself in the mirror, he decided he couldn't put off getting a haircut any longer. His own hair was getting much too long. It was too thick and wiry to lie down properly. He looked at his watch. The cable station should be very crowded by now. It would be a good time to pay a visit to the ski-rental shack near the practice slope.

Chapter 9

The sky was as blue as Slater had ever seen it, and the morning air was still crisp and new. He was glad for the weekend skiers, but he had to admit that Sunday was not the day to go skiing. Slater joined the crowd which filled the roadway and moved along with it like a chip in a stream. Beyond the railroad crossing, he shouldered his way toward the ski-rental shack.

Because of the excellent weather and the crowds, the rental skis were stacked outside; and the attendant of yesterday was not in sight. Slater approached the man in charge. He was wearing hiking boots and corduroy breeches. His brown turtle-neck sweater was torn and was becoming unraveled at the waist.

"My name," said Slater in German, "is Karl Nolker. I would like Herr Schlessinger's skis."

The attendant's face was the color of his corduroy trousers. His small, pale blue eyes regarded Slater carefully.

"The skis will be too long for you," he said slowly.

Slater remembered that they had been a little short for Wyman.

"Schlessinger's skis are exactly the right length for me," said Slater.

"One moment," he said and disappeared into the shack. He returned a minute later with a pair of Erbacher skis that looked like the ones Wyman had been given yesterday. The attendant held one of the skis up beside Slater, and Bill raised his right arm, and his wrist rested on the tip. He smiled at the attendant.

"Perfect," he said.

The attendant said nothing and put both skis on the snow. The bindings had to be adjusted. Wyman had big feet. Slater offered the attendant some money. He looked surprised and shook his head.

"Herr Schlessinger," he said, "has taken care of everything."

"I know," said Bill, "but take it anyway and bring me a pair of good poles."

The attendant took the money and brought Slater a brand-new pair of aluminum poles. Slater thanked him and, keeping his skis on, moved off in the direction of the cable station. He joined the crowd and then skied around in front of the cable-car docks and climbed up toward the woods. He didn't want to wait the hour he was sure it would take to get a ride to the top.

The climbing was slow, and he began to sweat long before he reached the trees, but the exercise made him feel good, and he didn't stop until he was almost a hundred yards above the line of trees. The evergreens were tall and straight; but they didn't offer much protection, for, like all the forests of Europe, the underbrush was cleared away, and the planting and cutting had been carried on scientifically for years. To Slater, being in these woods was like being in a maze. He took off his skis and stacked them behind a tree. He removed his mittens and began with the right ski, inspecting it carefully from the rounded tip to the plastic heel plate. He had no way of knowing whether these were the same skis that had been given Wyman. They looked the same and were the same length; but even if they were, that didn't prove anything. Maybe the skis had nothing to do with why Wyman was in Kitzbühel. Schlessinger could be the owner's real name. Slater had the feeling that the ski-rental people were not seriously involved with Wyman or Wyman's employers, nor was Rüdi or Anton, the desk clerk. They were merely hired to do a particular job, but had no connection with, and probably not even any knowledge of one another's roles. The thing that had made Slater pursue the ski angle was Webber's letter to Putnam. Slater treated all coincidences in the counterespionage business as suspicious.

He turned to the left ski and ran his fingers, which were getting cold in the shade of the forest, along the edges. Between the binding and the bottom, he felt a raised place and went back over the area. He tried, unsuccessfully, to get his fingernail under the edge. He felt around on the other side of the binding, felt what he believed to be a corresponding depression and pushed. The piece stuck fast for a moment and then pushed out on the other side. Slater pulled out what looked like a tiny drawer. If the previous user had been more careful in replacing it, Slater doubted that he would have discovered it.

Inside the drawer was a carefully folded piece of paper. When Slater unfolded it, he found it was much larger than he had expected. The message was short, and it was printed in ink. He was surprised that it was in English.

You were $170 short. I will pick it up thru Rüdi. Have made contact with I. W. If this is such an important job, I'd better have more information. Suggest you get me another contact and more money.
W.

I. W. must be Ilse Wieland. There was no longer any question of her involvement. Slater swore. If she knew that he and Carmichael were the same, he would really be in trouble. He had to keep Carmichael from her in the future, whatever else he did. And now the question was what to do about this note. It was obviously from Wyman, and the skis had to be returned as soon as possible. Schlessinger might already be trying to pick them up. He might even be waiting for the attendant in the shabby turtle-neck sweater to point Slater out.

Slater preferred, whenever possible, to leave his opponents' mechanism undisturbed, so he could monitor their operations or disrupt them through one of the weaker links. He had an idea for a substitute message that might work to his advantage, but he needed time, and he had neither pen nor paper. So he fitted the note back in where he had found it. Then he looked down through the maze of tall, straight-limbed trees at the crowd of waiting skiers below and tried to make a decision. He deliberately took a cigarette from the chest pocket of his black parka. He stood there in the snow and made himself finish the cigarette, a man in the woods facing an important decision—alone as always.

He threw the butt into the snow, put on the skis and skied down through the woods and the open field to the cable station. He observed the crowd carefully and for a long time. Then, pulling up the hood of his parka so that only his mouth, eyes and nose were visible, he approached a man who was waiting by himself on the edge of the crowd.

"Are you German?" Slater asked in German.

"Yes."

The stranger was about Slater's height and build. He had a black parka tied around his waist. It was much warmer here in the sun.

"Good," said Slater. "Then, perhaps, you will do me a favor." He smiled.

"Perhaps," said the stranger, but he didn't return the smile.

"I will pay you," said Slater, maintaining his friendly expression.

"What do you want me to do?" The stranger's eyes were a little more interested now.

"I want you to return these skis and poles to the ski-rental shack over there." Slater pointed to the small red building.

"Why don't you do it yourself?" The stranger's eyes were distrustful.

"I have my reasons. I'll give you ten American dollars." Slater took a ten-dollar bill from his wallet. The stranger hesitated.

"Do the skis belong there?"

"Yes, and they've been paid for," said Slater.

"What am I to say, if they ask me anything?"

"I don't believe they will ask you anything. If they do, say that you've changed your mind, that the line for the cable car was too long." Slater waited while the stranger tried to decide.

"And you'll pay me ten dollars to return skis that you rented?" The stranger was incredulous.

Slater held out the money, and the stranger took it.

"There are only two requirements," Slater said. "First, you must return the skis and poles, and second, you must forget that you were not the one who rented them."

The stranger stuck his own skis and poles in the snow, picked up Slater's and trudged off toward the shack. Slater watched him for a moment. The stranger's general outline and dark brown hair looked very familiar. He was in luck. The stranger's looks were surprisingly similar to his own. He would make an excellent decoy—for a while anyway. Slater smiled and walked toward the railroad crossing. By the time he had reached it, he had removed his parka. He waited by the track and watched as the stranger disappeared into the shack and came out less than a minute later and crunched back through the snow to his own skis. Slater turned and disappeared into the crowd.

Chapter 10

Slater would have liked to exploit his discovery of Wyman's message. Experience had led him to believe that Wyman and Schlessinger, or whatever Schlessinger's real name was, did not know one another. At least Wyman probably didn't know Schlessinger. After all, that was one of the basic reasons for establishing a net. The ideal was to have two-way communication, but at the same time have only one man aware of the exact identity of the other. That way, if Wyman were under suspicion by his government and subjected to a thorough interrogation, he couldn't reveal his superior's identity. If Slater's opinion was correct, he had to begin the slow and dangerous process of uncovering link after link in the chain of Communist espionage. If he were to dispose of the skis, for example, he might break Wyman's only means of communication with Schlessinger and force Schlessinger to get in touch with Wyman directly and reveal himself to Wyman. Then Wyman might be persuaded to tell what he knew. Slater had not disposed of the skis, because Wyman had already asked for a contact in his message, and to upset communications at this point would alarm the Communists at the wrong time, even if they never discovered who was responsible.

Slater returned to the hotel in time for lunch and went directly to the dining room. Ilse Wieland was seated with the Baron von Burgdorf at the corner table, his sausagelike fingers resting on her hand. The sight made Slater wince. As he passed her table, she nodded and smiled; and the Baron lifted his little, pig's eyes to look Slater over. The look conveyed a careful appraisal and implied in some strange way that Slater had been recorded as so much cash received is recorded in the window of a cash register. The amount appeared briefly and then disappeared, and the little eyes were as blank again as the windows of a vacant house.

"Please, Herr Slater." Ilse's voice stopped him just as he got past their table. "I would like you to meet the Baron von Burgdorf," she said.

"Charmed," said the Baron in English, his expression bland.

"Sehr angenehm," said Slater and bowed slightly.

"You speak German, Herr Slater. That is unusual for an American." The Baron had switched to German.

"When in Rome," Slater shrugged.

"Yes, of course." The Baron laughed, but only with his mouth. Any other reaction was smothered in his heavy flesh. He had not removed his hand from Ilse's.

"Won't you join us for lunch, Herr Slater?" said Ilse.

"Yes, Herr Slater," said the Baron a fraction of a second later than he should have to make the invitation sound completely genuine. "It would be a great pleasure to talk with an American who really speaks my language."

"I'd be delighted, Herr Baron, Fräulein Wieland." Slater gave another slight bow and seated himself next to Ilse.

"The Baron," said Ilse, "is having a big party at the Ehrenbachhöhe Hotel tomorrow night." Ilse smiled sweetly at the Baron.

"How nice," said Slater.

"The Baron was kind enough to invite me," she continued, "and when I told him I had a previous engagement, he asked me to invite my escort for the evening." Ilse turned to the Baron. "Since you have now met my engagement," Ilse laughed, "you may invite him yourself and have his answer now."

"But, of course, Herr Slater." His voice was smooth and filled with cordiality. "I was about to invite you in any case, but now that I know you will be bringing such a treasure," he patted Ilse's hand and smiled at her with his wet lips, "your attendance is essential."

Slater immediately wondered if Ilse knew that Carmichael had already been invited and was simply trying to put his alter ego on the spot, or whether she had made up her mind that the best way to watch him was to make him be her escort. He looked from Ilse to the Baron. She obviously wanted him to accept. The Baron wanted him to also now, but—for different reasons? Slater wondered, but even as he wondered, he heard himself accept.

"I have never been invited to attend the party of a baron before," said Slater. "I will be delighted to accept."

"Good! Very good!" The Baron nodded. "I am very pleased."

For the first time, the Baron removed his hand from Ilse's. Slater wondered if all of this had been engineered for his benefit, although he could see no reason why any man, particularly one like the Baron von Burgdorf, should have to pretend a lascivious interest in Ilse Wieland. The Baron just sat there and licked his lips, as if he found them continually chapped. Ilse's behavior, on the other hand, was out of character with last night's performance. Surely, he thought, she must have had enough of men like von Burgdorf.

"Ah, Baron, have you saved some lunch for me?"

Slater turned to see the pencil-shaped Englishman whom

he had met in the bar the night before. He was wearing perfectly pressed Jaeger beltless slacks, suède shoes and a Tattersall shirt, open at the neck with a Paisley scarf to cover up his thin throat.

"Sit down, sit down, Mr. Hormsby," said the Baron. "I assure you, you can have more lunch than you can eat." The Baron laughed.

Hormsby sat down next to the Baron. The contrast between the two men was incredible. Slater earnestly hoped that nothing would start Hormsby giggling again.

Hormsby turned to Slater as if seeing him for the first time. "I don't believe," he said to the Baron, "I've had the pleasure."

"Ach, please forgive me, gentlemen. Mr. Slater, Mr. Hormsby."

"Delighted," said Hormsby.

Slater nodded.

"You're an American, aren't you?" Hormsby said.

"Yes."

"You Americans are so droll," Hormsby continued. "I met a chap by the name of Carmichael in the bar last night. He had the whole place in an uproar. I tell you, I was fairly screaming."

And that's the truth, Slater thought, and then something Hormsby had just said jarred. He tried to remember carefully, but could not recall ever giving his name to Hormsby. In fact, that was the final stroke that had set Hormsby off. Hormsby had said, "What's yours?" meaning Slater's name, and Slater had replied, "Scotch and soda." And then everyone in the bar had gotten hysterics because of Hormsby's high-pitched giggle. Slater remembered he had left immediately afterward. Was Hormsby checking on Carmichael? Hormsby could have seen Carmichael talking with Rüdi.

Slater suddenly began to feel his nerves tighten. It was a reflex, conditioned by past experience. The only thing he could compare it to was his feeling as a schoolboy wrestler, when he had sat with his team on the bench and gotten his first look at his opponent from the rival school—but that had only been a wrestling match. Carmichael's hours were numbered. He had one more job to perform, and then Carmichael would be finished.

Slater made his excuses, thanked the Baron for his invitation and left the table. If he was going to keep that rendezvous with Webber, he had to start laying the groundwork immediately.

Chapter 11

Slater went out into the mid-afternoon sunlight. The sun, unimpeded by any clouds, had drunk heavily of the snow in the village, and the sidewalks and streets were beginning to dry out. There would be little slush left for the night to freeze. Spring was definitely on its way. He went to an outside pay station and phoned his hotel. He recognized Anton's voice.

"I would like a room with a bath," Slater said.

"For what dates, please?"

"For a week, starting tonight."

"Your name please, sir." Anton's patience was obvious.

"Oh, yes," Slater gave a nervous laugh. "Excuse me. You can't very well reserve a room for someone who doesn't give his name, can you?" Slater laughed again. There was a pause.

"Your name, sir." Anton's patience sounded endless.

"Oh, yes. I don't know what's the matter with me. Slater, William Slater. I'm an American," he added quickly.

"Yes, sir. Can you check in by five o'clock?"

Slater looked at his watch. It was already almost three. That didn't give him much time.

"Yes, I guess so. I'll be there."

"Very good, sir." Anton hung up.

Slater pushed open the glass door of the telephone station and walked back to the hotel. He headed in the direction of the men's room. He took the moment that Anton's attention was elsewhere and slipped up the stairs to his room.

He changed into Carmichael's clothing and packed his suitcase. After going over his room very carefully to make certain he had left nothing incriminating lying around, he went downstairs to the desk.

"I would like my bill, please. I'm checking out," said Slater.

"I hope you have enjoyed your stay with us, Mr. Carmichael," said Anton, "and you will remain longer the next time." His little speech sounded like a broken record.

"I appreciated your service, Anton," said Slater.

Anton's eyebrows raised. His eyes shouted a warning not to elaborate any further on his "service." The ten-dollar bribe for the room had certainly not gone to the hotel. Slater looked as if he were about to continue, and Anton presented the bill immediately. He didn't even count the change until Slater had left. When Anton finally counted the money, it was ten dollars short. Anton's dead face suddenly became apoplectic. He had to call the assistant and fortify himself with generous shots of Steinhäger in his room.

Slater got into the Volkswagen, tipped the porter too generously for bringing his suitcase and drove out of the village and onto the main road along the valley floor toward Kirchberg. He parked the car just long enough to get his shoes, pants and sport jacket from his suitcase and close it up again. He removed his hairpiece as he drove; and when he parked, finally, in front of a small restaurant, he changed his elevator shoes before leaving the car.

The restaurant was deserted, and he went straight into the men's room, washed his face and changed his clothes. When he emerged, there was still no one in sight! Apparently, the proprietor had decided, from long experience no doubt, that four o'clock was no time for business and had simply left the place unattended. Whatever the reason, Slater was just as well pleased not to bump into anyone, and he got back into the car and drove the rest of the way to Kirchberg.

He stopped the car once more, while he carefully packed away Carmichael's things and got out a canvas cover. He shut up the suitcase, locked it and zipped up the canvas cover. The suitcase now looked just different enough not to be obviously the same one Carmichael had carried.

Slater found a garage and asked the attendant, who looked more like a farmer than a mechanic, to keep the car for him until later that evening. The farmer-mechanic phoned for a taxi; and, eventually, a dilapidated old open touring car, which looked as if it would hold at least twenty people, arrived; and Slater, the driver and the machine, which sounded like a cement mixer, chugged back down the road to Kitzbühel. Slater slipped down in the seat as far as he could when they entered the village, reflecting that he was still five feet above the road and that this was the most spectacular entrance one of the United States' clandestine counterespionage agents had ever made into any town.

Several blocks past the Winterhof Hotel, he yelled at the driver to stop, jumped out quickly, paid the driver too much and, shaking his head, walked slowly back to the hotel. It was exactly five o'clock when he entered, and the Winterhof was packed with returning skiers. Everything went smoothly and he was given room 27 by Anton.

Slater got out his writing equipment and wrote a letter to George Hollingsworth, via Paris, giving the return address of William A. Slater, Winterhof Hotel, and explaining that Mahler might phone George to say that Carmichael was missing. If so, the phone call was to be believed. Slater arranged the names of the people he suspected into two columns and in the order of what he believed to be their importance and their function. It was rather early in the game to do this, but he had to arrive at some conclusion, no matter how tentative, so that his office and Hollingsworth would not be quite so much in the dark as they had all been when Webber disappeared. Slater asked his office to check on Herr Krüpl, knowing that so much was happening so fast the answer, if they had one, would probably be too late. He asked again for the identity of the German agent, and said that he would okay his office's giving his identity to German Intelligence. Their agent could identify himself to Slater by saying that he had a message from his friend Ben in Paris. Slater's reply would be that the only Parisians he knew were female.

Slater put down his ball-point pen. The letter in front of him was still, apparently, blank, and he had written four pages. He didn't want to have his real identity known to German Intelligence, but this whole affair was too complicated, and he would need their agent's help. The intricacies of international relationships were becoming more and more bewildering. Slater was certain he was working against the Communists. He was equally certain he had met some of the people involved, and he had as yet not met a Russian. It was American against American, against German, against an Englishman, against an Austrian. Nor was it simply a question of ideology. Some worked for power, for money, for adventure, and some because they were afraid. The only approach Slater had found satisfactory to unravel his opponents' networks was to attack them functionally from an organizational point of view. Since the signposts of nationality and ideology no longer had much meaning, Slater had to discern, from his knowledge of espionage patterns, his opponents' organization. Whenever two or more people worked together, they had to have organization; and the problems, inherent in all espionage activity, were such that all their operations necessarily followed the same general procedures. Slater knew these procedures, and many of their variations. His opponents were ingenious and ruthless, but they made mistakes; and the more people involved in an operation, the more room there was for human error. He watched for, and counted on, these errors. The trouble was they did the same, and he made mistakes. He had already made several. The one that worried him the most was his activation of Rüdi and the receipt of the $170. Slater should have gotten someone else to do that. He should get someone else to meet Webber tonight—Mahler, for example. The Russian Intelligence officers almost never did their own dirty work. Why should he? Suppose Mahler did get killed. Or, even worse, suppose he were to be questioned? He only knew Carmichael, not Slater. This was the dirtiest business in the world. An Intelligence officer's job was to accomplish his mission and keep out of the hands of the opposition. The end always justified the means. Slater winced. That was what the Communists said about their own aims.

Slater shrugged and smiled ruefully. After all, he was going to send someone else to meet Webber. He was going to send Carmichael.

Chapter 12

At eight-thirty that evening, Slater arrived at the garage in Kirchberg and picked up the car. It was already quite dark, but the night was clear and the moon would be up within an hour. Slater drove back toward Kitzbühel and turned off on a little side road about two kilometers from the village. He opened a paper-wrapped parcel beside him on the front seat and managed to dress himself as Carmichael. He had to get out of the car to change his trousers and realized, for the first time, how cold it was. His teeth chattered for several moments even after he was back in the car with the heater on. He knew it was more than the cold that made him shiver. He turned the car around and turned back onto the main road. After crossing the railroad tracks, he turned off the Schwarzseestrasse and drove into narrow streets that were little more than alleyways skirting the main section of town, across the Josef Pirchlstrasse and onto the Hornweg. He crossed the Ache river and the railroad, and started climbing up toward the Kitzbüheler Horn.

According to the map, Webber's farmhouse was on the left-hand side of the road, about halfway up the mountain, exactly two kilometers from the railroad. Slater took the mileage and switched on his bright lights. The road was steep all right, and icy in spots, but the Volkswagen skidded and lurched its way upward. According to the speedometer, he had less than four-tenths of a kilometer to go, and he kept his eye on the left side of the road. At exactly two kilometers he saw the farmhouse. It was about twenty yards above the road, and an ice-rutted driveway went up to the side door. Slater doubted that even the Volkswagen could negotiate that and he continued driving up past the driveway. He hadn't intended to drive in, in any case. He drove for another kilometer, up and around the hairpin turns that seemed to meet each other coming backward. He finally found a place in which to turn around and then, putting the car in low gear and dimming his lights, allowed the car to go back down the mountain. Just above the farmhouse, he switched off the lights and motor and braked the car very cautiously past the farmhouse, coming to a full stop at the middle of the looping turn immediately below.

Slater stepped out of the car quietly, tied crampons on his shoes, and started up the steep mountainside toward the farmhouse. He couldn't see it now, because it was set well back above the ridge. The tip of a crescent moon appeared above the range of mountains behind him and cast its reflected sunlight down into the valley, etching everything for miles into silver and black. The moon rose above the mountains faster than Slater could climb and was soon bright enough to cast his shadow before him. Slater swore, but continued to dig into the snow with the steel points of his crampons. He had little trouble keeping his silhouette low, as the bank was steep, and he was forced to hug it as he climbed. It was the ridge he was worried about. At the top he would stand out like a great dark shadow on the snowfield above. Why, Slater asked himself, couldn't he once be in a position where he could act like a sensible, normal human being? Why couldn't he accept Webber's letter as being genuine? It probably was, and the farmer might shoot him for an intruder or some wild animal, and who could blame him? Visitors with an open conscience didn't come steathily after dark across a snowfield. If Webber's letter was not genuine, then he would probably get shot anyway. It was, Slater knew, simply the result of a nervous past, which made suspicion of everything and everyone second nature. He was doing this crazy thing because it might give him a slight edge in the event something went wrong. Even the slightest advantage made it worth the effort. The only thing Slater had no choice about was whether to investigate. He had to do that, but hugging ice-encrusted snow on a moonlit night in the Austrian Alps was not his idea of the best way to stay alive.

Slater turned his head and looked down. The roadway was a black ribbon in the moonlight and seemed to curve downward forever. If he slipped now, his body would hurtle down the icy slopes until it crashed into an outcropping of ice-covered rocks or was smashed into bits at the bottom. Slater closed his eyes and dug in again with his feet. He shook his head to clear it and began to sweat. He waited for a moment for his heart to stop pounding and then started up again. He estimated that he couldn't be more than a few feet from the top of the ridge.

His head appeared above the top, and then his shoulders and chest. He reached his arms over the bank and tried to get a hold with his fingers, but the icy crust was too thick, and he had to push himself over the ridge and onto the sloping snowfield with his feet. He lay there, finally, all of him on the gentle slope, and panted heavily, his breath forming a halo of mist in the cold night air. He looked in the direction of the farmhouse and saw the pale lights in the downstairs windows. The farmhouse was steep roofed and loomed very large in the moonlight. Slater picked himself up and crunched through the snow, diagonally, toward the rear of the house. The crust held his weight and the walking was much easier, but Slater swore that he would go back via the road no matter what happened in that farmhouse. He got all the way to the rear of the main building before he heard a dog barking, and he waited in the shadow of a bare-limbed tree in the yard.

He didn't have to wait long before he heard a man's voice shouting at the dog to be quiet. Slater looked at the radium dial of his watch. It was nine-fifty. He was right on time. He heard the side door open and saw a man come out alone. The man was big and stoopshouldered, and was carrying a rifle. He walked carefully toward the front of the house and then turned back toward the rear. Slater jumped him as soon as the man was opposite the tree, chopping him in the back of the neck with the side of his hand. The man dropped to the snow without a sound. Slater took his rifle and gagged him with his scarf, then took the rawhide laces from his high boots and tied his wrists behind him with one and his ankles with the other. Slater dragged him behind the tree and looked him over carefully. The man was, undoubtedly, a farmer. If Webber was right, the farmer was slightly on the greedy side, but otherwise okay. If Webber was wrong, Slater had just reduced whatever odds might be against him by one man.

Slater looked over the driveway carefully for a moment, bent over and untied his crampons, and then went to the side door. He turned the handle and let himself in. He found himself in a poorly heated hallway. Coats and jackets were hanging from hooks along the walls. Cautiously, he opened the door at the far end and came face to face with the barrel of a Luger.

Chapter 13

Behind the gun was the man Webber had described as having a face like a waxed apple and whose name, according to Mahler, was Fritz Stadler.

"I came to see Herr Webber," said Slater.

"You are right on time," said Stadler, "but you were supposed to bring a car."

"I preferred to walk. It's such a lovely night." Slater smiled. "Where's Webber?"

"Herr Webber is no longer with us," said Stadler.

"You mean he's dead."

"He died for his country." Stadler's expression was very pious. "I have someone," he added, "who would like to have a talk with you. Come!"

The gun indicated the direction, and Slater led the way through a crude living room and into the family room. There was the tiled stove in the corner and a long heavy table with straight-backed chairs around it. At the far end of the table near the stove sat Herr Krüpl. The eye without the eyelashes looked enormous in the half light from the table lamp beside him, and the round indentation in his forehead gaped like an empty eye socket.

"Sit!" Krüpl indicated a chair at the opposite end of the table. When Slater hesitated, the Luger was pressed into the back of his neck. Slater sat down. Stadler remained standing behind him.

"I don't believe we have met," said Krüpl.

"No," said Slater.

"Your name?"

"There's a farmer tied up in the snow out there," said Slater. "He'll freeze to death if someone doesn't go and get him."

"There's plenty of time to get him," said Krüpl.

"Pretty cold out," said Slater insistently.

"Your name?" Krüpl's voice was steady.

"Jones," said Slater. "What's yours?"

"My name is not important," said Krüpl.

Slater could not understand why Stadler hadn't searched him. He would not find any identification papers, but Slater was a walking arsenal. Possibly Stadler had assumed, since Slater had entered the farmhouse without waving a revolver around, that Slater had come unarmed. He had not entered, revolver in hand, because he had been quite certain that, if it was a trap, whoever was inside would want to talk to him first to find out how much he knew. Had he entered with a gun, they might have been forced to kill him immediately. And why didn't Stadler go outside and release the farmer? It wasn't simply callousness, Slater felt certain. An ally with a rifle would be handy to have around. Slater decided that Krüpl must be unarmed and did not want to be left alone.

"Did you enjoy the $170, Herr Carmichael?" Krüpl smiled. The smile made his face look more grotesque than ever. "It isn't that we cannot afford the money, Herr Carmichael, it's simply that we like our people to earn it first."

"My name is Jones," said Slater.

"Your name," said Krüpl, "may not really be Carmichael, but it is unquestionably not Jones." Krüpl stared at Slater for a moment, as if trying to see through him. "Tell me," said Krüpl finally, "how did you discover our methods of payment?"

"I don't know what you're talking about," said Slater.

Krüpl drummed his fingers on the table and Slater felt the impact of the Luger as Stadler hit him a glancing blow across the back of the head. Slater's fingers went numb, and the light from the table lamp seemed to dance up and down for a moment, and then his head cleared and began to throb violently. He bit his lip to keep from yelling at the pain.

"Don't knock him out," said Krüpl. Slater said nothing.

"Answer my questions please." Krüpl's voice was dispassionate. "I understand your interest in the late Herr Webber, but like your friend, your curiosity may cause you considerable difficulty. Have you told your employers," Krüpl smiled at the word, "about our ingenious payment organization?"

"I have no employers," said Slater, "only friends. They know whatever I know."

Slater couldn't understand what Krüpl's connection with the $170 could be. He tried to think, but his head was aching so that he couldn't be positive. He thought that he had met Krüpl as Slater, not Carmichael, and that Ilse Wieland had made the introduction at the Café des Engels.

"How much did you pay Rüdi?"

Krüpl expected an answer, and Slater realized he had better give one. He couldn't afford another crack on the head. It would put him out of commission. The trouble was, Slater did not really know anything.

"Until I met you," said Slater, "I thought Rüdi had paid me." Slater steeled himself for another blow.

"I think, Herr Carmichael, that you are telling the truth."

The conceited fool, thought Slater. Krüpl has so much faith in his own ability that he can't believe anyone could suspect Rüdi of being anything more than a cog in the machinery.

"Why did you kill Webber?" asked Slater.

Krüpl hesitated.

"Because," he said, "he was too curious, and not valuable to us, but you, Herr Carmichael," Krüpl smiled, "are no amateur. I believe you have a history which would be of great interest to us. We are expecting some friends," again Krüpl smiled, "who will be here soon and who know how to persuade a man to give his entire history."

So that, thought Slater, was why there was no car in evidence. He had better move fast, while the odds were still only two to one. Slater felt in his coat pocket for his revolver. His hands were under the table, and he didn't believe Stadler would notice. The Luger went off, and a slug burned itself into the edge of the table in front of him. The noise in the room was deafening.

"Stand up! Put your hands above your head! Schnell!" Stadler's voice was as staccato as a machine gun.

Slater complied, and Stadler moved quickly into him and pressed the Luger into his stomach.

Slater was now standing away from the table with his back at a forty-five-degree angle to Krüpl. When Stadler started to reach for Slater's right-hand coat pocket, Slater suddenly twisted his body to the right, at the same time hitting the gun barrel with his left elbow. The Luger went off for the second time, and Slater smashed his fist into Stadler's jaw and went after the gun which was still in Stadler's hand. Slater grabbed the man's wrist, his thumbs pressing into the back of Stadler's hand, and twisted. The gun dropped, but Stadler threw his body across Slater's hips, and the two men crashed to the floor. Slater's hairpiece fell off as he wrestled to get free so he could get at his revolver, but his snub-nosed .38 fell out of his pocket; and when he finally rolled away and regained his feet, Stadler had done the same, and the two men stood facing each other across the room. The Luger and the .38 were lying on the floor between them.

"Krüpl" yelled Stadler. "Kill him! um Gottes willen!"

Both men looked toward Krüpl. Slater expected to feel a slug burning its way through his body, then suddenly remembered Krüpl was not armed. Stealing a brief glance at Krüpl, Slater saw that his face was all smashed and bloody. Stadler's bullet had hit him right in the middle of the face. Krüpl's hand was still holding a .32 automatic. Slater's calculations had been all wrong.

Stadler's face was wax white now, except for a bruise which was beginning to spread across its right side.

"We make a deal," he said. "I tell you what you want to know, you walk out of here alive."

"No deals, Stadler!" Slater knew the man was stalling for time until his "friends" arrived.

"I won't tell that you have brown hair instead of black." Stadler looked desperate.

Slater knew he would have to kill Stadler, if he could. Stadler had probably been the one who had killed Charlie Webber in any case. Slater took a step toward the weapons. Stadler did the same, pulling out a long pocket knife. He pressed the button and a thin, slightly curved blade switched out.

Maybe it was the click of the knife, the thought of Charlie Webber, or Wyman's treachery, or maybe it was the whole rotten business of ten years of fear, living a life of lies in which everything—even a beautiful woman—was denied him because of his profession; but Slater suddenly went berserk with a hate that would conquer any fear. Every muscle was as tight as piano wire.

Neither man said a word from that moment on. They circled for position, and nothing could be heard but their shuffling feet and the sound of the clock ticking in the corner. Slater watched Stadler's eyes. They were filled with fear and a hate that matched his own. Stadler was an old hand at infighting. He held the knife low and away from his body. Every time Slater feinted to get him off balance, he narrowly missed being cut. Slater backed toward the table, occasionally feinting, his arms wide like a football tackler's. His right hand closed over the top of the chair he had been sitting on, and he swung it in one powerful motion. The heavy chair slammed into Stadler's left side and carried him to the floor. Slater dived for his .38 and fired twice at close range into Stadler's body. The second shot was unnecessary.

Slater picked up his hairpiece, went over Stadler's body and removed his wallet, his passport and all his other identification. He did the same with Krüpl. He was surprised to find that Krüpl was an Austrian, and his home address was Kirchberg. Also Krüpl had a large number of American ten- and twenty-dollar bills.

Slater took a handkerchief from Stadler's pocket and went outside to the tree. The farmer was still there, and he was trying to move his body to keep it warm. Slater hit him over the head from behind, blindfolded him with the handkerchief, dragged him inside and left him, bound, in the hallway. He went back to the living room and dragged Krüpl's body out into the snow, beyond the driveway and about thirty yards from the back of the house. He didn't use the crampons, because he didn't want to leave any marks on the crust. He went inside the house again and repeated the process with Stadler. Stadler was heavier than he looked, and Slater found it hard going. He was getting desperate because time must be running out. He went back in the house for the last time, rummaged around until he found a shovel and a wooden bucket. He filled the bucket with water and lugged it and the shovel to the spot where the bodies were, and started to dig. Trying to get through the crust was like trying to dig through cement. He had to jam the shovel against it with all his strength and then jump straight-legged on the upper edge. It took him fifteen minutes to break through. The rest was relatively easy going. He dug a pit more than deep enough for the two bodies; and after shoveling the crusty part of the snow in first he dragged the bodies to the edge and rolled them in. He shoveled the snow in on top of them and stamped it down around them with his feet. Carefully, he smoothed the top layer with the back of his shovel. He turned to the bucket. A thin layer of ice had already formed over the top. He broke it with his shovel and poured the water evenly over the grave. In an hour, the top layer would freeze and it would meld with the unbroken snowfield.

Slater walked carefully back to the barn and put the shovel and the bucket inside the door. The moon had disappeared, and Slater groped his way along the driveway to the tree. He found his crampons and went, stumbling and slipping, through the frozen cart tracks to the road.

He walked as fast as he could in the darkness, prepared at any moment to fling himself into the snowbank at the side of the road. He reached the car, let off the brakes, and braked the car down to the bottom of the mountain. He turned on the ignition and put it in gear at the bottom, and drove, still without lights, until he had crossed to the other side of town. He drove halfway to Kirchberg, stopped the car by the side of the road, got out and silently retched into the snow.

Chapter 14

Slater's biggest problem at the moment was what to do with the Volkswagen. Carmichael had checked out, and from now on Carmichael was dead. But the car was signed into Austria in Carmichael's name.

Slater got back in the car and drove thirty kilometers beyond Kirchberg to Wörgl. He registered as Carmichael at a hotel near the railroad station and spent what was left of the night in a very small, but extremely comfortable, room. He was furious with himself for getting sick, but reflected that it was bad enough to have to kill one man without having to bury two corpses in the snow by the light of a waning moon. It was too bad Krüpl was a local. The police would double their efforts to find his body should the opposition decide to report him missing. Slater had no doubt that they would.

He took Krüpl's wallet from his coat pocket and emptied the contents on the bed. There were several hundred American dollars and Austrian schillings in large denominations. He didn't bother to count them. Krüpl had obviously been the paymaster, but how did he know when and to whom to make the payments? The obvious answer, and one that Slater immediately rejected, was that Rüdi had direct contact with

Krüpl and simply told him, but Krüpl was too smart for that. He knew Rüdi, but Slater doubted that Rüdi knew Krüpl, so how was the information communicated, and how did Krüpl know the exact amount to be paid the agents? Even Communists didn't pay all their agents the same amount. Slater thought he had the answer to the latter. He had performed the ritual with Rüdi on the 17th, and both he and Wyman had received $170, or $10 for every day of the month.

Slater had to find out how the communication between Rüdi and Krüpl was made. He knew he was counting on what might well turn out to be a very dangerous assumption, but there wasn't time to confirm or deny it. A group of disgruntled, unpaid Communist agents crawling around Kitzbühel would ordinarily be a very pleasing prospect to Slater; but if everything were to stop too abruptly, he'd have every spy and strong-arm goon in the area looking for the man who had caused all this; and he would not have the chance to find out what he really wanted to know, namely: the man who supplied Krüpl with the money. That man must be number one, and directly responsible to an Intelligence officer in the Russian Embassy in either Munich or Vienna. That was the way their organization worked. The Communists rarely gave any of their agents more than one job and, invariably, isolated them from the knowledge of one another and from their superiors whenever possible.

Slater counted on his theory that Krüpl received his supply of funds in some mechanical way through an inanimate channel, such as through the mails or some hiding place to which both he and his superior would have easy access, but at different times. He hoped that the communication of information was done only occasionally and by one of those two methods. If he was right, he might be able to continue the payoff until he could discover the identity of number one.

Slater shook his head. All of his assumptions might be correct; but if Krüpl had already alerted his superiors to his suspicions of Carmichael, Slater was about to put both feet into a worse trap than before. Slater believed that Krüpl's ego had made him decide to conduct his own investigation first. He could have known about Wyman, because he had paid Wyman before, and he might have been the one assigned to eliminate Webber. Krüpl had obviously known all about Webber.

Slater's head began to ache again, and he flopped onto the bed. He had to have help. He needed another man desperately. He could no longer trust Mahler.

The thought of Mahler brought him up short. If Mahler had been on the level as far as the letter was concerned, his life would be in danger from the Communists. If Mahler had set him up for this, Slater would kill him. Slater had told Mahler to get out of town by 6 P.M. tomorrow, if he had not received any word from Slater. Nothing like warning your double-crosser, if that's what Mahler was. Slater tried to plan the next day's activities, but he was too exhausted and he fell asleep.

When Slater awoke the next morning, the bedclothes were twisted and rumpled. The bed looked as if he had been having a fight in it. The throbbing in his head was gone, but his body ached all over and he was still unbearably tired.

He had a quick breakfast and checked out of the hotel as Carmichael and left the Volkswagen in a garage in Wörgl.

As Slater, he boarded a train back to Kitzbühel and returned to his room at the Winterhof without anyone's seeing him. He dressed in his ski clothes, tore up his bed, and went back down to the desk and turned in his room key.

"I don't know when I've had such a good night's sleep," he said.

"I'm very glad that you did, sir." Anton did not look as though he had had any sleep. Slater thought that Anton looked more tired every day.

"There must be something special about the air in Austria," Slater continued.

"There must be, sir." Anton looked bored.

"I mean," said Slater, rattling on, "I never go to bed early at home—in the States, I mean," Slater gave a nervous little chuckle, "because I'm always afraid I won't sleep, but last night I went to bed at eight o'clock, and I didn't wake up until half an hour ago."

"I'm very glad, sir," said Anton.

"You don't look as though you get much sleep, if you don't mind my saying so," Slater added the apology hastily.

Another guest came up and engaged Anton's attention so that Anton was spared the necessity of a reply.

Slater left the hotel, muttering something about getting a breath of God's clean air, and, once outside, headed for a nearby hotel and went into one of the pay stations near the lobby. His number rang several times before anyone answered.

"Good morning, Pension Eggerwirt."

Slater recognized the voice of Herr Nadler, the "old" young proprietor.

"Good morning," said Slater. "Is Herr Mahler there?"

"One moment, please."

Slater waited several moments. He put a handkerchief over the mouthpiece.

"Herr Mahler here. Hello." It was Mahler's voice.

"We got your friend Herr Carmichael. Thank you for your co-operation." Slater's accent was very thick.

"I don't know what you're talking about. Who is this?" Mahler's voice was very excited.

"We take care of you later," said Slater.

"Wait! Who is—"

Slater hung up and remained seated, his hand still on the receiver. Of course, it didn't necessarily mean anything positive, but Mahler's excitement did seem real enough. On the other hand, Krüpl, Stadler, or someone else could have prearranged a code for the opening of any telephone contact, in which case Mahler would have immediately been on guard. Slater tried to imagine what his next move would be if he were Mahler and really innocent of any collusion with Krüpl and company. There were only two things Mahler could do. The first would be to get out of Kitzbühel as fast as possible. The second would be to get to a pay station and call Hollingsworth. As far as Slater knew, Mahler had no car so he would have to take the morning train. Slater looked at his watch. Mahler had an hour to make it to the station—provided he was innocent.

Slater stepped out of the telephone booth and out of the lobby into the street. He crossed the street and joined the skiers on their way to the cable car. The sky was overcast and bleak, and there were not as many skiers as would be normal, even for a Monday morning. Slater took up a position at the corner of the railroad station platform nearest the crossing gates, positive that he could not miss Mahler, if Mahler appeared.

A half an hour went by and it started to snow. The snow came down heavily, and the skiers on their way to the cable station stopped and turned back to their inns and pensions. Slater turned for a moment and looked up at the mountain. The top was shrouded in a cloud, and a cable car suddenly emerged from the mist, coming down to the valley station. Apparently, only one was still running, and that was empty except for the attendant. Possibly the skiers already up at the top preferred to remain, hoping the snow would let up and allow them a day's skiing.

From where Slater was standing, it did not look as though the snow would stop at least until the evening. He stood there on the edge of the now deserted platform and, protected by the eaves of the station's roof, watched the visibility close down as the snow increased. He had never seen such a quiet snowstorm. The big flakes fell straight down by the thousands, one on top of the other, and would soon blanket every man-made thing and smooth out the rough edges of the world around him.

Slater peered through the curtain of snowflakes toward the road. Mahler should have been there by now, if he were coming. He must have been one of Krüpl's men after all. And then Slater saw the figure of a man trudging through the snow. He was lugging a suitcase, his eyes straight ahead looking toward the station. By the time Slater could make certain it was really Mahler, he heard what sounded like a shot, and he saw Mahler pitch headlong into the snow.

Slater ran across the tracks to Mahler. He tripped on one of the now invisible railroad ties and fell on his face ten yards from Mahler's suitcase. The fall undoubtedly saved his life, for he heard another shot which seemed to come from nowhere. The snow made sounds impossible to trace. Slater cursed, his mouth full of snow, and waited. A man finally appeared and approached Mahler cautiously. He stopped about fifteen yards from the other side of Mahler's body and took careful aim with what looked like an automatic. Another shot sounded, and the man toppled into the snow, a bullet in his throat.

Slater waited another minute, put his .38 back in his parka, got back on his feet and crouched down beside Mahler. Mahler was still face down in the snow. There was a bullet hole underneath his left shoulder blade. Slater rolled him over gently, and Mahler opened his eyes and looked up, his mouth open and his eyes vague and puzzled.

"Heinz," said Slater. "This is Carmichael."

"You," Heinz gasped for breath. "You don't look like Carmichael."

"I know," said Slater, "but I am. I was wearing a black wig. Don't you recognize my voice, Heinz?" Slater's voice was urgent. It was, suddenly, terribly important to him that Heinz believe he was a genuine person. "My name is really Slater, Bill Slater."

"Why—" Heinz nearly went under "—did you shoot me?"

"Dear God!" said Slater, frantic now that Mahler, who had really been a friend, would die thinking he had shot him. "I didn't. I just killed the man who shot you. Look, Heinz, please! Listen to me! It was I who telephoned you this morning. I was suspicious of you because I got mousetrapped last night." The tears were streaming down Slater's face.

"Mousetrapped?" Heinz' eyes were vague. "Trapped by—a mouse. What—" Heinz Mahler never finished the question.

Slater remained on his knees in the snow and stared through his tears at Mahler's blood, as it spread slowly into the whiteness. He could not be sure, of course, but he thought, he hoped, there was just the trace of an impish smile on Mahler's dead face.

Slater lifted Mahler's body up by the shoulders, trying not to realize how really slight he was, and then turned him so he was facing the dead stranger, and laid Mahler down on his stomach in the snow again. He took out his .38, wiped it clean and put it in Mahler's right hand.

Slater walked over to the body of Heinz' assailant and removed all the personal papers from inside his corduroy jacket. The face meant nothing to him, but the clothing did. He was dressed like a local citizen of medium circumstances. He must have been Stadler's partner. Slater turned away and groped through the snow back toward the town. In an hour, when the snow had covered up his tracks, he would call the police from a phone booth. They would discover an unidentified body, a gun with two shots fired and his friend Mahler with a

.38, the serial number of which had long ago been removed with acid.

Slater never looked back. There was too much back there he wanted to forget, but it would take more than a heavy snowfall to smooth the rough edges of his world, and more than acid to eat the memory of Heinz' death from his brain. It was truly a rotten world he lived in, which prevented him from personally acknowledging the death of a friend. Slater's outline disappeared from the scene behind the lacy curtain of soundless snowflakes.

Chapter 15

When Slater reached the Bichlstrasse, he found it almost deserted. It was still early, and the skiers were not yet aware that they were to become shoppers because the snow was going to continue through the day. The public lounges, the library, the cocktail bars and cafés were going to be filled. Possibly a few of the vacationers would suddenly realize how tired they really were and would take the opportunity to catch up on their sleep while the world around them turned whiter and, somehow, newer again.

As Slater scuffed through the snow, he tried to keep down the feeling of hate which was stealing its way, unwanted, into his consciousness. It was a feeling he had had often. It was the one bulwark which kept out, momentarily at least, the more shameful emotion of fear. But to Slater, whose career had been made from man's fear and hate, this was no solution, because his hate was fast extending to the world—a world in which no nation could entirely trust another, which in turn reflected itself in the actions of its citizens. Economic idealism, thought Slater, which brought death to the Webbers and Mahlers and paid the wages for more than a million people like himself all over the world to further exploit, foster and develop still more hate. Slater believed in his country, but no longer on a right or wrong basis. He detested the politicians who made political capital of the misery of others. Worst of all, he felt trapped. There was no honorable way out for his conscience. He hung on to his sanity by believing that he, at least, was attacking what he knew was bad. He was not forced to spread lies or half-truths about the perfection of his own nation, nor did he directly encourage enslaved peoples with the visions of a Utopian democracy to hurl their defenseless bodies against steel tanks. Slater was still able to cling tenaciously to the conviction that what he was assigned to fight was inherently bad. The Krüpls and Stadlers were pawns of the most inhuman political machine the world had ever seen; and this was what kept him fighting his fears and, consequently, the enemies not only of his nation but of the people his enemies pretended to represent.

But Slater had had too much experience in the international scene not to be a realist; and he was continually plagued with the feeling a climber must get when, on a shale-covered mountainside, after two steps upward, the slippery rocky soil slides out from under him, and he is carried, against his will, one step backward. Slater was a sensitive man, an idealist, a man who wanted to believe; and because of his ability to feel, to sympathize, to fear, to understand even his enemies, he was a dangerous, effective counterespionage agent and not simply a thug or a brainless adventure seeker. For ten years he had worked, not for pay, but because he had believed. But there had been too many casualties for his beliefs—too many Heinz Mahlers. Now Slater felt he, too, was becoming a casualty—the way he had to live, full of suspicion that turned to fear and then, as a bulwark against his fears, into hate. Slater knew there must be something better for him. He was becoming sick with the politicians' and militarists' glib discussions of expendables in the big picture. He hadn't known Webber and had only just begun to know Mahler, but he had known many others, men and women of character, who had lost their lives for a cause. They were not expendable. There are never enough of those kinds of people to go around. And now, thought Slater, I'm about to call in another—for the cause.

He opened the glass door to the sidewalk telephone station. The door left a fan design as it pushed back the snow. Slater called Zurich, identified himself to Hollingsworth and requested clear conversation immediately. George had been about to leave for the Consulate.

"Bankers' hours, George?" asked Slater.

"I was up a little late last night." George sounded embarrassed.

"Your hours are your own affair, George." Slater hadn't meant to sound sarcastic. "Charlie's been killed. I didn't see the body," he added, "but I've no reason to doubt that he's dead." Slater cursed inwardly. There just wasn't any gentle way to break that kind of news.

"I'm sorry, Karl," said Hollingsworth after a moment. "I'm sure you did all you could."

Slater was grateful for that remark.

"I've made some progress down here," said Slater, "and I think I'm about to make some more."

"Good," said George. "Isn't W supposed to leave today?"

"Yes," said Slater, "but I'm quite certain he won't. If he asks for an extension of his leave, make certain he receives it."

"Right."

"I'm going to present you with a choice, George." Slater knew it would only sound like a choice. "Either you get my office to send me a man or you can come down here yourself."

"When do you want me?" said George without any hesitation. Slater cursed again, but he was pleased.

"As soon as possible."

"Right," said George. "I'll be there this afternoon. Shall I take the train?"

"Yes."

"Where will you meet me?" said George.

"Don't worry. I'll pick you up after you leave the station. You know the two places not to go. If for some reason," Slater added, "I don't contact you, find an inn and go have a drink and dinner at the Café des Engels."

"Suppose I run into W?"

"Act surprised," said Slater, "but don't overdo it. Remember, this time, unlike Charlie, you've got a friend."

"Right" said George.

Slater wished Hollingsworth didn't always say "Right!" with that eager-beaver inflection, but he made no comment.

"One more thing," said Slater. "Contact my office before you leave. Tell them to send all the information I requested to Salzburg and hold any mail. Just say Annie doesn't live there any more. I'll phone Salzburg tonight."

"Right!" said George. "I'll see you this afternoon. I'm glad you want me to come down. Oh, by the way, your office refused to expose you to our Saxon friends. They think you're too important."

"Well, I'll be damned," said Slater and then added, "Be prepared for a little surprise when we meet. Auf wiedersehen."

Slater hung up. He had wanted to mention Mahler so that Putnam could do something for Mahler's family, but his name might be picked up by an operator and connected with the corpse lying out in the snow.

Slater phoned the police, gave them the information about Heinz and hung up. He left the phone station and returned to the hotel and checked the train schedule. He still had several hours. He started on the way upstairs to his room to work out some way to get Rüdi alone when he felt a hand on his arm. He turned and there stood Ilse Wieland, her green eyes smiling up at him.

"Hello, Bill Slater," she said. "You haven't forgotten our engagement tonight?"

"No," He smiled in spite of himself, "I haven't."

"You will take me then?" Ilse looked up at him anxiously.

"If you want to go," said Slater.

"It was the only way I could think of to have your company." She continued to look directly at him, but she was no longer smiling. "It was obvious you were not going to ask me anywhere."

"Why don't we go somewhere else then?" Slater was convinced she would object to that.

"But that would not be polite," she said. "The Baron has asked us, and we have accepted. We must go."

She's more than a match for me, Bill thought. She's too lovely and too appealing.

"Very well," he said. "The Baron's it is."

"Are you going upstairs to visit someone?" she asked.

"No," said Slater, "I'm going up to my room."

"You have moved, then?" she said.

Slater just stood there and looked at her, remembering all at once that when he had brought her back to the hotel from the Café des Engels he had left her on these stairs. She had remembered and noted that he had not, at that time, been a guest of the hotel.

"They didn't have a room here when I arrived," he said. "I wasn't able to move in until Sunday afternoon."

"I see," she said.

Slater had to find out immediately who this woman really was and what she knew about him. Too much had happened for him to let her destroy his position—if she hadn't already done so.

"Why," said Slater, feeling strangely embarrassed, "why

don't you come up to my room and have a quiet drink with me?"

He could have cut out his tongue. He knew he had said it too fast. No woman would accept such an awkwardly put proposition on a staircase in a hotel lobby filled with people who had nothing better to do on a snowy day than eavesdrop. Much to his surprise, she accepted. She took hold of his hand and accompanied him upstairs. He couldn't think of a thing to say, and it made him furious. He had always considered himself a man of the world.

He unlocked his door and stepped aside to let Ilse enter. He pointed to the easy chair and picked up the house phone. His own voice sounded strange.

"Please send up some Scotch, soda water, ice and two glasses to room twenty-seven, right away."

Slater was, suddenly, desperate for a drink. He turned, expecting to see Ilse seated in the chair. To his consternation, she was standing right behind him. They were now face to face, their eyes almost on the same level.

"You Americans are so strange," she said.

"I guess I am acting kind of crazy," said Slater. "Why don't you sit down?" It sounded more like a plea than a simple request.

"Because," she said slowly, "I prefer to stand." She paused and looked into eyes almost as green as her own, tense, wary, tired eyes. "And because," she continued, "I want you to kiss me. You want to. I know you do—and you need to. Please!"

Slater took Ilse into his arms. Her lips were unbelievably soft and willing. She stood up close to him. Her arms went around his neck and she returned his embrace. They stood close and kissed each other over and over again. She kissed his eyes, the corners of his mouth, his neck, and neither said anything intelligible until the bellhop's knock on the door interrupted them, and they were forced to separate.

Slater thought the boy would never stop fussing around the room, pointing to the ice, commenting on the brand of Scotch, asking if there was enough soda water, until Slater was ready to throw him out. Slater locked the door after him, when the boy finally left. He turned back to Ilse.

"Who are you, for the love of God? If you're something else I can't believe in, I'm going to go crazy! Maybe this is an everyday thing in your book, but it's not in mine."

"I know." Ilse's voice was soothing. "I could see it in your eyes, Bill Slater, Bruce Carmichael—or whatever your real name is."

Ilse started toward him again, but Slater backed away and she stopped.

"Who are you?" said Slater.

"I am Ilse Wieland. I have a dress shop in Munich. I am on a special assignment for the West German government," she said. Her statements seemed mechanical.

"And just who do you think I am?" Slater's eyes were still tense.

"I think you are here for your government to meet a Hungarian colonel by the name of Imré Dinar."

Slater had finally regained his composure and concealed any reaction to the name.

"Have you any way of identifying yourself?"

"No," she said. "Have you?"

Slater did not answer, and Ilse took another step in his direction.

"Please, Ilse," he said, "sit down and let me think."

The one time in his life when he had wanted his office to expose him they had refused. Lord knows, they had done so, inadvertently, enough times. The Germans had already refused to reveal their agent's identity. That was the real reason for his office's refusal, Slater was certain. It wasn't because they didn't believe he was not expendable. And now what?

Her knowledge of Dinar proved only that she was either what she claimed, a member of German Intelligence, or in the employ of the Communists. This tender scene might be a perfect provocation to take him off his guard, to find out what he knew. The Communists couldn't have picked a better instrument. Ilse was, without any doubt, the most compelling woman he had ever known. He refused to admit any more than that. Nor could the Communists have chosen a more opportune time. In that crazy, emotional outburst, he might have— Slater snapped his mind shut and looked across the room at her.

"Care for a drink?" he asked. His mind was steady, but his hands were not.

"I would be delighted, Liebchen," Ilse smiled slowly. She was now sitting on the bed. "You can think what you like, but you will not be able to close your mind to me, Bill Slater. I will wait."

Chapter 16

Bill Slater handed Ilse her drink and retreated across the room. He sat down in the chair and took a long swallow of his drink.

"Just let us suppose that you are working for your government," he said slowly, not looking at Ilse. "How do you expect to find this Hungarian colonel?"

"I have a picture of him and identification signals to exchange with him," she said. "The difficulty is that the Communists have captured my predecessor and may have the passwords also—as well as better pictures."

Slater took another long swallow of his drink.

"Do you have a prearranged meeting place?"

"Yes," she said. "The Colonel has only been to Kitzbühel once in his life before. At that time he stayed at the Ehrenbachhöhe Hotel. I am to meet him there."

"When?" Slater tipped his glass, but it was empty, and he got up to pour himself another drink.

"I was supposed to meet him," she said, "the day I met you and Herr Wyman; but if you remember, Herr Wyman accompanied me to the hotel, and we had coffee together. If the Colonel was there, I didn't see him."

"Does the Colonel know what you look like?" Slater watched her face carefully.

"No," she said. "How could he?"

"I just wondered." Slater frowned. "Tell me, do you think that the Colonel will be at the Ehrenbachhöhe Hotel this evening?"

"I don't know."

"Do you think that the Baron's party tonight is a coincidence?"

"I don't know what to think." Ilse appeared to look thoughtful. "I have only known the Baron since I am here."

"What about the thin Englishman, Hormsby?" Slater asked. "Had you known him before?"

"No."

"What do you think of Wyman?"

"Herr Wyman is a very handsome young man," said Ilse. Slater felt himself becoming angry. "But," she continued, "he is a weakling."

"He's an excellent skier," Slater said, torturing himself.

"Not any better than you, Bill Slater." Ilse's reply was very quick. "He cares more about showing off than he does about his neck."

"He wanted you to admire him," said Slater, wondering why he couldn't get off the subject of Wyman.

"I don't admire him, Liebchen." Ilse looked at Slater with such gentleness in her eyes that he nearly went over to her and took her in his arms.

"Why did the Baron invite you to his party?"

"Because I am an attractive woman." Ilse's reply was matter-of-fact.

"You are a beautiful woman, Ilse—whatever else you may be." Slater had not meant to say that. It just slipped out.

"Oh, Liebling!" Ilse started to get up again.

"Sit down!" Slater shouted, and Ilse sat very still. "If you are what you say you are, Ilse, you must realize that you are in danger."

"Not until I have established myself with the Colonel," she said. "There is just the possibility that my predecessor did not give the Communists the identification procedure."

"You called me Carmichael a few minutes ago. Why?"

"Your height can change," she said, "the color of your hair—even your voice, but not your eyes or hands." Ilse smiled and then looked at him, her face suddenly quite serious. "Don't you know, William Slater, that you cannot fool a woman in love?"

Slater poured himself another drink.

"Help yourself, if you'd care for another," he said. His voice was gruff.

He seated himself in the chair again and watched her as she moved across the room. She was in her ski clothes, and her motions were as smooth as a cat's.

She made herself a drink, her back toward him, and then turned and raised her glass.

"Prosit" she said and drank. "I don't think anyone else realizes your dual identity," said Ilse. "I thought at first that Wyman was the American agent. It was not until I realized your double identity that I was convinced you were the one."

"What made you think there should be an American agent?" asked Slater.

"My superiors told me your government had sent someone down here."

"Tell me, Ilse, if you meet this colonel, what then?"

"This," said Ilse thoughtfully, "is a problem." She turned to Slater and smiled. "I had thought you might help me with that."

"I see."

Slater turned his mind inward and tried to think. Ilse had still not told him anything that the Communists might not want him to know. That the Ehrenbachhöhe Hotel was the meeting place might or might not be true, but the possibility would be enough to guarantee his presence there, and that was probably what they wanted. On the other hand, the party might be an excuse to get everyone under suspicion under one roof, where the Baron or someone else could take care of them. Slater knew the questions to ask Ilse which might establish her identity, but he was strangely reluctant to do so.

"Ilse?"

"Yes." She was back on the bed.

"What is the identification procedure?" Slater hung on her answer.

"My orders are not to reveal it," she said quietly. "I can't," her face was suddenly contorted, "not even to you!"

"Why not?" Slater knew why. It was because she was his enemy.

"Because they might capture you and torture you for it, Liebchen! It is safer that only one of us knows!"

"What about the picture?"

"I haven't got it with me," she said. "I would show it to you tonight, but I think it might be dangerous to take it with me."

"I see."

"No" she cried. "You don't see! You are so full of suspicion, you can no longer see anything!" Ilse stood up. "You can't even see love when it looks at you."

She moved across the room and stood in front of Slater's chair. "You are so full of fears, and you are so tense inside, you are going to blow up in a million pieces" Ilse's eyes filled with tears. "It isn't wrong to kiss a woman, even if you think she is your enemy. You want too much from life, William Slater."

She started for the door and unlocked it. "I can't love a bunch of stretched wires, a tortured creature who is no longer human and is even afraid of a woman's kisses. Good-by, Herr Slater!"

Ilse slammed the door behind her.

Chapter 17

Slater poured himself half a water glass of whisky and drank it down. He stared at the closed door for a moment and shook his head. He did not have much time to discover the things he had to know before that party tonight. It was one party he could not afford to miss.

Slater picked up the house phone and called the dining room.

"Is Rüdi on duty now?"

"No, sir," said a voice that Slater had never heard. "Rüdi does not come on duty until four o'clock today."

"Do you know where I can reach him?"

"Just one moment please, sir."

Slater waited patiently until he heard the receiver being picked up again.

"He lives on the Hornweg, number twenty-five." The voice gave Slater Rüdi's phone number in addition, and the conversation was at an end.

Slater left his room, went downstairs and out into the snow. He turned left on the Bichlstrasse and left again down some stone steps and into the first of the back streets of the village. The snow was still coming down thickly from a motionless gray sky. He stopped for a minute and stood at the corner of a narrow street and listened. There was no traffic of any kind, and the absolute quiet was unnerving. The snowflakes gathered on his bare head and coated his eyebrows. He tried to peer through the snowflakes and penetrate the wall of gloom around him, but he could not see more than a radius of twenty feet. It was not, he admitted, that he had heard anything suspicious, but he had the uneasy feeling someone was watching him. If Kitzbühel was, as he suspected, the pay center for Communist agents, eliminating all possible pursuers would be like trying to dig a hole in the ocean.

Slater started walking through the snow again, a little faster this time. He rounded a corner and stopped suddenly, his back against the wall of a house. He waited and held his breath, but no one appeared around the corner. Ilse was right. He was a bunch of stretched wires. Hollingsworth had noticed it, Slater knew, but how much of this sort of thing could a man take—even a man without fear? He resumed his walking, turned into the Hornweg and followed it, until he came to number 25. The tracks going up to the front door were partially filled in. There was only one set of footprints, and they definitely were going into the house and not away from it. Slater stepped into the prints. His were slightly larger. He was wearing his ski boots, and there was no way of knowing what the person who had made the tracks had worn. He knocked on the door and waited.

The door was opened by a short stout Hausfrau with grayish hair. She looked surprised.

"Ja? What do you want?" she asked.

"Is Herr Rüdi Petsch at home, please?" Slater smiled. "I would like to talk to him."

The woman hesitated a moment. "I will see if my husband is awake yet. He works late, you know," she added. "Wait here."

She closed the door and left Slater standing in the snow. It was several minutes before the door opened again and Rüdi stood on the threshold. He was only half dressed. His night shirt was bulging over his pants. He no longer looked like the immaculate headwaiter whose body strained against every button, but he was still dough-faced and shapeless.

"I," he hesitated, "I don't believe we have met, Herr—?"

"No," said Slater still speaking German, his tone peremptory and very businesslike, "but my name is not important. I must have a word with you—inside."

Slater entered the house without waiting for an invitation. Rüdi stepped aside to let Slater in and then just stood there and looked at him.

"Close the door, please," said Slater.

Rüdi did as he was told.

"Herr Krüpl has disappeared," Slater began watching Rüdi closely.

"Herr Krüpl? Who is Herr Krüpl?" Rüdi seemed honestly puzzled.

"That's right, of course," said Slater heartily. "You didn't know Herr Krüpl. You were recruited by Herr—, I mean, by someone else."

"Who is Herr Krüpl, and why should I care if he has disappeared?" Rüdi looked annoyed.

"Herr Krüpl is the man who pays you, of course," said Slater patiently, as if Rüdi was being very slow to understand. "I have been ordered to take his place. There are people to be contacted, and I don't know who they are, because, unfortunately, Herr Krüpl disappeared without telling us your method of contact."

"I knew it!" said Rüdi. "It was that Herr Carmichael!"

"Who?" Slater appeared excited. "If you know something which might help to explain Krüpl's sudden disappearance, please tell me at once."

"This man, Carmichael, he is a guest at the hotel," Rüdi explained. "He tried to make contact with me at the bar instead of the dining room."

"Why did you pay any attention to him?"

"Because he said the right things and explained that he didn't want Herr Wyman, with whom he had been dining, to know he was one of us. I don't believe Wyman is considered altogether trustworthy. Anyway," Rüdi added, "you know how carefully we are separated from each other. This was the first time in two years I had two men on the same day."

"But I don't understand," said Slater. "Didn't you communicate your suspicions to Krüpl?"

"Yes, naturally. I put a question mark on the menu after the information." Rüdi was indignant.

"Well?" said Slater.

"Yes. Well, Krüpl must have tried to investigate Herr Carmichael and gotten in trouble."

"What room does Carmichael have?"

"Room twenty-three, but he checked out Sunday," said Rüdi, "Anton told me."

"I see," said Slater. "That is not good."

"The menus were an excellent idea, Rüdi," said Slater. "Was it yours?"

"Mine, and the man who hired me." Rüdi stopped talking and, suddenly, looked with suspicion at Slater. "Why didn't you know about the menus?"

"I told you," said Slater patiently. "Krüpl has disappeared, and your recruiter is not even in Europe at the moment. Your work is essential, Rüdi. It is important that you continue. Now, explain what you do with the menus. I think I know already."

"It's really very simple," Rüdi began. "After the contact has established himself at the evening meal, and he has signed his name and room number on the check, I take this information and transfer it to the next day's menu."

"Which," broke in Slater, "you then post outside to the left of the entrance to the hotel."

"Exactly, sir."

It was clever all right. Anybody and everybody could be passing the hotel after dinner. It wouldn't attract attention for someone to stop and have a look at the menu.

"I assume," said Slater, "that the individual's name is not important."

"No, only his room number, and the place he is staying." Then Rüdi added, by way of explanation, "One cannot always get a room at the Winterhof."

"No," said Slater. "The Winterhof is a very popular hotel."

He wanted to smile, but he didn't think Rüdi would appreciate it.

"How do you indicate," Slater asked, "which hotel the individual is using?"

"It can only be one of three," he said. "If it's the Winterhof, I make no mark. If it's the Grieswirt or the Alpenblick, I place a very small A or G at the bottom right-hand corner. For the room number I place a period directly above the digits."

"Do you do this in sequence?" asked Slater.

"Pardon?" Rüdi looked confused.

"If the room number," said Slater, "is twenty-nine, for example, do you dot the first figure two you find on the price list for that day, and then dot the first figure nine after that?"

"Exactly," said Rüdi.

"From now on," said Slater, "I want you to do just the opposite. Dot the first nine first, and then the first two after that."

Slater had to explain in some detail, and, finally, ended up telling Rüdi to reverse any room number he received and enter the result the same as he had done before. Thus, twenty-three would become thirty-two, etc.

Slater mopped his brow. This Rüdi, he thought, was certainly not the smartest man in Kitzbühel.

"Do you know," Slater asked, "what happens after that?"

"No, sir!" said Rüdi proudly. "I'm not supposed to know, and I don't."

"You were quite free with Wyman's name just now." Slater looked at Rüdi coldly for a moment.

"I am very sorry, sir, but he has been here two times in the last three weeks. I was told not to put down his room number. Anyway, he is the first man who has contacted me twice, so, naturally, I remembered his name. I have forgotten all the others, believe me, sir!'

"How much are you paid, Rüdi?"

"Twelve hundred schillings a month, sir—on the first day of the month."

Less than fifty American dollars a month, thought Slater. He was always shocked at how little it cost to buy an agent in Europe. Was this fat little man a Communist, or was he simply shortsighted like so many of their other employees? After all, fifty dollars a month, tax free in Austria, plus his hotel salary and tips would constitute a pretty good haul. Rüdi undoubtedly considered himself a wealthy man—and shrewd, very shrewd.

"Do you always discuss your suspicions and assignments with Anton?"

"No, sir," Rüdi seemed horrified at the idea, "but he is in a position to know the names and room numbers of the guests. I use him occasionally. He will do anything for money," Rüdi added.

And you won't, Slater thought, marveling at the almost blissful inconsistency of people.

"You must not discuss me or give my description to anyone, you understand?"

"Yes, sir, of course," said Rüdi.

"I will not be here long. I will pass the new communication procedure along to my replacement. You are not to try and contact me in any way except through the medium of the menu. If you suspect trouble or are interrogated by anyone, put a small triangle in the lower left-hand corner of the menu. That will mean that you want to meet me. I will phone you and tell you where and when we can meet."

Slater did not want to set up any meeting place in advance from which he might be ambushed. Should anyone get to Rüdi with a convincing or more lucrative proposition, Slater didn't want to give him time to get his new friends to the meeting place first.

Slater started to go. He stopped at the door and turned back to Rüdi.

"You have done an excellent job, Herr Petsch. We are grateful to you."

"I've tried to do my best, sir." Rüdi bowed, and his chins hung loose, like the crop of a turkey, as he did so.

"I will try to get you a small bonus," said Slater. Rüdi's eyes glittered. "Although," Slater added, "a job well done for the party should be its own reward."

"But, of course, sir!" The expression in Rüdi's eyes did not match his stated enthusiasm.

"Still," Slater mused aloud, "a little extra money never hurt anyone, nicht?"

Slater permitted himself a little smile and put his hand on the door. Rüdi rushed up eagerly to open it for him.

"Perhaps," said Slater putting his hand against the door, "I should leave by the back entrance."

"Oh, yes," said Rüdi. "I will show you the way."

Slater stepped out into the snow again, put up the hood of

his parka and trudged through the whiteness along a narrow back street which ran more or less parallel to Bichlstrasse, the main street of the town.

Apparently Krüpl had really taken matters into his own hands without the knowledge of his superiors. He had employed Stadler to help him, and yet, Slater frowned, something didn't quite fit. Slater tackled espionage nets organizationally, and he had already formed a picture of this net's organizational outline. Normally, he did not believe in preconceptions. They could be as misleading to the counterespionage agent as to the scientist. Slater was almost positive he had his fingers in two pies. Rüdi, Krüpl, the money, all pointed to a payoff organization. Wyman and Stadler must be part of an action net or an active espionage organization. It was a serious deviation from classically tried and proven clandestine procedure to dovetail the two organizations except at the top echelon, and it was a sound principle, rarely violated. If the two organizations worked together with full or even partial knowledge of each other, the activities of one would be a serious threat to the other. They should be kept separate, so that the exposure of one would not mean the end of both.

Two things came to Slater's mind. The first was that if there was any dovetailing, the Communists must have considered the present situation extremely important and have given Krüpl unusual authority. What could be so very important about a Hungarian colonel's defection? Such defections were common. Slater thought back to the article he had read in Zurich at the Baur-au-Lac Hotel while waiting for Wyman. The writer had discussed the possibility, which he apparently considered imminent, of an organized satellite rebellion. Slater's reaction, then and now, was that such a thing would be impossible, would be foolhardy in fact—unless the Western democracies were alerted by the revolutionaries beforehand

and were persuaded by their organization and determination to join the timetable and begin World War III.

Was it possible that Imré Dinar had left Hungary to ask for Western military aid in exchange for full particulars as to the satellites' revolutionary organization and military timetable?

Slater wondered what his office really knew. They frequently thought they knew more than they actually did. More to the point, they often withheld information from Slater, for his own protection, they said; but he knew that was not always the case. The withholding of vital information was usually for his country's protection, not his. What he didn't know, he couldn't tell. Slater was a realist. More important, he was a professional, who did the same with those who worked with and for him. He told them only what they needed to know to do their job effectively.

But he wondered whether his government knew for a fact what he, so far, was only beginning to suspect about Imré Dinar. And, if his superiors did know, what would they really want him to do about it? Slater didn't want his country to start another world war, not even in support of people who loved freedom more than their own lives. It was a terrible thing to admit, but he had to be honest, at least with himself. He believed in individual freedom as much as any man he knew. He had fought the Nazis and had been a prisoner for two years for his beliefs, but he knew that the next war would bring such total misery for everyone that he didn't believe it would settle anything. He had been working for ten years to prevent any further penetrations of the West by the Communists. His one hope was that the Communist party in Russia would lose face in the world of nations and in Russia to the extent that the Russian people would revolt and repudiate their government. He had to admit that he was losing faith in such a possibility.

Suppose Dinar was what Slater now suspected? If he contacted the West, would even the hotheads at home throw their armies into another world war? Slater didn't like the idea of presenting them with the opportunity.

From the point of view of the revolutionaries within the satellites, Slater knew his course was quite clear. He had to prevent the Communists from getting hold of Dinar and forcing him to reveal names, dates, military stockpiles, organization, numbers—all the information he must have to convince the West.

But if he did manage, somehow, to get to Dinar, he would have to try to convince him to maintain the organization, increase it if he could, but hold it in abeyance until Russia actually attacked the Western world, and then use it as a guerrilla force to sabotage Russia's efforts and to strike suddenly from within their countries but only in co-ordination with an all-out Allied offensive. If the revolutionaries struck now, they would be crushed immediately by the Russian armies.

Slater knew that telling this to Dinar would probably be useless. How could you tell a people not to revolt against slavery when the very reason for their organization was because they could no longer tolerate their existence in a total dictatorship?

And this, thought Slater, might be the "big picture." It was no wonder the Western leaders of character were confused and upset. How could anyone make a wise decision with such alternatives?

And when the Hungarian underground had gotten Dinar across the border into Austria, with what instruction had they left him? They could not let a man with information which could ruin them, loose in Europe for too long. They had to know that he was alive and free from Communist hands. If they believed he had been captured, they would strike immediately, before the Russians could learn of their plans and destroy them. Dinar must be maintaining communications somehow. When those communications stopped, the revolutionaries would attack immediately, and thousands of lovers of freedom would lose their lives.

If the Russians had the smallest suspicion of all this, they would not hesitate to kill anyone who might stand between them and Dinar. It was no wonder they had recruited Wyman. An American government official stood a far better chance of getting Dinar's information than the Russians did.

Slater turned the corner and began the crossover to the Bichlstrasse, which would now be the Josef Pirchlstrasse. It would have been a lot simpler, he thought, if the Kitzbühelers had called it Main Street and been done with it.

Slater shook his head, and the snow which had accumulated there fell on his shoulders and onto the ground. Krüpl, he thought, must have notified somebody of his intention to trap Carmichael, but whom? It would only be a matter of time before Slater's connection with Carmichael would be discovered. Had Ilse Wieland been assigned to confirm that connection? Would the Communists wait for proof or was the situation sufficiently serious to warrant his immediate destruction? They had murdered Webber. Murdering Americans, particularly those with diplomatic status, was not their mode of operation, but only, Slater knew, because up until now it had not been necessary.

Chapter 18

The electric train from Salzburg droned through the storm and sent the snowflakes spinning crazily in its wake, but nothing could prevent their piling on top of the already deep snow. So far, the train had made good time in spite of the whiteness in the high mountain passes. Fortunately, there was still no wind to create the impassable drifts so common to the Tyrol. The air was unbelievably dry, and the snow was light and fluffy. It was as though the great cloud bank, drifting slowly into western Austria, had stopped, hemmed in by the Alps, and was now trying to shake off its tons of snow in order to raise itself high above the peaks that held it captive and drift on again into the heart of Europe and beyond.

Gregor Slazov gave up trying to see out of the train windows and looked at his wrist watch. He should be in Kitzbühel within the hour. He smiled to himself. It had been a long time since he had been in the decadent West and particularly with such an important assignment. True, he shrugged, all his assignments were the same, but this one would mean a great deal to his career. The Comrade Stottoff must indeed already think much of Gregor Slazov to have given him such a mission; besides, the Comrade General was slipping. He had been too soft. He, Gregor Slazov, had told him that. No, Slazov thought, Stottoff had not picked him for this assignment. The Comrade General did not like Slazov's methods. Slazov smiled. The Comrade General did not, in fact, like Slazov. He is afraid of me. One day soon, he may have good reason to be afraid. Comrade General Gregor Slazov. How did that sound? Slazov laughed, and his laughter was deep. It sounded good.

Gregor Slazov had come a long way in the party. He knew that because he knew people were afraid of him. He would be one of the real leaders someday. He had tried to prepare himself for this responsibility by attempting to eliminate all traces of his peasant background. He had tried to refine his speech, to read only what were considered the best books in Russian and even Western culture. He had become a student of music and art. He had even tried to lose weight. His thick short body and heavy, slab-sided, peasant face with its small, almost slant eyes were a source of much discouragement and despair. He tried to hide his stockiness with expensive clothes, but they always looked unpressed and pinch-waisted. Comrade Gregor Slazov was a snob.

The Comrade General had not told him much, but, Slazov reflected, it was not really necessary. Perhaps, even the Comrade General did not know very much. Anyway, the job was simple. All he had to do was find an American named Carmichael and kill him. Slazov interested himself mildly in what this American called Carmichael had done. It must have been serious. One was not ordered to kill an American every day. If one was successful, then one would make more progress in the party.

Slazov knew better than to try and plan the execution at this time. The method had naturally been left up to him. The Comrade General had not been so generous with the element of time. Carmichael had to be disposed of immediately. He would be pointed out to Slazov at the Hotel Winterhof; and if, for some reason, the two men missed connections there, Slazov would be introduced to him later.

Gregor Slazov settled back in the seat and closed his eyes. Murder was a good career for a man. It kept him stimulated and made his life sweeter. When he could see, at first hand, how easily men died, it made the breath of his own life fresher, the touch of a woman more exciting, the taste of food more satisfying, the aroma of wine headier. He looked upon game hunters with contempt. They knew nothing of the hunt. The most exciting game of all was man.

The train slowed gradually to a stop at the Kitzbühel station. The valley floor was relatively flat, and there was little danger, but it was a matter of pride with the engineer that his train never skidded, no matter what the weather conditions.

Slazov reached for the expensive suitcase in the rack above his head. It was quite a stretch for his short body, but he finally got it down. The leather bag was heavy, but he handled it as though it weighed no more than a piece of balsa wood. He left the compartment and moved along the corridor. He climbed down the steps to the platform and landed neatly in the snow. Slazov was surprisingly light on his feet.

In spite of the weather there were a number of people at the station. The train from Zurich was just pulling out. Slazov looked at as many of the faces that he could see distinctly. He noticed a tall, young, dark-haired man who was obviously American. He watched closely as the young man started off into the storm toward the town. This could not be Carmichael, thought Slazov. This man is just arriving. He looks like a young diplomat. Gregor Slazov prided himself on his ability to spot certain types at a glance. He decided to follow the young American.

George Hollingsworth was excited. Meeting and talking with a man like Carmichael had been a stimulating experience. When Carmichael had called on him, he felt that he was, at last, going to participate personally and actively in this cloak-and-dagger business. Every diplomat should have firsthand experience in at least one such affair. It would enable him to have more savoir-faire in diplomatic negotiations. It should give him a feeling of latent power to know that he could handle these clandestine forces. Maybe one day he could employ some of his own. George was elated. He would show Carmichael that an amateur could learn fast.

George put his head down and stepped out into the world of thickly falling snow. He walked slowly, not able to see more than a few feet ahead, wondering just how Carmichael would pick him up in this storm, when he felt a sudden bump in his right side and heard someone say, "Excuse me. Didn't see you in all this snow." Hollingsworth turned, fully expecting to see Carmichael. Instead, he saw a ruddy-faced man in ski clothes who must be heavier than he appeared because the bump had given George quite a jar. He could not immediately determine the color of the stranger's hair because it was covered with snow. When George looked at the green eyes, the wary, tense eyes, he knew it was Carmichael.

"Hello, Bruce," said George, proud of himself at having known him almost immediately.

"Hello, George," said Slater, surprised at Hollingsworth's quick identification but relieved that he wouldn't have to go into any lengthy proof.

"If I'm that obvious," said Slater, "the Carmichael routine was a waste of time."

"Not at all," said Hollingsworth. "It was because I was expecting you. I couldn't see you too well at first, and I recognized your voice."

That much was true, thought George, but it's his eyes. They'd give him away to anyone who took the trouble to look. George could not get rid of the impression that Slater was really a man with black, not brown hair. Slater would always be Carmichael to Hollingsworth. Possibly it was because he had met him first as Carmichael. The sun-tanned man who now stood beside him looking like a person who lived out of doors would appear to the casual observer to be a free spirit whose facial lines, those around the outer corners of his eyes and mouth, had been caused by smiling into the sun and wind, and laughing at the rain. Maybe, thought George, when this is all over, those eyes will relax again.

"I've got a reservation at the Zima," said George. "I believe it's the last place over toward the practice slope."

"We might as well turn around," said Slater. "That's as good a place to talk as any. Here, let me take your suitcase."

Slater took the bag before Hollingsworth could protest that it really was not very heavy and led the way back toward the station and across the railroad tracks. Hollingsworth slipped in the snow but managed to keep his feet. His shoes and ankles were wet, and he suddenly realized how poorly equipped he was to be plowing through a snowstorm. He hurried to catch up with Slater. As Hollingsworth moved up, he noticed a short stocky man coming, head down, straight for Slater, apparently totally unaware that there was anyone in this blurry white world but himself. The stocky man bumped into Hollingsworth's suitcase.

"Excuse me," said Slazov, looking carefully up at Slater's face. "I guess I couldn't see where I was going. The snow is so thick."

Slazov's English was heavily accented, but very smooth.

Hollingsworth had come up to the two men. He noticed that Slater was looking Slazov over very carefully.

"That's quite all right," Slater said slowly, but he didn't smile. He glanced at Slazov's suitcase. Neither man seemed disposed to move along, and George was beginning to feel the cold.

"I am going in the correct direction for Winterhof Hotel?" asked Slazov.

"Yes," said Slater.

"When is white like this, everything looks the same." Slazov smiled. "Thank you."

Slazov tipped his hat and disappeared behind the thick curtain of snowflakes.

Slater started off again toward the Zima, trying to remember whether he had ever seen the stranger before. He had obviously just arrived.

Slater had to admit he was disturbed. A collision in a snowstorm was not too unusual, but a collision with a newly arrived Russian, who was definitely more interested in what Slater looked like than he was in finding his way to the Winterhof, was upsetting. There were other Russians in Kitzbühel, but Slater had not met any of them, and, so far, the dirty work had all been done by the locals. Slater shrugged. He was entirely too jumpy, and there were more important things to attend to at the moment.

Chapter 19

They arrived at the Zima Hotel, and Slater waited impatiently while George registered. The lobby and public rooms were almost deserted. The guests must be in their rooms reading and writing letters. The place would be jammed this coming weekend because of the new snow.

George's room was very simply furnished, but it was spotless, and the casement windows were facing out toward the practice slope. On a clear day the view would be lovely. Slater remembered that the white exterior of the inn was covered with murals in vivid colors. Slater stretched out on the bed while George unpacked and changed into his ski clothes.

"Why don't you take a nap for a little while?" said George. "You look beat."

Slater closed his eyes. A nap was a wonderful idea. He needed more than a nap to recover from the last twenty-four hours.

"Thanks for the suggestion," he said, his eyes still closed, "but there's a lot to be done, and I'm afraid there isn't enough time to do it in."

Slater heaved a sigh, squeezed his eyes shut, and then

snapped them open, and pushed himself up to a sitting position. He fished some papers out of the chest pocket of his parka and spread them out on the bed.

George put on a heavy ski sweater and walked over to the bed.

"What are all these?" he asked.

"I need a fresh approach, George," said Slater. "These are the personal papers and personal effects of a man by the name of Krüpl."

Slater reached again into his parka and brought forth a cigarette lighter and a small leather notepad.

"Who is Krüpl?"

"Well, for one thing," said Slater, picking up Krüpl's sand-colored passport and handing it to George, "Krüpl is an Austrian. He lives in Kirchberg; and he is, if my suspicions are correct, the Communist paymaster in this area."

He picked up Krüpl's wallet and showed Hollingsworth the sheaf of bills.

"From the looks of the money he must at least be in the black market," said George.

"So is everyone in Europe," said Slater. He sounded very tired. "Somewhere in this mess," he continued, "there must be a clue to Krüpl's contact."

George looked puzzled.

"Again," said Slater, "if my surmises are correct, Krüpl receives this money from a person he doesn't know, probably through some blind or other, or maybe some hiding place to which both he and the man who pays him have access. I've got to find out where, when, and how Krüpl got this money, and who the man is who pays him. You see, George," Slater looked up at him, "I want you to take Krüpl's place."

"What about Krüpl?" George frowned.

"Krüpl is dead."

"Dead?" George swallowed nervously.

"He was killed last night," said Slater calmly. "I buried him and a man named Stadler at about midnight."

"You mean—" George suddenly found it necessary to sit down on the bed. This wasn't turning out at all the way he had expected. "You mean you killed two men last night?"

"Not exactly," said Slater. "I killed Stadler, and Stadler's bullet killed Krüpl. They are the men who murdered Charlie Webber," he added, "if that makes you feel any better."

It should, thought George, but it didn't. It made him awfully damned nervous.

George took another long look at Slater. How could this man sit there, so calmly for once, and talk about burying two men? He took a handkerchief and wiped his forehead. He wasn't cut out for this sort of thing. Furthermore, he was uncomfortably aware of how little he really knew of this man Montague, Carmichael, Slater, and God knew how many other names.

Slater was aware of the sensational effect his calm announcement was having on Hollingsworth and decided that, for the present, he had better not mention Mahler and Mahler's assassin. There was no need for Hollingsworth to know. Slater proceeded to bring Hollingsworth up to date and then turned once again to Krüpl's personal effects, which he handed to George one by one, requesting him to examine them carefully.

George took the lighter and looked it over. He did something which Slater had not done. He tried to light it. The lighter did not work.

"I'm probably grabbing at straws," said George, "but not only is this lighter out of fluid—there are no flints in it."

"Which leads you," said Slater, "to what conclusion?"

"Well," George said thoughtfully, "I don't know exactly, but this is an unusual lighter. Looks like an American Zippo, but this design was done by hand."

"What do you make of the design?" asked Slater.

George held up the lighter and examined the engraving. "Looks almost oriental."

Slater nodded. "Have a look in Krüpl's notepad."

George took the notepad and thumbed through the pages. "All I can see are some addresses, phone numbers, and what appears to be a shopping list." George looked at the inside back cover. "This was bought at the Kitzbühel Buchhandlung—the Kitzbühel Book Exchange." He frowned. "I didn't know Kitzbühel had one."

George stood up and looked down at Slater. "I wish you would tell me what I'm looking for. It would be a big help."

"I'm glad I didn't." Slater smiled. "I know what to look for. At least I should by this time," he added. "But you're the one who may have found it."

"I found it?" George looked bewildered. "Found what?"

"George, let me ask you a question," said Slater. "If you had the problem of giving money, in fairly large amounts, to someone you didn't want to discover your identity, but someone you'd like to keep an eye on from time to time, how would you do it?"

"Well, I—"

"Wait a minute," Slater broke in. "There's another important condition I left out."

"What's that?" asked George.

"You also wish to make certain the money is delivered, and to the right person."

"Must this delivery take place in Kitzbühel?" asked George.

"Not necessarily in Kitzbühel, but somewhere in this general area."

"What about mail, c/o John Smith, General Delivery?"

"Yes," Slater nodded, "that's possible. However, there are some disadvantages to that method, not the least of which being that the Austrian government could decide to investigate. Of course," he added, "there are inadequacies in any such setup. These are what the counterespionage agent counts on."

Slater pushed himself off the bed and onto his feet and began to pace the small room slowly as he talked.

"That, George, is precisely the greatest difficulty with all espionage activities. Because they are not normal, because almost all such activity is based on distrust and fear, even between associates working on the same problem, rather than on a normal exchange between co-workers, the individual agents frequently give themselves and each other away. Theoretically, the clever organizer does his best to make all communications between his agents appear normal, but they almost never come off that way."

Hollingsworth sat on the bed fascinated and, once again, bewildered by this many-sided individual who was now holding forth, in the language a professor would have found suitable, on the theory of espionage.

"Perhaps," Slater continued, "if some espionage organization were to adopt the revolutionary policy of having all of its agents know and trust one another implicitly, a real aura of normalcy might be established; but," he paused, "I assure you, no organization ever will adopt such a policy."

"What have I discovered that may have given you a clue to Krüpl's contact?" asked Hollingsworth.

"You noticed two things that I didn't, George."

"I did?" George was obviously pleased.

"First, that Krüpl's lighter was not used for lighting cigarettes. In fact, I don't believe Krüpl smoked."

"I didn't know that." George sounded downhearted about discovery number one.

"No," said Slater, "you couldn't have. I could have. I never saw him smoke. He had neither cigarettes nor pipe on his person, but," he shook his head, "I didn't." Slater smiled ruefully. "The other thing you noted that I overlooked was the name of the store where this notebook was purchased. I'm inclined to think it's important because it is so obvious as to be overlooked, and a store is not only a good place to be able to deliver goods but also makes an excellent observation point for Krüpl's boss to keep an eye on Krüpl."

"Where does the lighter fit in?" asked George, completely carried away by the academic side of this counterespionage problem.

"Probably for identification," said Slater. "I've never seen one like it before. I seriously doubt that there are many others —maybe only one other."

"And that," said George excitedly, "is in the possession of Krüpl's boss."

"Possibly," said Slater, "but don't count on seeing it. Whoever has one will not be likely to display it under any but the most unusual circumstances. Here," he said, handing the lighter back to Hollingsworth, "from now on this is yours."

George took the lighter again, this time handling it gingerly. He had the distinct feeling that the academic side of this affair was about to come to an abrupt end. He was right.

"Here's what I want you to do, George," said Slater. His tone was now very businesslike. "I want you to go to the Kitzbühel Buchhandlung and go up to the counter. When you get one of the clerk's attention, I want you to put the lighter on the counter and ask if there is a book for you."

"Suppose I don't get any reaction?" said George.

"Leave immediately," said Slater. "If you do receive a package, bring it back to your room and wait here for a call from me. Do you have a gun?"

George sheepishly pulled a .32 automatic out of his pocket.

"Why look embarrassed?" asked Slater. "You may need it before you're through. Don't forget to make me identify myself before you let me in."

George laid the automatic gingerly on the window sill.

"If I get this money, am I supposed to go around making the payoff?"

"No," said Slater. "I've changed my mind. I don't think there's time for that. If there is, I will have someone local take care of it. I've made some other plans which I won't tell you about just now."

Slater went over to the window sill and picked up the automatic. He examined it a moment and then turned to Hollingsworth.

"Don't you think," he said slowly, "that this gadget would work better if you put some shells in the clip?"

George's face flushed. His mouth moved a couple of times, but nothing came out.

"Weren't you ever in the service?" asked Slater.

"I was too young for World War II, and the Foreign Service has kept me out of the army. To tell you the truth, I've never fired a revolver."

George was embarrassed, but he was glad he had admitted his ignorance of firearms. Slater was amazed that there was a young man anywhere in this crazy world who did not know how to handle an automatic. He concealed his annoyance.

"Actually, George, carrying a revolver is sometimes more dangerous than not carrying one. However," he added, "when you do need one, you usually need it bad; and there's usually no adequate substitute, believe me."

Slater filled the clip, put an extra shell in the chamber and locked the automatic.

"You now have all the fire power this thirty-two will give you. Never fire at a target less than twice; point the automatic as you would your finger; make your own silhouette as low as possible; always keep some distance between the gun and the target; and never," Slater smiled, "point the gun at someone you don't intend to kill."

George put on the safety and stuck the .32 in the right-hand pocket of his ski pants.

"When do you want me to try and make Krüpl's contact?" he asked.

"In half an hour," said Slater. "Wait here fifteen minutes after I leave, and then head for the bookstore. I'll be there before you. Don't acknowledge me, but return here as soon as you have finished your business, and we'll have another little talk."

Slater left the Hotel Zima and stepped out into the snow. It had finally stopped snowing, but the fresh wind, which was breaking up the clouds, was whipping up the snow and kiting it crazily into drifts. As Slater approached the station, he could see the plows in action. A snowfall, no matter how unexpected, was an old story to these mountain people, and Slater reflected that the main roadways would be cleared by this evening. He smelled the wind. It was surprisingly warm and moist. He looked up at the Hahnenkamm and shook his head. March was a strange, unpredictable month. The weather could turn unseasonably warm. It had been almost balmy three days ago. He didn't like the warmth of the wind. A sudden change in temperature at this time of year after a heavy snowfall could mean avalanche weather, and with the passes blocked, many of the villages, even entire sections, would be cut off for days. He could imagine himself, Hollingsworth, Dinar, if he was still in the community, and the Communists all shut up in this happy valley. He muttered something to himself about life being just a bowl of cherries and entered the Kitzbüheler Buchhandlung.

The bookstore was crowded, and Slater joined the people who were browsing. The Europeans in general and the Germanic people in particular were very book conscious, and the publishing companies vied with each other to see which could turn out the most attractively bound and illustrated editions. Slater had had little time for much reading, and he turned now to his browsing with real pleasure. He looked up occasionally to see if he could recognize any of the staff or customers. He had not been there more than ten minutes when Hormsby entered, slipping smoothly through the crowd like a sharp knife through warm butter. Slater marveled at Hormsby's thinness. He should have moved like a crane, but he was as smooth on his feet as a professional dancer.

Hormsby went over to the counter, handed the girl a package and said something to her. Slater moved in Hormsby's direction. He wanted to have a closer look at the package. It certainly looked like a book. Hormsby was still talking to the girl when Slater stepped up behind him.

"Good day for reading, Mr. Hormsby," said Slater, his mouth almost touching Hormsby's right ear.

Being suddenly addressed from the rear apparently unnerved Hormsby, for he wheeled around. He had something in his hand which he was not quick enough to stuff in his pocket. Slater saw it just before it disappeared. It was the duplicate of Krüpl's lighter. Slater had to get Hormsby out of the bookstore in a hurry. If Hollingsworth walked in there and tried to pass himself off as Krüpl with Hormsby looking on, George would be in for more trouble than he would ever be able to handle.

"Ah, Mr. Slater, isn't it?" said Hormsby. "What a pleasant surprise." Hormsby's accent was very clipped.

"Now that," replied Slater affably, "is just what I was thinking. How about letting me buy you a drink?"

"Excellent," Hormsby smiled. "And then, I'll buy you one."

Hormsby was apparently as eager to get out of there, now that he had an audience, as Slater was to get him out.

"And then," said Slater, "I'll buy you one."

"And then," Hormsby began his high-pitched giggle, "I'll buy you one."

"And then—"

"And then," Hormsby cut in, "we'll be as squiffy as a couple of owls."

"Squiffier," said Slater. "Here's to a couple of squiffy owls."

The two men went out into the street arm in arm and walked through the snow into the Winterhof. They entered the bar, still chattering away like long-lost drinking pals. They argued over who was to buy the first drink, and what the poison should be. Hormsby held out for a gin and lime, and Slater for a lime and vodka combination he called a skazzerak.

"My dear fellow," said Hormsby frowning, "you're not going to drink a Russian product?"

"Why not?" said Slater. "I like vodka."

"I wouldn't drink anything made in Russia!" Hormsby was vehement. "And as a good American, you shouldn't either."

"It's their politics that I don't like, not their alcohol."

Slater had to admit that this dapper cadaver sitting opposite him was most convincing in displaying his dislike of anything Russian, even though he was unquestionably the Communist paymaster for the area.

"Are you going to the Baron von Burgdorf's party tonight?" Slater asked.

"I wouldn't miss one of the Baron's parties for the world. Terribly interesting—always."

"You don't think all this snow will make the Baron decide to call it off?" asked Slater.

"Definitely not." Hormsby added, "Anyway, it's stopped snowing. Bit of a wind, but I believe they'll run the cable car all the same. Baron's a very important man."

"You English are more impressed by royalty than we Americans," said Slater dryly.

"That's funny," said Hormsby, "I've had just the opposite impression."

Slater reflected that Wyman was undoubtedly partly responsible for that. Now was no time to antagonize Hormsby, but Slater was on edge and his temper was very nearly out of control. He could not get the idea out of his mind that Hormsby was responsible for Mahler's and Webber's deaths. Hormsby was certainly at least number-two man in the area, if not number one. It was odd that these discoveries were frequently such an anticlimax, but that was the way this business worked. It was not like apprehending criminals. Unless, in this case, Hormsby had violated Austrian law and Slater could prove it, there was nothing he could do except notify his office of Hormsby's role and let someone unknown to Hormsby monitor his operations.

Slater hated these mercenaries. A citizen of the West, particularly of England and the United States, should know better than to sell himself to the Communists. It was obvious that Hormsby was in this for the money, and he probably did not get much of that now that they had him in their power and could blackmail him. There had been times, too many times in the past ten years, when he had actually helped Communist agents to escape the law of some European nation because in his professional opinion, and that of his office, the guilty person had been more useful alive, his espionage role known, than in prison or executed as he deserved and replaced by another unknown.

Slater's impulse was to try and get Hormsby alone someplace and beat him until he told who number one was, and what their plans were to get Colonel Dinar. But to get the maximum intelligence "take" out of this, it would be smarter to get to number one through Hormsby without the knowledge of either and then alert his office to monitor all their future actions. Slater was very much afraid that Carmichael had already upset the apple cart, but Carmichael had not had much choice.

Eliciting information from a fellow professional made a

subtle and charming dialogue for the movies or a spy novel, but it rarely paid off. Still, Slater realized, he had almost nothing to lose. They were on their third "and then I'll buy you one" and Hormsby appeared to be mellowing.

Slater pulled out a cigarette, offered one to Hormsby and asked if he had a light. Hormsby fished around in his pockets and produced a package of matches. Failure number one.

"I'm going to get a lighter one of these days," said Slater. "I'm always running out of matches."

"If you get a lighter," said Hormsby, "you'll always be running out of fuel. Anyway, I've never found one that worked yet."

Failure number two.

"Ah, Fräulein Wieland!" Hormsby's thin face brightened, and he stood up. "Won't you join us? You are just what a couple of old bachelors need."

Ilse stopped at the table and, without a glance in Slater's direction, seated herself beside Hormsby.

"Sorry, Slater," said Hormsby, "I was speaking for myself. I don't know whether you're a bachelor or not."

"I am," said Slater looking at Ilse. But I wouldn't be for long, he thought, if she were real—or if I were real, for that matter.

"Are you coming to the Baron's party tonight, Fräulein Wieland?" Hormsby asked.

"Yes, Mr. Hormsby." Ilse still ignored Slater. "As a matter of fact," she continued, "I was told to tell anyone I might see, whom I knew was invited, that the party will be informal because of the snow."

"You've told him," said Slater, exasperated in spite of himself at her attempt to ignore him. "Now, why don't you tell me?"

"You have already admitted you heard, Mr. Slater."

Ilse looked at him then, and Slater decided, spy or no spy,

she was the most beautiful woman he had ever seen. You could not refer to Ilse Wieland as a girl. There was too much knowledge behind her eyes—the kind of depth and knowing that would seem promiscuous in a young girl, but promising in a mature woman.

Hormsby looked from Slater to Ilse and back to Slater.

"What's this, a lovers' quarrel?" Hormsby looked at Slater's somber expression and began to giggle. "This is priceless! I thought you two were coming to the party together."

"Apparently, Fräulein Wieland would rather go alone," said Slater.

He was acting damn childish and he knew it, but he couldn't seem to help himself. Ilse made no reply.

"Oh, Fräulein Wieland will not be alone, I assure you," said Hormsby.

"I'm sure she won't," said Slater and stood up. "If you'll excuse me, please, I have some things to attend to."

As Slater was leaving the bar, Hormsby called after him.

"I'll buy you a lighter as a consolation prize, old boy, although I assure you they never work." Hormsby giggled again.

Slater never turned, but his broad back felt twice normal size and very exposed. It could have been an innocent enough remark, but it probably was not. The elicited, as usual, had probably learned more than the elicitor.

Chapter 20

Gregor Slazov checked in at the Winterhof and had a private conversation with Anton Reisch in Slazov's room.

Slazov was seated in the armchair. His short stubby body filled the chair, and the arms creaked almost every time he breathed. Anton was standing respectfully.

"Normally, Herr Reisch," Slazov said, "we would not have contact, you and I, but when you told me at the desk that Mr. Carmichael had checked out, this was indeed bad news."

"I'm very sorry, Herr Slazov," said Anton. "I should have gotten a forwarding address. But—"

"I doubt that it would have been a real one." Slazov looked thoughtful. "Tell me about this man Carmichael. What did he really look like?"

"He was tall with straight dark hair, strong features, high-bridged straight nose and green eyes."

"How old?" asked Slazov.

"In his thirties," said Anton. He was getting tired of standing.

"What were his habits?"

"Very conservative," said Anton. "Very," he added remembering the ten dollars. "He spent a lot of time in his room."

Slazov was angry. For a man who spent so much of his time in his room, Carmichael had apparently caused considerable trouble. How could he, Gregor Slazov, find a man he knew nothing about? As usual, the party had not told him enough. The only contact thay gave him was this idiot Anton, who looked as if he was about to fall asleep.

"Have you any suggestions how I can find this Mr. Carmichael?"

"I have the license number and description of the car he left here in yesterday. I have made some inquiries of the various hotels west of here." Anton paused.

"Well!" Slazov said emphatically. "Continue."

"A man by the name of Carmichael spent last night at a hotel in Wörgl," said Anton.

"Then he has probably left Austria by now," said Slazov disgustedly.

"I don't think so, Herr Slazov," said Anton. "You see, Wörgl is less than one hour's drive from here, and Carmichael did not check in there until three in the morning. He left here at about three in the afternoon. Also," added Anton, "he left Wörgl very early this morning, but I don't think he left Austria. I think he is here in Kitzbühel."

This was news! Slazov looked at Anton with grudging respect.

"I think I have met Carmichael. He arrived on the train this afternoon. He is very tall and has straight dark hair, but," Slazov frowned, "I would swear he looked more like a diplomat—a very young diplomat not over twenty-five, at the most twenty-nine. He was met," Slazov added, "by a husky American with green eyes and," Slazov paused, "strong, prominent features."

"A man of about thirty-five, with strong even teeth and very short, brown, slightly wavy hair," Anton added. "That would be Herr Slater. He checked in the hotel after Carmichael checked out. Both Carmichael and Slater appear to know Fräulein Wieland."

Gregor Slazov pushed himself out of his chair. "Are you trying to tell me that Carmichael and Slater are the same?"

Anton hesitated. "I think so, but I'm not sure. Herr Slater has been out all day, since nine o'clock this morning. I didn't get the report from Wörgl until after that, but Herr Slater made a great point of telling me this morning how well he slept last night. When I see him again, I will know."

Gregor Slazov paced the room, It could be so. Disguises were rare in this business, but they were used. Slazov had a pair of elevator shoes to make him taller, but he knew it was useless to try and change the face of a peasant. If Carmichael was Slater, Slazov was sorry he had exposed himself. Such a man as Slater would be dangerous, but, Slazov smiled to himself, it would also make the game more interesting.

"If Carmichael and Slater are the same, who was the tall, dark-haired young man with him near the station?"

Anton shook his head. "I don't know but I will find out."

"Who is this woman that knows both Carmichael and Slater?" asked Gregor.

"Fräulein Ilse Wieland," said Anton. "She is a member of German Intelligence."

"They are working together then?" said Slazov.

"I don't think so," Anton said thoughtfully. "Anyway, not yet. This is what we wish to avoid."

Slazov looked at Anton closely. Somehow, Anton Reisch did not look quite so tired or so completely fit the role of desk clerk. Reisch was a smart man. Maybe Gregor Slazov should find out more about this man. It was time Slazov became more than an assassin.

"From whom do you take orders, Herr Reisch?" Slazov's question sounded like a command.

"Not from you, Herr Slazov," said Anton quickly. He drew

himself up to his full height. He was six inches taller than Slazov.

"No," said Slazov. "Nor from anyone else in this area." He hated anyone who was taller than he.

"You may think what you like, Herr Slazov, but you must keep your thoughts to yourself. You have been sent here to dispose of a man named Carmichael. I will help you to find him, if he is here. Who I am, what my job is, why Carmichael is to be eliminated is not your affair."

Gregor Slazov grumbled. This man was as bad as the Comrade General Stottoff.

"When Herr Slater returns," said Anton, "I will let you know my opinion. In the meantime," Anton took a calling card from his pocket and handed it to Slazov, "remain in your room until I phone you."

Anton opened the door and left.

Slazov looked at the card. He read the message on the back first.

MY DEAR HERR SLAZOV,

Any friend of Adolph's is a friend of mine. I would be honored if you would come to my party tonight. It will be at the Ehrenbachhöhe Hotel. Please dress in ski clothes because of the heavy snowfall.

E. v. B.

Slazov frowned and turned the card face up. Engraved in neat German script was the name Baron Erich von Burgdorf. Slazov continued to look puzzled for a moment and then smiled slowly. Apparently Carmichael or Slater was expected to attend. Slazov hoped so. A murder was much easier at a party where there were a lot of people. Carmichael would not be the first corpse Slazov had disposed of in the snow.

Chapter 21

Slater knocked on Hollingsworth's door at the Zima, and George let him in.

"I got it!" said George. "I got the book!"

Slater had to smile at George's enthusiasm, but he was surprised.

"You mean you simply went up to a clerk, laid the lighter on the counter and asked if there was a book for you, and it worked?"

"Yes," said George. "Well no, not quite. At first she looked at me kind of funny."

"I should think she might have," said Slater dryly.

"Yes," said George, "she did. But then I told her I was picking up the book for a man who looked like Krüpl. I mean," he said, "I described Krüpl, and then she gave me this."

George held up the package. "I've been dying to open it."

Slater ignored the package and rubbed his chin thoughtfully. Depending on what was in the package, he had certainly gotten a break this time.

While Slater was obviously lost in thought, a thought struck Hollingsworth. He put the package on the bed and sat down heavily himself.

"You never expected me to get this package," he blurted out, "did you, Carmichael?"

"No." Slater still looked thoughtful. "I thought that if you stumbled into the store like an amateur, showed the lighter, and asked for a package, you would be followed by the paymaster, if he were there, or by someone else. Then," Slater added, "I could have followed him right to your room."

Slater was saying all this calmly, academically, completely unaware of the devastating effect his words were having on George.

"I would have invited him inside," Slater continued, "for what would probably have been a very rewarding chat. You see, the lighter was only additional identification. Undoubtedly the procedure Krüpl used for getting the package was simply to ask if there were a package for a Mr. Blank. The trouble was I didn't know the name. I don't think you would have gotten the package if the paymaster had not just delivered it in person and, for some unexplainable reason, had been checking his own lighter. We really got a break for a change."

"Why you cold-blooded devil!"

Hollingsworth suddenly jumped Slater and tried to get his hands on his throat. "I'll kill you!"

Slater was taken completely by surprise. All he could think was that the young fool had gone crazy and was a hell of a lot stronger than he looked. Slater clamped his left hand on Hollingsworth's left wrist, pushed his right hand just under the left shoulder, twisted suddenly, and unceremoniously threw Hollingsworth across the room. Hollingsworth's back crashed into the wall and he landed, face down, on the floor. Slater rubbed his throat and looked over at Hollingsworth. George was still conscious, but his eyes did not seem to focus very well.

"What in hell's the matter with you?" Slater said. "Have you lost your mind?"

George got his eyes to focus again, and he struggled to his feet.

"You deliberately used me as a decoy! I might have been killed! I'm no dirty spy, damn you! I'm a Foreign Service officer."

"I see," said Slater. "Neither was Charlie Webber a dirty spy."

He nailed Hollingsworth with his eyes, and the eyes were hard, almost glassy. "It isn't a very nice job being a dirty spy, is it?" said Slater. "Hardly the sort of job for a gentleman."

"I thought you were a gentleman," said Hollingsworth. "At least that you would behave that way where I was concerned—show some human decency toward someone on your own side." He looked sullen.

"Okay, George," said Slater quietly. "You can take the night train back to Zurich. I'll get someone else to use as a decoy."

George walked awkwardly across the room to the bed, giving Slater as wide a berth as the size of the room would permit. He picked up the package and started to unwrap it.

"Put down the package, George."

George paused, still holding the package in his hand.

"But I got it. I want to see what's in it."

"Whatever it is," said Slater, "no longer concerns you. Put it down!"

George dropped the package on the bed.

Slater went over to the side of the bed opposite Hollingsworth and calmly unwrapped the parcel. Inside it was a book. Slater riffled the pages and found a neatly folded paper. He carefully unfolded it and took it over to the window.

Could not contact you personally as was my original intention. If Carmichael didn't show up last night, forget him. Have sent for specialist who will dispose of him tonight. There will be no more payments until further notice due to presence of Carmichael in area. All employees have been notified to stay away. Will be paid elsewhere. I will contact you personally very soon. S.

Slater read the message over several times. S must be Schlessinger, and Schlessinger was undoubtedly Hormsby. Slater tried to think what all this meant in terms of his immediate problem.

If Carmichael was still a threat to their operation, Dinar must still be a free man. If this message was to Krüpl, the Communists still did not know he was dead. If Hormsby did not suspect the relationship between Carmichael and Slater, Slater was still in the clear, and one other suddenly very important point, Ilse Wieland must really be a German agent. Slater looked thoughtful, for a moment almost wistful. Now, more than ever, he had to come out of this mess alive. He hoped he had not become so much of a "dirty spy" that he could no longer enter a life on the outside.

Slater turned to look at Hollingsworth, and then looked at the note again. Hollingsworth was busily getting dressed in his street clothes, obviously in a hurry to get out of that room, out of Kitzbühel, and as far away from this business as possible. Slater didn't really blame him. He wished that his own reaction had been the same ten years ago, and he had run away from this crazy, stone-rolling, useless life; but at least, when he had made a commitment, he had always managed to find the guts somewhere to finish the job. Maybe it was his sense of the dramatic, or perhaps it was an inner loneliness, but the sudden desire to have someone know what he was walking into overpowered his better judgment.

"I'm going to read you this note, George, after all. That is," Slater added, "if you still think you'd like to hear it."

George nodded. He stood in the middle of the room, fully dressed, and all packed. He listened carefully while Slater read the message. When Slater finished, Hollingsworth said, "And now, I suppose, you're going to go to this party tonight, just as though there was no paid assassin waiting to kill Carmichael."

"I have no choice, Hollingsworth," said Slater.

"No," Hollingsworth's voice was full of anger, "but I do. You get paid for taking these kinds of risks. I don't. I thought you were tense and worried because you didn't like the job of deceit and murder, but I don't think so any more. I think you thrive on it, so go ahead. Kill or be killed. You won't get sympathy from me."

"I don't need your sympathy, Hollingsworth." Slater was furious. He had to clamp his hands on the back of a chair to keep from laying them on Hollingsworth. He was furious with himself because he had asked this Foreign Service fop for sympathy.

He let go of the chair and moved to the door. He turned to face Hollingsworth.

"If you're not out of Kitzbühel tomorrow—"

"Don't worry," Hollingsworth cut in. "I want to keep my amateur status. I don't want to turn into something like you."

Slater slammed the door. He looked at his knuckles. They were still white. It was too late to get anyone else. Ilse was disgusted with him. Hollingsworth had run out. He would just have to finish this job alone. He squared his shoulders and stepped out into the snow.

Chapter 22

The warm March wind held the promise of spring. It scudded the late-afternoon clouds across the sky, caressed the snow with its warmth, created moisture in the snow and kept it from drifting. The wind billowed out Slater's ski pants as he walked before it and pressed flat the loose clothing of those who moved against it. And the wind was impulsive; taking sudden turns, funneling full force around buildings and, unexpectedly, up side streets until it dissipated itself in alleyways and small courtyards or was caught up again in the main currents.

Slater pushed down the hood of his parka and leaned his back against the warm wind, content for the moment to let the elements carry him along. Where did not seem very important at the moment. He needed time to think. He also needed food and some sleep. Tonight would be long, he was certain. The Communists had cleared all their agents not directly involved with Colonel Imré Dinar from the area. They had kept Ilse Wieland alive only so that she could lead them to the Colonel. They had brought in an assassin to murder Carmichael, and it was just a question of time before they would discover that Carmichael was Slater. The stage was set, and Slater wondered what, should his assassin be successful, he had accomplished so far which could be considered useful to his country.

He had been sent to find Webber and bring him back. He had failed on both counts, but he had killed Webber's murderers, and at the same time eliminated three Communist agents. He tried not to think of Heinz Mahler. To Slater, Heinz' death was his greatest personal failure. It had been so unnecessary. If only this business had not made him so suspicious, he would have covered Mahler immediately and given him protection, at least until reinforcements arrived.

And what about his second assignment to determine Wyman's place in this setup? That he had done to his own satisfaction, but to prevent Wyman from carrying out his job was the problem that faced him now. He had the feeling he would be either a success or a failure, alive or dead, within the next twenty-four hours.

Slater passed through the lobby of the Winterhof, nodded to the desk clerk and climbed the stairs to his room. Once inside, he called room service to send him up a meal. He got out his writing equipment and sat down at the table to write.

As he laid page after page of still apparently blank paper beside his left hand, he smiled and shook his head slowly. Writing this letter was a little like writing a last will and testament. Slater reflected sadly that, after all, it was all he had to give, and he wanted to be as thorough as possible. He described the networks as he believed they operated—or had operated. Because of his own actions, much of this was history, but it all would go into the Intelligence archives as valuable folklore on the technique of clandestine communications. The menu system was clever. The Communists might reactivate it here and, if not here, then elsewhere.

When Slater finally put down his pen, he felt somewhat better. His time in Kitzbühel had, after all, been quite brief; yet he had been able to break their communication setup, and he could name every agent in the Kitzbühel operation but the number-one man. The last page had been a diagram of the local apparatus as he saw it.

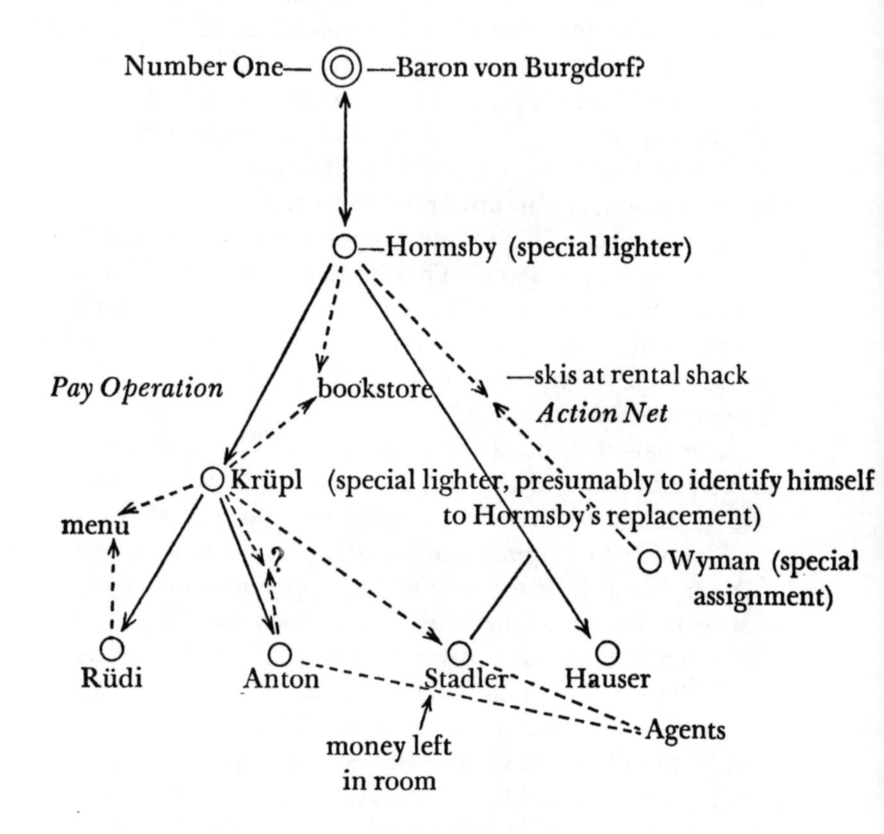

He also enclosed the passports of Stadler, Krüpl and Hauser, the man who had killed Mahler, and ended his report with his future plans and an analysis of what the Communist plans might be. Almost as an afterthought, and because he realized it was his duty, he added Ilse Wieland's name as the German Intelligence agent. Who could tell when the United

States and Germany might be on opposite sides of the fence again?

He wrote his cover letter, filling the blank pages with innocuous thoughts on the beauties of Kitzbühel, the length and comparative difficulty of the various ski trails, the reasonableness of the local prices, and the general Gemütlichkeit of the area. He signed it again, "As always, Ben," and sealed the heavy Manila envelope, knowing that Paris would be upset when they saw the big envelope. An agent who thought he still had a fighting chance almost never sent anything bigger than a conventional, personal letter.

The dinner arrived just as he was clearing everything away. The waiter was very solicitous and, to Slater's mind, a little too curious for comfort. Slater had to be rude to get rid of him.

The food was well prepared, but Slater had to force himself to eat. He knew he needed the nourishment, and he finally managed to get everything down. The wine was the easiest. He would have liked to drink himself into a stupor. Tired businessmen frequently took a little too much alcohol, and even sleeping pills, to relieve tension and often with their doctors' blessings. Slater could not permit himself such luxuries, not even one of those new "happy pills" his fellow countrymen were lately taking by the millions. He had to sit there alone with his nerves. He tried to rub the back of his neck to loosen the tightening muscles and start the circulation going again, but he got a cramp in his right arm from doing it. That made him more nervous so he gave up.

He stood up and stretched. He had to get out of his room or go berserk from claustrophobia, waiting there, all shut up and tense, for someone to come and murder him. He also had to get rid of the letter as soon as possible. It was his only legacy, and he wanted it to get into the proper hands.

Slater left the room and went downstairs into the lobby.

"Mr. Slater!"

He turned and saw Anton beckoning him over to the desk.

"Yes?" Slater approached the desk.

"I wonder, sir," said Anton, "if you could tell me Mr. Carmichael's forwarding address?"

Slater felt as though he had been struck across the face. He struggled to withhold any emotion.

"Mr. Carmichael?" he said. "I don't think—"

"The night clerk tells me you were looking for him the other night," Anton said smoothly.

Slater suddenly remembered that Anton had not been on duty when he had gone up to his room the last time. Slater had nodded to the night clerk.

"Oh yes, I remember," said Slater, trying desperately to make the best of it. "Tall, dark-haired fellow. I only met him once. Invited me to have a drink. You know, fellow American on a foreign soil." Slater knew he was talking too much, and he stopped too abruptly.

"Yes, sir," said Anton, "that's the man. He left here owing the hotel two hundred and sixty schillings."

"That's a shame," said Slater. "Didn't seem that sort of a fellow to me." He shook his head. "That just shows you, you never know."

"No, sir,' said Anton. His voice sounded tired again, and Slater noted it with something approaching relief.

"Do you know where we can reach him, Mr. Slater?"

"I'm sorry, but I only met him once. I have no idea where he went to. Guess it's just as well."

"Thank you, sir."

Slater left the hotel and went to the post office to mail the letter. He knew it was just a question of time now, and all because what he had at one time considered a smart move had now turned out to be a bad blunder. You could not foresee everything in this business. How was he to know, when as Slater he had asked the night clerk for Carmichael, that Slater would register at the Hotel Winterhof? If Anton were suspicious of the connection, he at least knew now that Slater had been in Kitzbühel before he had registered at the Winterhof. Some phoning around would reveal that Slater had not been registered anywhere else.

Anton Reisch looked after Slater's broad back and watched him until he disappeared through the front door and into the now slushy main street. He picked up the house phone and asked for Slazov's room.

"Hello, Herr Slazov."

"Yes."

"Anton here." Anton put his mouth close to the mouthpiece. "The person we discussed is the right man."

"Are you sure?" asked Slazov.

"There is no question," said Anton.

"Where is he now?"

"He has just left the hotel."

"Good. I will be right down. Thank you for your help."

"Don't thank me," said Anton. "Just do your job."

"I always do," said Slazov.

Chapter 23

After mailing the letter, Slater entered the nearest public telephone station and called his office in Salzburg. After he had properly identified himself, he was connected with a voice he had not heard in three years. The voice was deep and slightly accented. It belonged to an old friend and an old hand in the business, Lazlo Kartovski, an overfed gourmet who raised cymbidiums and looked like Farouk.

Lazlo was a man of many talents. He spoke five languages besides Polish, the language of his parents. His chief drawback as an operator was his chimeric disposition, which went in rapid succession from a state of high-living frenzy to the blackest despair, from a most affable expansiveness to an uncontrollable rage.

"Hello, you handsome devil!" exclaimed Lazlo. "I suppose you have all the women at your feet down there."

Slater winced. Lazlo was in one of his most affable moods, and now Slater knew he would hear nothing but the wildest compliments about his supposed amatory achievements.

"It's wonderful to hear your Slavic voice, Farouk. How many wives have you had since I saw you last?" Slater laughed. It had been a long time since he had talked with anyone he knew well enough to ask such a question and know the answer in advance.

"You think I will never marry, you rascal, but I did find a beautiful girl in Ankara. She is like a princess, my charming friend, and I will marry her someday."

"Why wait, Farouk?" Slater chuckled. "Even Farouk cannot keep a princess waiting."

"Oh, I would! I would, but I am so broke all the time. It takes money to be married."

Slater wished he could keep their conversation going on like this forever, to stay in this world of pleasantries with an old friend, but he couldn't. It had served its purpose, and now he had to ask for the report.

"Listen, moneybags," said Slater, "have you bureaucrats up there got a report for me?"

"Moneybags!" Lazlo yelled. "I am broke, flat, busted, kaput." He paused. "Yes, but it will not be much help, I'm afraid. We know nothing about any of the people mentioned —except the beer merchant with the title."

Slater shook his head. He had been afraid of that. Well, he had added a whole new list to the rogues' gallery.

"I guess I hit the jackpot, all right," said Slater. "All but three, who are no longer with us, will be worth further acquaintance. The young lady is an associate of" and Slater mentioned a code name for German Intelligence.

"So you have been up to your old tricks," said Lazlo. "I am referring to the three who have retired. Sounds to me as though you need a friend."

Slater was deeply grateful for the offer, but he decided to ignore it. Lazlo was about as subtle as a herd of elephants—besides, there just was not time enough.

"Tell me more," he said, "about the merchant of distinction."

"He is real enough," said Lazlo, "but he is as misguided as

some of our inheritors of great wealth. He has championed the cause of the common man about whom he knows nothing. He is used for his money, and the front he can put up. He throws parties for them. He has a double-sized belly and an undersized brain."

Slater laughed at Lazlo's description.

"Don't laugh, my handsome friend," said Lazlo. "The man is a moron, but he is dangerous."

"I liked your choice of words," said Slater soberly.

"But not my big feet and heavy hands, eh?" said Lazlo.

"What are you talking about?"

"You know very well. You don't consider me an appropriate friend just now. You don't want my big feet tromping all over the place down there." Lazlo paused, and Slater knew he would be hurt, but there was nothing to say.

"All right! All right!" said Lazlo finally. "But you are my friend, all the same, you slayer of women. And if anything happens to you, you will never forgive yourself."

"You're so right, Lazlo," said Slater.

"When will I hear from you again?" asked Lazlo.

"Tomorrow, I hope."

"If I don't hear from you by tomorrow afternoon, I will bring the marines and crush a few skulls."

"Do that," said Slater.

"Auf wiederschauen, mein schöner Freund," said Lazlo.

"I hope it won't be another three years."

Slater hung up. He hoped he could call Lazlo tomorrow. He shuddered to think what Kitzbühel would look like after Lazlo got through turning it upside down. Kartovski had been the despair of the Office on several occasions when he had taken things into his own hands. He had been kicked out over and over again, but he was so valuable most of the time that he was always immediately rehired.

Slater left the phone booth and headed back for the hotel.

It was a fortunate circumstance for him that the main street was neither crowded nor empty. Slazov liked crowds for his work, and Slazov was following Slater, impatient to get his job over with. If there had been no one, he would have shot Slater from a distance from the cover of a doorway. Had the street been crowded, Slazov would have punctured Slater with a sharp needle, and Slater would have died in agony within five minutes. The hunted never has the advantage that the hunter does, particularly when man is the subject of the hunt.

Slater was at a tremendous disadvantage. He was not out to kill, but to stay alive and accomplish his mission. He did not realize he had seen the face of his murderer; but, even if he knew Slazov, his only chance to even the odds would be to turn murderer himself.

Slater entered the lobby. Anton was at the desk. Slater stared at the clerk and wondered not only what he knew, but what his position in all this really was. The diagram had obviously been wrong. If the Baron was not top man, who was? Someone, thought Slater, as yet unknown, or the tired, greedy Anton Reisch? He was in an excellent position to be the principal agent. The problem of communication and observance was solved for a man in such a job.

Slater suddenly felt reckless. A crazy impulse moved him over to the desk.

"Yes, sir, Mr. Slater?" Anton was unusually cheerful.

"I kept thinking," said Slater, "about the fellow Carmichael."

"Yes?" Anton was wide awake. "What about Mr. Carmichael?"

"Well," said Slater, trying to talk in the style of the ingenuous, somewhat absentminded character he had created for Slater, as far as Anton was concerned. "Like I said, I've been thinking over what you said about Carmichael, and, well, it's a damn shame that an American would come over here and cheat on his hotel bill. I mean it creates a bad impression." Slater frowned and looked at Anton. "I'm not going too fast for you, am I? I mean," Slater looked embarrassed, "you understand my English okay?"

"Oh yes, sir," said Anton.

"Well, you know how it is," said Slater smiling awkwardly. "I sprech a little deutsch, and I guess my accent's pretty good because right away the guy I'm speaking to floods me with a whole lot of German in a row, and I'm lost."

"I assure you, sir," Anton said very gently, "I can understand your language very well."

"You people," said Slater admiringly, "sure are clever when it comes to picking up all those foreign languages."

"What," said Anton, no longer quite so patiently, "did you wish to say about Mr. Carmichael?"

"Oh, yes, sure." Slater gave an embarrassed laugh. "Well, when you asked if I knew where Carmichael might be now, at first I didn't think I had any idea; and then when I remembered something he'd said to me in the bar, I decided not to say anything about it. You know, seeing that he was a fellow American and all that."

"That's quite understandable, Mr. Slater," said Anton sympathetically.

"Yeah, I mean, you know," said Slater shrugging his shoulders, "you don't like to tell on a fellow countryman, so to speak."

"No, of course not," said Anton expectantly.

"Well," Slater sighed, "that's a load off my mind. Thanks very much for listening, and I sure hope you catch up with him."

Slater started to move away from the desk.

"But, Mr. Slater," Anton called after him.

Slater turned. "Yes," he said, looking blank.

"You haven't told me where I can find Mr. Carmichael."

"Oh" Slater raised his eyes upward, shook his head disgustedly at himself. "I don't know what's the matter with me sometimes. I'd forget my head, if it wasn't connected to you-know-what."

Anton looked puzzled. "No, what?"

"My neck." Slater laughed. "By golly, I got you that time."

Anton looked as if he were in great pain. He waited until Slater had subsided. It took quite a while, for Slater was almost hysterical. He had played his part too well, and the pressure, plus Anton's reaction, was almost too much.

"Mr. Slater," said Anton very quietly, as if he were afraid any distraction might set Slater off course again, "please, tell me where you think Mr. Carmichael might be."

"Well," said Slater, "I think he might still be right around here someplace."

"What makes you think that, Mr. Slater?" Anton's voice actually sounded eager.

"Well, you see," said Slater, "I met him Saturday here in Kitzbühel." Slater paused. "The thing is, I got confused and got off the train at a place called Wörgl. I meant to come here instead. Anyway, I found a room in some peculiar little place in Wörgl, Saturday night; but there was nothing to do there, so I spent most of the day and that evening here. When I met this fellow Carmichael in the bar and told him about my predicament, he told me he didn't think I could get a room anywhere in Kitzbühel on a Saturday night."

"It is very difficult," said Anton, and right away regretted it.

"You're telling me!" said Slater. "I must have tried a hundred places. Every one of them filled up. Standing room only, so to speak."

"Please, Mr. Slater," said Anton. "Go on."

"Yes, well, that's it."

"What's it?" asked Anton.

"Carmichael told me I could share his room for the night,

but I never could find him in, so I had to go back to Wörgl."

"I'm very sorry, Mr. Slater," said Anton, "but I don't understand what that has to do with Mr. Carmichael's present whereabouts."

"Oh yeah, I forgot," said Slater shaking his head again. "Carmichael also asked me all about Wörgl. He said he had a girl friend there he was planning to visit the next day. He wanted to know what kind of a town it was, what there was to do." Slater shrugged. "Of course, I couldn't tell him much."

"No," said Anton with more feeling than the small word justified. "Well, thank you very much, Mr. Slater."

"Think nothing of it," said Slater. "I don't want you to think that all us Americans are like that fellow Carmichael."

"I don't," said Anton, "I assure you."

Slater went up to his room; and Slazov, who had been watching the whole performance, went over to the desk.

"What was all that about?" Slazov asked Anton.

"I'm not sure," said Anton thoughtfully. "If that man is an agent, he certainly knows how to perform exactly like an idiot. I will do some checking. Don't do anything further until you hear from me. If you don't get him now, you can take care of him at the party tonight."

"I wish," Slazov looked very annoyed, "you'd make up your mind."

"I will," said Anton. "In the meantime, don't let him out of your sight."

Slazov moved away from the desk and took a seat at the far end of the lobby where he could observe the stairs.

Slater bolted the door to his room, put a chair against it and walked over to the bed. He picked up the house phone and left a call for seven o'clock. He had made a play for time. Time in which to sleep. He prayed that he had won; because if he didn't get some sleep immediately, he didn't think he could go on. He took his gun from his waist holster and placed it on the bed. He removed his boots and stretched out on the bed. He fell asleep immediately with the revolver lying on his open right hand.

He was suddenly awakened two hours later by a heavy pounding on his door.

Chapter 24

Slater began the struggle back to the world of reality. He had the feeling of pushing his way through layer after layer of thick mist to a small orange-colored light. When he finally opened his eyes, he found himself on his back staring at the ceiling, his body bathed in sweat, and his right hand holding the clammy butt of his .38.

"Who is it?" Slater called.

"It's the room clerk, sir. The operator tried to call you at seven o'clock, and then at a quarter past, but you didn't hear so I was sent up to find out if you are all right, sir."

"What time is it now?" asked Slater.

"Twenty-five minutes past the hour, sir. Are you all right, sir?"

"I'm fine, thank you. I'm glad you called me."

Slater was suddenly alert. He had heard that voice before, but he could not remember where. The accent was peculiar. Whoever was out there was no Austrian. He checked his watch. It was 7:25. He had, unquestionably, overslept. Slater looked at the door. The man had been trying to break in. If his assassin was out in the hallway, this was as good a time to have a showdown as any.

Slater slipped out of the bed quietly and went over to the door in his stocking feet, removed the chain and slid back the bolt. He stepped back about five feet and, keeping the revolver well out in front of him, said, "Come on in. I would like to thank you for your consideration."

Slater waited tensely, prepared to fire at the slightest sign of trouble, but there was no answer.

"Come in," he called again, trying to sound cheerful and friendly. "The door is unlocked."

There was still no answer, and Slater could feel his heart beating in his throat. He lowered the revolver and wiped the sweat from his eyes. He stood there, breathing heavily, still five feet from the door. Had the man gone away, or was he waiting out in the hall for Slater to open the door, too smart to be the first one to expose himself?

Slater clamped his jaw tight, and the muscles rippled in his cheeks. He knew he couldn't just stand there and do nothing. The whole thing was probably a result of his overworked nerves. He looked around the room, knowing beforehand it was useless. There was no other way out of the room. Slater tried to collect his thoughts. He did not want to step out into that hallway until he had somehow satisfied himself that there really was no one here. He went to the phone and picked up the receiver.

"Room service, please."

"Yes, sir." The operator's voice sounded very reassuring.

"Room service," a voice answered.

"Please send up a bottle of Scotch, some ice, and soda water to room twenty-seven, right away."

"Yes, sir! Right away, sir!"

Slater replaced the receiver on the cradle, walked over to the door, bolted it again and started putting on his ski boots. His fingers were clumsy, and it took him quite a while to lace them up. He opened his suitcase and pulled out a clean shirt and a Paisley scarf. He was in the process of knotting the scarf around his neck when he heard a knock on the door. He picked up his revolver and stepped behind the door.

"Who is it?" he called.

"Room service with your order, sir." It was a different voice.

"Come in. The door is unlocked," said Slater, sliding back the bolt.

The door opened slowly, and Slater waited until he saw the man appear with the tray. He put the gun in his pocket and asked the waiter to put the tray on the table.

"Was there anyone in the hallway as you came in?"

"Why no, sir."

Slater picked up the house phone. When the operator answered, he asked her if she had called room twenty-seven at seven.

"Yes, sir," she said immediately, "and I called you again at 7:15, but you didn't answer either call. I'm very sorry, sir," she added. "I was about to try again."

"That's all right, miss," said Slater. "The extra sleep did me good."

"I'm glad, sir." The operator sounded relieved.

"By the way," said Slater, "you didn't send anyone up here to wake me, did you?"

"No, sir."

"Thank you."

Slater hung up and turned to the waiter, who was standing by the table respectfully.

"Shall I make you a drink, sir?" the waiter asked.

"Yes, please," said Slater. Anything to keep the man here, he thought. "Tell me," said Slater, "do you have any foreigners on your staff?"

"No, sir. All the employees of this hotel are Austrian. Most of us were born right here in this valley." The waiter carefully poured the whiskey over the ice into the glass and then filled the glass with soda.

Slater turned back to his suitcase and closed it.

"Do you like Scotch whiskey?"

"Oh, yes, sir," said the waiter, "but it's too expensive for me."

"Pour yourself a drink," said Slater. "We'll drink a toast to Kitzbühel, and then we will go down to the lobby together."

Slater went to the bathroom door. "Please excuse me for a moment."

He closed the door and checked his equipment. An informal party would nevertheless indicate wearing a sport jacket above the ski pants. Many Germans and Austrians wore sport jackets while skiing. Slater was glad to have the cover for he preferred to wear his revolver in a belt holster. He believed the revolver was less conspicuous and easier to get at than if it were kept in his pocket or in a shoulder holster. Part of it, he realized, was purely a matter of habit and personal preference, but the position of the gun was also largely determined by his build. He was deep in the chest and slim in the waist. Consequently, all of his jackets were loose at the waist and offered more than enough room for a gun. Slater bent over and felt the inside of his calf. The knife was there and so was the thin file on the other side. He had grown so accustomed to wearing them he could forget they were there. He checked his pipe lighter to make certain the .22 long cartridge was in place and the firing mechanism was functioning. He pulled the small white handkerchief from his breast pocket and gently unfolded it. Two round, transparent gelatin capsules, which were filled with a watery substance, lay in the palm of his hand. One of them would kill him within a matter of seconds. He looked at them for a moment and shook his head. He knew he could never stand up under torture, but he wondered if he would have the courage to take one of the pills. The gelatin was purposely thick. A man could put one in his mouth, and the temperature of his body would not melt it. The idea was that if an agent believed himself in immediate danger of capture, he could put one into his mouth and save it until all possibility of escape was gone. At that time, he could bite down on it, and the poison would kill him immediately. One of the chemists who prepared the "L" tablets had told him never to bite unless he really wanted to die because there would be no turning back.

Slater checked the Belgian .32 in his right jacket pocket and then pulled on his parka. In the chest pocket was a regular Smith & Wesson .38 revolver, a weapon of which he was particularly fond. The barrel was long enough to make it accurate in practiced hands, and a .38 slug would stop a man cold. In the chest pocket also were three Swiss chocolate and fruit bars, and in his right hip pocket was a small flask of brandy.

Slater had long ago gotten over any feeling of self-consciousness at loading himself with so much equipment. There had been too many times when he had had occasion to use every item but the "L" pills. Maybe, he thought, looking at his face in the mirror, they are what I will have to use this time.

He emerged from the bathroom, completely dressed and ready to go. The waiter had poured his own drink but was waiting politely for Slater.

Slater picked up his glass. "To Kitzbühel," he said. "And to your success and mine."

"A long life to us both, sir," said the waiter.

Slater looked at him over the rim of his glass. Now why, he thought, should anyone wish me a long life—now of all times.

The two men finished their drinks simultaneously. The waiter preceded Slater out of the room, and Slater turned the key in the door. It wasn't until then the realization suddenly dawned on him that, besides bolting his door and putting a chair against it, he had also locked it from the inside. Whoever had tried to break in had either had the key or known how to pick the lock. Slater accompanied the waiter downstairs, wishing he had taken another drink, somewhat comforted by the fact that the bottle of Scotch would be waiting for him when he returned.

When the waiter and Slater had disappeared around the corner and down the stairs, a door at the end of the corridor opened, and Slazov's short thick body stepped into the hallway and moved unhurriedly to Slater's room. Slazov knocked and then waited and listened. After the second knock, he took out the key Anton had given him and opened the door. Closing the door quietly behind him and bolting it, he stood in the middle of the room and, rocking back and forth gently on his feet, looked carefully at everything. He went over to the bottle of Scotch, unscrewed the top, lifted it to his lips, and tasted it cautiously. He put down the bottle and made a face. He did not like Scottish whiskey. He pulled a small vial from his coat pocket and removed the stopper. It looked like a perfume bottle. He carefully poured the contents into the whiskey, shook the mixture and replaced the empty vial in his pocket, leaving everything as he had found it. Slazov tried to open Slater's aluminum suitcase but gave up in disgust after five minutes of fruitless effort. He did not really care what Slater had in there. Anton could pick up the suitcase later and open it with a blowtorch. Slazov put back the bag and left the room, locking it again from the outside, and headed downstairs to the desk.

And now for the Baron's party, thought Slazov, smiling to himself. There was nothing he liked better than to mix business with pleasure. The poison in the Scotch was, after all, only just in case something should go wrong. Slazov laughed. Nothing had ever gone wrong before.

Slazov turned in his keys to Anton.

"He has gone?" said Slazov.

"Yes," said Anton reproachfully. "I thought he wouldn't be able to attend."

"Our friend," Slazov shrugged, "is too nervous. He is high-strung. Someday, who knows," Slazov added, looking at Anton, "he may die of ulcers."

Slazov moved off, his heavy laughter filling the lobby behind him.

Chapter 25

Slater moved along the freshly plowed streets toward the cable-car station. The snow was piled high on the sides, and the road was the only place to walk. The air was chilly again, because the night sky was clear and there was not the smallest cloud to catch the new warmth of the earth and hold it against the ground. If it got any colder, Slater was certain there would be great thick patches of advective fog. He hated to drive in that kind of weather. It was frustrating to be moving along briskly in the clear open air one minute and then, suddenly, plunge into a still, thick mist and have to throttle down to a crawl, knowing all the while that six to ten feet above the roof of the car the visibility was perfect. He wanted to put up his hood, but to do so would cut down on his visibility and hearing, and he had no doubt that either he was being followed or someone was waiting for him along the way. There was a crowd of party-goers up ahead, and he caught up with it as fast as he could, but did not join it, preferring to remain a few paces to the rear.

Slater broke off from the crowd as it turned beyond the railroad crossing toward the cable station and walked over to the red ski-rental shack. He had counted on its being open because of the big party at the top. He was relieved to find he was not the only one of the guests who thought that a moonlight ski, especially if well fortified with alcohol, would be an exciting adventure.

There were about ten peoplc in the shack. Slater looked at them carefully. They were young, mostly, and European. He did not recognize any of them, and no one showed any apparent interest in him. He got his skis and poles without incident and, putting skis and poles under his left arm, moved awkwardly across the hundred and fifty yards to the cable car.

There is a certain amount of anonymity that ski clothes give a man, particularly at night. There was nothing distinctive about a black parka above black ski pants. As he approached the ring of light around the cable house, Slater saw at least twenty people who were dressed identically. There was a little rickrack on one parka, possibly an identifying ski patch on another, but at any distance they all looked pretty much alike.

Slater entered the basement, purchased his ticket and walked along the corridor to the side door. He looked up at the sky. There would be a moon before long, not a full one, but it would be too bright for comfort. He decided to remain in the shadow below the big wooden platform until his number was called. He could hear the shuffling feet and laughter of the people above him. Most of the conversation was in German, but there were so many voices he could pick up only an occasional phrase.

While Slater stood there in the darkness beneath the platform, he tried desperately to think, oppressed by the conviction that all the pieces to this puzzle were now in his possession. They must be, or the Communists would not have sent an assassin to murder him. The pieces were there somewhere in his mind. Up to now, he thought he had put them together very nicely, but something was radically wrong, for the pieces had apparently only appeared to fit because the picture was a preconceived one—one he had set up. Now, suddenly, they had all fallen apart.

Slater resorted to the one technique which experience had taught him was, if not infallible, at least the best method for solving any problem. It was a process, he suddenly realized with painful surprise, he had not employed nearly as much as he should have. He began to question himself. What did he really know? He must forget for the moment the functions of the people he suspected. Who were they? Slater was positive that Hormsby, Anton Reisch, Rüdi Petsch, Krüpl, Stadler, Hauser, von Burgdorf, Wyman, all of them were members of the Communist organization in Kitzbühel. What, he asked himself, was his proof that each of these men was a working member? He took each of them, one by one. He eliminated the most obvious ones first. Rüdi was guilty by his own confession. Krüpl and Stadler had tried to trap him. Hauser had killed Heinz Mahler. Hormsby had delivered a package in the bookstore and owned an unusual lighter, identical to the one in Krüpl's possession—a lighter which he had refused to produce in the bar in spite of all Slater's provocations. Anton had positively revealed himself when he had asked Slater if he knew Carmichael's whereabouts. No desk clerk would try to collect on a guest's bill when the shortage was the exact amount of the bribe the guest had found it necessary to offer to secure his room in the first place. Von Burgdorf was, at the very least, a front man for the Communists. The Office of Security, through Lazlo Kartovski, had told him that.

Slater's body stiffened, and he withdrew deeper into the dark protection of the space beneath the veranda. He heard Wyman's voice, loud and aggressive, as Wyman passed out of the exit from the ticket office. Wyman stood in the light from the doorway, turned and called back to someone inside.

"Come on, Ilse," he said. "It's beautiful out here." He

looked up into the night above him. "There are nothing but stars. Not a cloud anywhere."

Ilse Wieland appeared, and Slater noticed she was carrying skis.

"Here, I'll carry those," said Wyman, "although I can't see why you wanted to bring skis along."

Wyman seemed annoyed, but he took the skis and poles from Ilse, and the two disappeared around the corner of the uprights supporting the veranda and joined the crowd on the steps.

And then there is Wyman, thought Slater. There was more evidence against Wyman than anyone else. Slater tried to keep his personal feelings out of his assessment of Wyman. It was difficult. To Slater, Wyman was a social opportunist, apparently without conscience, who would do anything to get the money to realize his social ambitions. He traded on his good looks and athletic ability. Slater frowned. He knew he had to forget his own opinions. Opinions did not often trap spies. He reviewed the damning evidence against Wyman.

First, there was the bogus bank account in Zurich in the name of Martin Hazel. A bank account opened over the telephone and created by a postal money order. Hollingsworth had checked that. What was it George had said? Slater tried to remember exactly. George had called the bank clerk mentioned in Webber's letter and asked if there was an account in the name of Martin Hazel. There was, and it had $835 in it. Eight hundred thirty-five dollars was the amount of the money order. Hollingsworth had neglected to ask if Martin Hazel and Wyman were the same man.

Second, there was Wyman's girl friend in Zurich, Trude Kupfer. George had gone to see her, and she had shown him some of Wyman's expensive gifts. Slater began to wonder. Was a Trude Kupfer the kind of a girl a social climber like Wyman would go for? Slater wished he had interviewed her when he was in Zurich. Now that it was too late, he could think of a few questions he would have asked.

The new hypothesis which was beginning to force its way into Slater's mind was badly damaged when he considered the third bit of evidence. Why, he asked himself, had Wyman purchased a round-trip ticket to Munich and then changed trains? No, thought Slater, I must be losing my mind. He had followed Wyman, when Wyman had asked for Schlessinger's skis. He had intercepted the message in those skis. The message had said that Wyman would collect $170 from Rüdi. Slater stopped abruptly. He forced his mind back to the interview with the waiter. Rüdi had said that he had received orders not to put Wyman's room number on the menu. At the time, he had not questioned the remark. He had immediately decided that Wyman had become too greedy, and the number-one man had given orders to turn off the golden supply. That could still be the reason, but was it? Slater smashed his fist into his open palm. The only things he had actually seen himself which incriminated Wyman were his purchase of the Munich ticket, his asking for the skis, and his routine with Rüdi. By that time, thought Slater savagely, my mind had already been conditioned, but the whole idea was fantastic. The bitter, hard-earned lessons of ten years told him that nothing in this world was impossible. The greatest single mistake a man could ever make was to underestimate the enemy or accept any bit of evidence at face value. He knew this as well as any operator alive. He had been a fool, a blunderer of the worst kind, and that was the reason he was now standing alone in the cold darkness underneath the veranda, knowing his life might be the price he would have to pay.

The number of his car was announced over the loudspeaker. The blaring sound startled him. He had to make his appearance now. Slater tucked his skis and poles under his left arm again and moved quickly into the light of the exit, walked around the platform and started up the stairs. The platform was crowded and he was extremely uncomfortable. He didn't want anyone too close to him. He was well aware of the advantages a crowd could provide an assassin. He also was familiar with some of the techniques.

Slater handed his skis and poles to the attendant and entered the cable car. He pushed his way to the far side and stood with his back against the window, facing the center. Wyman and Ilse would not be able to get a car for another twenty minutes. At that moment, Slater would have given almost anything to have Ilse beside him. It was a selfish wish, he knew, but two pairs of trained eyes were far better than one, and he had something he wanted very much to tell her. He hoped he would have the chance, but in the meantime, for her sake, he would have to keep away from her when anyone else was around. If Slater's calculations were correct, any obvious partnership between himself and Ilse would endanger her life. He was now firmly convinced that Colonel Imré Dinar must be at the Hotel Ehrenbachhöhe. Dinar was probably one of the guests of the hotel. This much the Communists were undoubtedly sure of. What they apparently did not know was exactly which of the guests he was. Somehow, they had discovered that the Ehrenbachhöhe Hotel was to be the meeting place. Possibly the previous German agent had told them that much, and they were now counting on Ilse to identify Dinar. A plan was taking shape in Slater's mind. He wished he had persuaded Ilse to show him Dinar's photograph.

The cable car was jammed. In Slater's opinion, it was too full. The operator had permitted too many people on board and had definitely exceeded the safety limits. Moreover, the occupants were excited at the prospect of a big party. Undoubtedly, some of them had been drinking. They moved and jostled each other restlessly, and there was a great deal of laughter. The voices called to each other in the semi-darkness, as they swung high up into the starry night. Slater could hear the inevitable comments about broken cables and swaying cable cars. One clown expressed the hope, in a state of high glee, that the snow was as soft as it looked, because it was a long way down.

Slater was unusually conscious of things he did not normally notice: the beauty of the night outside the windows, the black bulk of the mountains opposite, the ever increasing vista of the valley below. For once he did not want to see these things. He was afraid to take his attention from the activity immediately around him, but these things outside were real. They were the wonders and beauties of life, to be enjoyed and appreciated; but even these simple pleasures were now denied him as he forced his attention back to the people around him.

The light was poor, but of those individuals he could distinguish, none looked familiar; and no one appeared particularly friendly, except in that inept way that strangers have when meeting one another at a party—a look of innocuous cordiality which went no deeper than the vapid smile that represented it. If he were killed in their midst, they would get away from the unpleasant reality of his corpse as fast as they could, angry at him for trying to spoil their meaningless party. They would rush to the hotel, hold the center of the stage for a brief period as the bearers of sensational tidings, and then be the gayest of the gay as compensation for their brush with death. All but a few, thought Slater grimly, who would solemnly question the why of it all and philosophize on the impermanence of life.

How he envied them at this moment But he hated them too, because they could offer him no help. They didn't know this party, about which they were so excited, was a front behind which the Communists intended to capture and destroy a man dedicated to a small nation which demanded freedom from slavery, a man whose capture might mean the annihilation of thousands of people. Slater wanted to shout at them, to shake them, to tell them what was happening, but it would be useless he knew.

The cable car slowed and nudged its way between the cement piers. Slater breathed a sigh of relief. He was at the top, and he was still alive.

Chapter 26

Ilse had seen Slater pass without so much as a glance in her direction. She watched him step on board, and the other passengers close in behind him. She kept her eyes on the car as it was pulled up and away into the night.

He is so stubborn, she thought, so afraid to believe in anyone. This life is bad for us.

"Are you sure," said Wyman, "that you never knew that fellow Slater before?"

Ilse was startled, but turned calmly to Wyman. Apparently he had been watching her.

"Yes," she said truthfully.

"Obviously, Mr. Slater is a fast worker," said Wyman dryly.

"What does that—fast worker—mean?"

Ilse frowned. She knew what it meant. She looked up at Wyman again for a moment. His remark surprised her. It indicated that he was more intuitive than she had expected. She had better watch herself carefully from now on. Herr Wyman must be more dangerous than she had thought.

"Forget it," said Wyman, picking up her skis and poles, which were leaning against the railing. "That must be our car. Let's move up so we can be among the first inside. I'd like to be by the window to watch the view."

Wyman led the way and Ilse followed him. She was as anxious as he to get to the top.

They were not the first, but Wyman's broad shoulders managed to secure a spot by the front window. Ilse found herself wedged in between Wyman and a short chunky man whose body was as unyielding as a slab of marble. She was annoyed and turned to ask him to please move over, but his attention was elsewhere. She started to grab his sleeve to get him to notice her when something about the man's appearance made her hesitate. He looked vaguely familiar. Ilse tried to remember where she had seen him before. He was dressed in street clothes and was wearing a felt hat. His face, what she could see of it from the side, was heavy—the face of a peasant. Ilse shook her head. What did he look like without a hat? He was probably bald. She shrugged, started to turn back to Wyman, and then she became conscious of the smell of bay rum. It was a scent all its own that she could never forget. She turned her head again; but this time it was not necessary. She knew who he was. He had been pointed out to her at a party at the Russian Embassy in Vienna and had later danced with her. She had been told that his name was Gregor Slazov, and he was an assassin for the Communists—a paid killer who had murdered more than one member of German Intelligence. He was also used as a hatchet man within Russia.

Ilse shivered and tried to make herself as small as possible. At first she thought he might be here to dispose of her, but she did not flatter herself that she would be that difficult to eliminate. Then she thought of Dinar, but rejected that idea because of her conviction that the Communists wanted to take him alive. Suddenly she knew. It was Slater he was after, and Slater would not come near her so she could warn him. He didn't trust her. Ilse closed her eyes and bit down on her lower lip to keep herself from crying out.

As Ilse and Wyman stepped out of the car and out of the

building which housed it, they were met by a pony-driven sleigh and whisked away, up along the ridge to the hotel. It was a wonderful way to be taken to a party, to be carried to the accompaniment of sleigh bells along the ridge of night with a small crisp moon just beginning to silver the snow on the mountains all around.

The hotel looked like a great ship in the middle of an open sea. The moon was not sufficiently high in the sky to pale the brilliance of the hundreds of lights in all the windows. Ilse allowed Wyman to help her out of the sleigh, and the driver stacked her skis and poles into the snow by the wide wooden veranda which served as a balcony from which the guests could observe the valley far below between them and the range of peaks beyond. Ilse had never been up there at night before, and the view was breath-taking. The porch was deserted as it was quite cold, and Wyman hurried Ilse inside.

An orchestra was playing American music, which was now so popular in Europe; and the main floor was jammed with couples. Ilse reflected that most of them had more enthusiasm than rhythm. About half of the people dancing were wearing ski boots. Judging by all the skis stacked outside, a good many of them planned to ski down into Kirchberg when the party broke up at dawn. Maybe, she thought, some will even try to ski by moonlight. She decided to keep her boots on. They were somewhat awkward to dance in until you got used to them, but she didn't believe she would be doing much dancing.

Ilse checked her parka separately from Wyman's, which, she noted, seemed to annoy him, and turned to inspect as many of the older men as she could see.

"Let's dance," said Wyman, starting to take Ilse in his arms.

"Oh, please," she said, "not yet. Let's look around first and see everything the Baron has provided us."

Ilse took Wyman's hand and walked along the wall the length of the main dining room. She could not see Slater anywhere. She led Wyman, protesting every inch of the way, into the other public rooms. A bar had been set up in the smallest room at the far end of the building. Judging by the crowds, it should have been set up in the biggest room. It was there that she spotted Dinar. There could be no question. He looked exactly like his picture: thick gray hair, stocky, ruddy complexion, bushy mustache and eyebrows—a powerful-looking man whose years as a soldier had etched fine lines around his eyes and deep lines in his cheeks. He looked, at the same time, older than fifty and yet more fit than the average man of that age. Ilse liked his face. She would have liked to have the opportunity to paint him some time. She turned and looked up at Wyman. It was too bad that this healthy, rugged-looking young man was a Communist. She could have used such a man.

"Will you get me a drink, Herr Wyman?"

"Why can't you call me Ronnie, Ilse?" He shook his head. "Mister is pretty formal, don't you think?"

"All right, Ronnie." Ilse laughed. "Now, may I have a drink?"

"You certainly can. Wait here, and I'll bring it to you."

Wyman shouldered his way into the crowd around the bar, leaving Ilse alone in the middle of the room, but directly in the Colonel's line of sight.

It was fortunate for her, since she was not a man, as her predecessor on this assignment, that the Baron had asked his guests to wear ski clothes, because her next move would have been too conspicuous otherwise. She hoped Dinar would notice and interpret it correctly. She started to take a step forward but stumbled. She looked down at her feet in surprise and immediately bent over to tie her boot lace. It took a second or two as she had to undo it first and then retie it. She straightened up, looked around the room as if embarrassed at her clumsiness, and her eyes rested for a brief second on Dinar, just long enough to see him pick up an ivory-stemmed cigarette holder from the table and start to fit a cigarette into it. Ilse held her breath and looked anxiously for Wyman. She was too excited. Dinar had seen her, and now she was afraid to look back.

Wyman arrived with the drinks.

"Sorry I forgot to ask what you wanted," he said. "I brought you a Scotch and soda. I hope that's all right."

Ilse nodded and took the glass. She glanced quickly at Dinar. The holder, with the cigarette now in it, was in his mouth, but it was still unlighted. He had returned her signal.

She turned to Wyman. "Yes," she said, "that was just fine. I love Scotch and soda." She did not need to look at Dinar again. She knew by now that the cigarette would be lighted.

Now, she thought, we know each other. What shall I do next? How am I to get him out of here? If he is seen with me, they will kill us both. She was frantic.

"There's your friend Slater," said Wyman. "I suppose he's going to ask you for a dance, and," he added bitterly, "I don't imagine you'll refuse him."

Ilse looked expectantly toward Slater as he approached them from the next room. He walked past them with nothing more than a curt nod and headed into the crowd around the bar. She turned back to Wyman, trying not to betray her exasperation.

"You see, Ronnie," she shrugged. "He does not even know that I breathe."

Ilse looked over Wyman's shoulder and saw Slazov moving casually toward them.

He is going into that crowd after Slater! I know it, she thought. He will kill Slater there. Well, let him! Slater is only an American. It is my duty to get the Colonel out of here. If I interfere now, it will only endanger my mission.

Before Ilse realized what she was doing, she found herself in front of Slazov, blocking his way.

"Oh, Herr Slazov!" she gushed. "What a wonderful surprise. I haven't seen you since that Embassy party in Vienna." Ilse took his arm. "I remember what a wonderful dancer you are. You must dance with me immediately. Come!"

Ilse turned Slazov around and led him to the main dining room.

Her action caused quite a stir in the bar. There was more than one man who had already noticed the copper-haired woman and envied her handsome American escort. Now, as Wyman stood, confused and angry, in the middle of the room, they wondered why such a lovely woman would prefer the company of an ugly, bald Russian. Slater had not apparently noticed a thing. He had been too busy edging his way into the bar.

"It is not very gracious of me to say so," said Slazov in German, "but I cannot remember where we met."

"We met at a party at the Russian Embassy in Vienna, two years ago."

Ilse smiled. She tried to look at him without looking down. Slazov was not much shorter than Ilse, but he had almost no neck, and his eyes were lower than hers.

"I don't blame you for not remembering me, Herr Slazov. You danced with so many women that night."

It was the truth. Slazov was an excellent dancer, in spite of his thick body, and he had danced almost every dance.

"So!" said Slazov, visibly flattered. "I always like to be remembered by a beautiful woman."

She is lovely creature, he thought. Is too bad I am not here for pleasure.

He frowned. He had already waited too long to get rid of the American.

The music stopped, and Ilse did her best to keep the conversation going, but this dance with Slazov had had an effect contrary to what she had wanted. Slazov left her abruptly, determined to finish off the American in a hurry and come back to Ilse a free man.

Ilse stood there on the edge of the dance floor, where Slazov had left her, and stared after him. She watched him turn suddenly and start out toward the main exit. She looked ahead of him and saw Slater open the door and disappear outside, apparently completely unaware that anyone was following him. Slazov followed at a leisurely pace. He reminded Ilse of a small steamroller—the pace was slow but inexorable. Ilse closed her eyes. Was there nothing she could do to stop Slazov? Turning, she went as fast as she dared to the coat room. She got her parka and went outside onto the veranda. She looked around for some sign of Slazov or Slater. There was nothing out there but the wind. The moon was considerably higher and brighter, and the stars had lost some of their brilliance. The place was as deserted as the moon above her. Ilse shivered and slipped cautiously down the veranda stairs.

Chapter 27

The snow was granular, and the tiny crystals of ice reflected the light from the moon. It looked as if someone had scattered a thousand diamonds over the white expanse.

Ilse started carefully down toward the cable station. The snow and the thinner atmosphere at six thousand feet deadened the night sounds. She could barely hear the crunching of her own footsteps. Ilse thought she could make out two dark figures moving along the ridge below. They seemed very far away. If they were Slazov and Slater, she would never catch up in time to be of any use. She turned back to get her skis. The sight of the small hotel immediately above her, nestled just below the summit, its bright lights paled by the moon's reflection, created momentarily an eerie sensation within her. She was less than fifty yards away from the music, noise and laughter of over a hundred people, yet the building was apparently as silent as a tomb.

Ilse moved quickly now, convinced that she would be too late, no longer caring about her mission or her country. She had to try to save Slater.

After putting on her skis, she pulled a Belgian .32 from her parka and skied without poles to the ridge and started down.

She did not want poles to interfere with her aim. She bent her knees until she was in a very low crouch. That way her silhouette was lower, and she could build up more speed.

She found herself unaccountably angry, not at Slazov—she despised him—but at Slater. As her skis began to pick up speed, all she could think of was that Slater was nothing but a stubborn, high-strung fool who had rejected her offer of love. She would show him who was a Communist! No man was ever going to spurn her affections and get away with it! He would owe his life to her, and then she would make him pay. The cold night wind stung her eyes and made them water. She blinked them so she could see.

The two figures ahead were almost life-size now, and the farthest was still at least fifty yards from the cable house. It was Slater, all right, and he was standing up as straight and conspicuous as a tree in a desert. Slazov was moving along steadily about sixty yards behind. His walk seemed as confident as a person out for a Sunday stroll through the park. Suddenly, the picture of what was about to happen flashed in her mind. Slazov was almost above the marker for the Streif ski run. In less than a minute he would be below the ridge, and he could fire and lean up against the mountain for protection. In that minute Slater would be in the open space below, completely exposed. If she were going to do anything, she would have to do it now.

She took aim with her .32, knowing she was too far away for accuracy. She squeezed the trigger three times and screamed at Slater to run for cover. Then she pointed her skis straight down the mountain and deliberately fell into the deep snow twenty-five yards below Slazov. From her position, she could not see either man, but she could hear shots coming from her left and from above her. Slater had at least had a chance to fire. Unless Slazov was pressed against the ridge, he must have been hit. Ilse knew without any doubt that Slater must be a crack shot. She unfastened her harnesses and began to crawl slowly up toward the spot where Slazov had been. As she climbed higher, she could hear shots coming from the direction of the cable house. When she was finally high enough to see, she lay flat in the snow, her automatic in front of her, and waited for Slazov to appear. She waited at least a minute, but nothing happened. She could see Slater's body lying on the snow immediately in front of the cable-house door. She could not be certain whether he was still alive. If Slazov were still above her and alive, he was taking great pains to keep out of sight. Another minute went by, and her right hand was almost numb from the cold. Suddenly, a whole series of shots sounded thinly above her. Slazov appeared, she fired twice, and his body fell forward and sprawled head downward in the snow. Ilse remained where she was, motionless, waiting for some movement from Slazov. Then she heard somebody yelling in English at Slater and, lifting her head, saw a tall young man appear above her where Slazov had been. Ilse looked in the direction of the cable house and watched Slater get to his feet and climb, almost casually, up to the Streif trail marker. She decided he was the handsomest, most wonderful man alive. She turned and let herself slide down to her skis. She put them on and began edging her way back up to the ridge. When she got to the top, after crisscrossing twice, she was exhausted. She stood on level ground and her legs trembled.

Slater went over to her and took Ilse's face in his hands. They looked at each other for a moment, and neither said anything. Slater must have noticed her trembling, for he bent over quietly and started to rub her legs vigorously. Ilse felt the circulation returning and with it, a grateful warmth. The trembling stopped.

"Let me see your right hand," he said, and he took off her

ski mitten and proceeded to massage her hand. The feeling began to return.

"Have you any more shells?" he asked.

Ilse nodded and pointed with her left hand to the chest pocket of her parka. He unzipped her pocket and brought out the .32 and a small box of shells. He reloaded the automatic and returned it.

"You may need it again, Liebchen." He had been speaking to her in German, and he had been using the familiar "du" form.

"What about your hands?" she said.

"Maybe you'll warm them for me later," he said.

The tall young man approached them. Ilse had noticed that he had been busy with Slazov's body.

"I got all his papers," he said. He appeared extremely nervous.

"Good," said Slater, turning to the young man. "We'll dispose of the body, George."

"No, no!" said George. "I killed him," George hesitated, "the least I can do is get rid of him."

Slater smiled. "I've something else for you to do, George."

"Well," George hesitated, doubtfully, but he was obviously relieved.

"I want you to get back down to the village as fast as you can and get hold of a car. I want you to have it waiting at Klausen, headed for Kirchberg, at the foot of the Fleck Trail. Make certain there's plenty of gas in it and start the motor as soon as you see or hear any activity on the trail."

George still hesitated.

"Well, what are you waiting for? Let's get with it!"

"You sure," he said, "everything will be all right here?"

"I hope so," Slater smiled. "And, George."

"Yes."

"Thanks a lot for everything."

Hollingsworth grinned. "Right," he said. "I'll be there waiting."

Hollingsworth turned and headed for the cable house.

Slater turned to Ilse. "That Hollingsworth is crazy. He's never fired a gun before, and I told him not to fire less than two shots at a human target." Slater shook his head. "He must have fired the entire clip!"

"Who is Hollingsworth, and how did he get up here?" Ilse was confused.

"He's in the Foreign Service," said Slater. "He's been helping me here." Slater frowned. "We had a little argument this afternoon. Told me he was checking out of this whole business. I told him to go ahead, and I thought he would. He phoned me at the hotel up here while you were flirting with the Russian. He asked me if there was anything he could do. My first thought was to tell him to go to hell. It's awfully easy, Ilse, to forget the sensibilities of someone new to this business. Ever since I told him to get out of Kitzbühel, I was worried about his wandering around loose. The only thing he knew which might have been useful to the opposition was my real identity, but I knew it wouldn't be long before they'd figure it out anyway. The thing is there have already been too many innocent victims, and I had called George to come down here in the first place. He obviously wanted to help and he was ashamed of his performance this afternoon.

"I needed help. There was no question about that. Even amateur assistance I thought would be better than nothing. I had spotted our bald friend just before you asked him to dance. I knew they had sent someone to dispose of me and I remembered seeing him by the station. I figured he was following me then. I asked Hollingsworth if he remembered him. When he said he did, that decided me. I told him to come on up to the ridge above the Streif trail marker; and as soon as I passed below it, he was to fire at the Russian. I made him promise to fire." Slater added, "And I thought he would."

"But you told me he'd never fired a gun in his life."

"I know, but I didn't really care whether his shots were accurate. I hoped they would be, of course, but the main thing was for Hollingsworth to create a diversion long enough for me to turn and shoot."

"But I fired first."

"Yes, and that confused me. I couldn't decide at first whether my assassin had another ally. That was when I scrambled for cover."

"I heard shots coming from your position."

"They didn't do much good. All I could do from there was to keep him hugging the side of the ridge."

"Apparently Slazov tried to climb up the ridge and get you from above."

"That's when George emptied his clip." Slater looked over Ilse's shoulder at Slazov's bulky form, lying face down in the snow, his head downhill. "You haven't looked at the body," he said quietly.

"No."

"Your first three shots threw off the Russian's aim, and mine pinned him to the ridge; but the two shots that killed him were from the front, not from the rear." Slater looked at Ilse and smiled. "You see, Liebchen, Hollingsworth missed."

"Oh, no!"

"Oh, yes!" Slater put his hand on her shoulder. "So you see," his smile was gentle, "I owe you my life. Are you going to make me pay?"

Ilse looked up at him, trying to make her eyes noncommittal.

"I think so," she said slowly.

She wished this moment could be prolonged somehow, but she knew that was impossible.

"Let's bury this monster." She said it in a whisper. "Even in death he frightens me."

Slazov was extremely heavy and awkward, and it took both of them to carry him along the ridge. They buried him as deep as they could and packed the snow in above him. Even in the cold moonlight, the burial plot was fairly obvious, but there was no time to do a better job.

"I have spotted Dinar," said Ilse when they had finished.

"I know," said Slater. "I was watching you untie and retie your boot. That's why I sent George for the car."

"But how did you know which man was Dinar?"

"I was given his description. Are you certain you have found the right one? Did he give the proper signal?"

"Yes," said Ilse, "but now that I've found him, I haven't one idea how to get him away from there."

Slater and Ilse discussed the problem on the way back up the wide slope to the hotel. Ilse went inside first, and Slater waited for about ten minutes and then entered.

George Hollingsworth had to wait fifteen minutes for a cable car to arrive. The cars ran on demand instead of on schedule, and he became more and more impatient and apprehensive as the time passed.

He was alone on the concrete pier. The machine operator had disappeared upstairs into the warmth of the control room. George stood there, staring out into the night, wondering where any man could have found the courage to turn his back on his murderer and lead him alone into an uncertain ambush. Hollingsworth heaved a heartfelt sigh. He felt so terribly inadequate beside Slater. His country should thank God for such a man. George was suddenly ashamed. He knew he had missed Slazov. The girl had shown more courage than he had, and they were both counting on him now. He frowned. He would not let them down this time, if he had to steal or kill to get that car.

A black speck appeared below him and grew rapidly larger, until the cable car was near enough for him to see the moonlight reflected by its windows. George stepped gratefully into the car, and the attendant, who was the only other occupant, closed the door, gave the signal, and the car started slipping down quietly to the village below.

Chapter 28

When Slater entered the hotel, he saw Ilse dancing with Wyman. He edged his way toward them through the dancing couples. He stopped long enough to watch her for a moment. He decided they made a very handsome pair. Ilse followed Wyman effortlessly and smoothly. Wyman was as good on the dance floor as he was on skis. The thought angered Slater, and he cut in sooner than he had intended.

"Your hands," said Ilse, "are freezing."

She put her left arm around his neck and pushed up very close to him. He could smell the fragrance of her hair and feel the warmth of her body. They could have been any young couple who had just discovered they were in love. They should have been able to dance all night, to confess their love, to drink a toast to one another, to escape on skis into the village at dawn as many others at the party obviously planned to do. They should have but they were not just any young couple, and they could not act as others would. But the love was there all the same for anyone not totally blind to see.

The guests were too busy with their own merry-making to notice them, or care one way or the other—all but a few, and they cared a great deal.

"I can see Hormsby," said Ilse in Slater's ear.

"What's he up to?" asked Slater.

"He's talking to Wyman. I think he's going to cut in. Please," said Ilse, "let's go to the bar now."

Slater took Ilse's hand, and they left the dance floor. Ilse looked along the wall and saw Dinar again, still sitting at the same table.

"He's a fine-looking man," said Slater. "I hope he can ski."

"He's been here before at this hotel. He must be able to ski," she said. "Anyway, he's wearing ski boots."

If he can't, she thought, we haven't a chance.

She stole a quick glance at Slater. We've got to get out of this alive, she thought. I have waited too long for this man to lose him now.

Ilse and Slater moved into the crowd by the bar.

"You're right, you know," he whispered. "If either one of us is observed talking to him, it's the kiss of death."

Ilse nodded and Slater got the attention of a bartender long enough to order two drinks.

"Have you ever seen the man at the table next to him?" he asked.

"No," she said. "Can't you think of any other way?"

Slater shook his head. "But I'm wide open to suggestions."

"I don't like it," she said.

"Neither do I," said Slater, looking the man in question over carefully. He was not very big, but he was big enough.

Slater picked up the drinks, gave one to Ilse, and led the way out of the crowd.

"Are you going to do it now?" Ilse asked anxiously.

"Why wait?"

They both knew the answer to that.

"Have you got it?"

"In my right hand," he said.

"Well," Ilse pressed his hand, "good luck."

Slater left her, took a gulp of his drink and started uncertainly over to the table beside Dinar's. His walk was that of a man not completely drunk but well on the way. He blinked his eyes and then opened them wide as if that would help him to see the world as it really was. He held his head awkwardly, a little forward and to one side, as if to tell the world that his head was all right, as any fool could see, and the rest of his body would follow one way or the other. When he was opposite the table, his eyes fastened on a very pretty young German girl seated with a heavy-set young man who was speaking to her with almost dignified ardor. Slater approached the table, stopped and looked down at them with uncertain eyes. He tried, unsuccessfully, to take a swallow of his drink, but he could not get his mouth and the glass together. He stared at the glass as though it were a naughty child that would not behave properly.

The young couple looked up at him uncertainly. Slater looked down on them, tried to put out his arm to steady himself, missed, and ended up on his knees with his arms on the table. He remained there, looking vaguely at both of them.

"You," he said to the man slowly but very distinctly, "are in love with her." He nodded for emphasis.

"And you," he said turning slowly and trying very hard to focus on the girl, "are in love with him." Slater nodded again.

The girl tried a tentative smile. Her escort did the same.

" 'S a toast to love!"

Again Slater tried to get the glass to his mouth and failed miserably. He managed to get to his feet. He looked at the offending glass again, frowned, and then calmly poured the contents over the head of the man.

"I can't drink it," he said thickly, "but you can."

The young man swore as the liquor trickled down his face and into his collar. He stood up, grabbed Slater by the front of his sweater and struck out with his fist. Much to his surprise, Slater twisted suddenly, and the young man's fist smashed into Slater's shoulder instead of his jaw; but Slater went down heavily on his right side, almost at Dinar's feet. In that brief second, Slater tugged Dinar's trouser, pulled his shoelace and left a piece of paper on the floor beside Dinar's shoe. Slater immediately rolled his body away from the table into the center of the room and tried to get up.

The enraged young man, encouraged by his success and feeling the power of delivering a crushing defeat while his girl friend was looking on, rushed over to renew the attack. Ilse intercepted him.

"You bully!" she shouted. "You leave him alone. Can't you see he is drunk? He meant no harm. Go away!"

The young man was no match for those flashing green eyes, and he retreated as Ilse helped Slater to his feet.

"You were wonderful, Liebchen," she whispered in his ear. "You should have been an actor. You were so funny."

"Did he get the note?" asked Slater.

"Yes," she said, leading Slater over to a vacant table on the far side of the room.

"I hope he believes it's genuine."

"Here, Liebchen," said Ilse loudly, "sit here, and I will get you some coffee."

Ilse sat him down and ordered a waiter to bring a pot of coffee.

"Do you think anyone saw me deliver the note?"

"No, your shoulder was in the way."

"Where were Hormsby, Wyman and the Baron at the time?"

"I don't know; I didn't see them."

Slater was suddenly angry.

"You know that guy would have taken another swing at me, if it hadn't been for you!"

Ilse looked surprised. "What did you expect after pouring a glass of whiskey over his head?"

"But I was drunk," Slater grumbled. "As far as he knew, I was defenseless."

"That's what you get for being drunk," said Ilse primly.

Slater looked at her and she gave way immediately and smiled.

"Well?"

"Well," he said slowly, "I guess we'll just have to wait."

"What time is it now?" asked Ilse.

Slater looked at his watch. "Ten minutes to one," he said. "We've got all night. This party won't break up until after dawn."

"Maybe the party won't, but I don't think we will be permitted to stay that long. Somebody will miss Slazov."

"Yes," said Slater thoughtfully. "Who do you think it will be?"

"It could be any of them—Hormsby, Wyman, the Baron. Possibly, all of them," said Ilse.

"I don't think so," said Slater. The waiter brought the coffee, and Slater pretended to have difficulty drinking it. "Maybe one of them, maybe not. But certainly not all three."

"Why not all three?"

"You know, Ilse. That's not the way they work. Only the top man will know Slazov. Even he," Slater added, "may not know him by sight. Slazov may have been told to contact one of the lower echelon in Kitzbühel. After all, the assassin's identity must be protected from potential informers within his own organization. He is the one man in this crazy business who is committing a legal crime."

The truth of this statement hit Slater with a strange force. After all, what crimes had Hormsby, the Baron, or even Wyman committed for which they could be prosecuted? He could not even prove that Wyman was a traitor to his country—anyway, not in a court of law.

"And the number-one man," said Ilse, "might very well not choose to reveal himself to an assassin who might one day be used to eliminate him."

"Exactly," said Slater. "This very need for secrecy, for compartmentation, is the weakest link in espionage activity. The one man who knows Slazov by sight may not be here."

"But, Liebchen, the very fact that you're still alive may bring him up here immediately—if he's not already here."

"That's the chance I had to take," said Slater. "We had to give Hollingsworth time to get that car."

"How far is it from the cable car to the bottom of the Fleck Trail?"

"Only about three miles." Slater frowned. "The trouble is that Slazov saw me with Hollingsworth. Undoubtedly Slazov will have tried to put someone on Hollingsworth. I hope George can get hold of a car."

"Do you think he'll make it?" asked Ilse.

"He's got to," said Slater evenly, looking thoughtfully at Ilse.

She returned his look and smiled gently.

"I know," she said finally and very quietly. "He's got to."

"I'd like very much to dance with you right now," he said.

"You're still too drunk to dance." Ilse smiled. "Besides, we might get separated that way. We're safer together."

Slater nodded in agreement, reflecting that the solid wall at his back felt reassuring. Ilse was not a bad ally for many reasons. She had courage, probably more than he had, and she certainly knew how to handle that .32. Hollingsworth had been gone for over an hour. He must have gotten to Klausen by now.

Slater looked at the entrance to the bar. A familiar figure was standing in the doorway. He was talking urgently to another man who was only partially visible, but who also looked vaguely familiar. Unfortunately, the brighter light was behind them, and Slater could not see them distinctly. He put out his hand and squeezed Ilse's arm, nodding in the direction of the doorway. Ilse gave a sudden start and turned back to Slater.

"That's Anton Reisch, the desk clerk," she said.

"Yes," said Slater, "and he's not here as an employee. I was quite certain," he said slowly, thinking back to that afternoon, "that Anton must be the one who knew Slazov by sight."

"We don't have much time then," said Ilse. Her voice was calm, but Slater thought that her eyes looked greener than he had ever seen them.

Slater frowned. He could not be certain, but he thought Anton appeared somewhat the worse for wear.

Chapter 29

"Have you ever seen the other man?" said Slater. "The one Anton is talking to."

"No," Ilse shook her head. "I don't think so. He looks like an American."

Slater frowned. "Maybe he is."

An American, thought Slater, that's it! He wished he had brought along a certain passport-sized photograph to be sure.

"Ilse," he said urgently, "I know that man, not personally, but I'm almost positive I know who he is."

"Is he important?" Ilse looked alarmed.

"Important!" Slater whispered. "If I'm right, he's the number-one man in this operation. Not only that," he added, ruefully, "but possibly the most diabolically clever agent it's been my misfortune to run across—a man who has ruined the reputation of a possibly innocent associate, and deliberately sacrificed the lives of three members of his own organization for the success of his mission."

Slater shook his head. "He is the living personification of the theory that the end justifies the means."

Ilse was caught by the urgency of Slater's voice. "What are you going to do about him?"

"I don't know," he said. "That's the frustrating part of it. I may not be able to do anything. Either we win or lose, as far as our lives and Dinar's are concerned; but unless I'm way off base, when the results are in, plus or minus, that man will be safely behind the Iron Curtain. In the meantime, the odds are still at least four to two against us. And at the moment it doesn't look as though we're in any position to fight back."

Slater looked up at the doorway as Anton moved into the bar and found a seat at a table near the door. He could not miss them when they went out.

Slater whispered to Ilse, "Is there any other way out of here?'

"There's the servants' exit on the far side of the bar," she said. "I believe it leads to the kitchen behind the main room."

"I'm afraid we'll have to use it," said Slater. "Anton's got the main door covered."

Ilse pressed Slater's hand, and he followed her glance. Hormsby had just entered the room and was talking with Anton. The conversation was brief. Then Hormsby walked to the far end of the bar and stationed himself there.

"Well," said Slater dryly, "I see the boys are finally getting acquainted."

"And," Ilse added, "all for our benefit." She tried to match Slater's tone, but her voice faltered.

At that moment the Baron von Burgdorf appeared, his gross body completely filling the entrance. He looked around the room for a moment, licked his lips absentmindedly, and moved in the direction of their table. Before Ilse was aware of what was happening, Slater had her in his arms, kissing her. Ilse automatically returned his embrace.

Slater whispered in her ear, "Even the Baron will think twice before interrupting lovers. Anyway, our time has run out. We had to give the signal."

Slater underestimated the Baron's persistence.

"I hate to break up such a tender scene, my dear," he said, looking at Ilse. His eyes were so small Slater could hardly see them in the half-light. "But," he licked his lips again and smiled, "I have come to claim a host's privilege—a dance with the loveliest lady at my party." His voice was gentle and deep, but there was power behind the request.

Slater released Ilse, but his hand closed over the edge of the table, and the blood drained from his knuckles.

"Oh, Baron," said Ilse. Slater could feel her body tremble, but her voice was steady. "You are so kind, I would be honored to dance with you." Her smile was enchanting. "But I am afraid to let this American out of my sight. I am a very jealous woman, and you have invited so many lovely ladies."

"Now, now, Ilse," said Slater soothingly. "You have no need to be jealous of any woman." Slater made himself smile up at the Baron. "Nicht wahr, Herr Baron?"

"Come," said Slater, getting to his feet and pulling a confused and unwilling Ilse up with him. "I will accompany you and the Baron," he bowed at the Baron, "to the dance floor. After all," Slater continued, "the Baron is our host, a most charming host."

Ilse glanced at Slater sharply. The man is a chameleon. What idiocy is this?

Slater took her left arm, the Baron her right, and the three of them promenaded out of the bar. As he left, Slater looked over at Dinar's table, but the table was empty. Dinar had gone. He had received and understood their signal.

When the three had disappeared into the next room, Anton signaled Hormsby, who moved quickly from his position by the bar over to Anton's table. They had a brief conference and followed Ilse, Slater and the Baron.

Once inside the ballroom, Slater turned to the Baron.

"I've changed my mind, Baron," he said quickly. "I think I'm the jealous one. Come on, Ilse, let's dance."

Before the Baron could do anything, Ilse had disengaged her arm and was dancing with Slater.

It was a strange sort of dance. Slater was continually whispering, almost fiercely, into her ear. He steered her first into the center of the crowded floor and then toward the main entrance. At the cloak room, just to the right of the door, he ordered her to get their parkas; and he faced the crowd, his hand staying just above the revolver resting in his waist holster. Ilse thought he looked a little wild. She managed to get their parkas and tugged at Slater's jacket.

"You leave first," he said quickly. "Dinar should be waiting just below the Fleck Trail marker."

Ilse hesitated.

"Get out!" he said. His voice was low, but it was intense.

"We'll wait for you on the trail," she said.

"You'll do nothing of the kind—and don't wait at the bottom for more than ten minutes. If I don't show up, drive to Zurich as fast as you can get there."

Slater could see Wyman walking along the edge of the dance floor toward them.

"Here comes Wyman," said Slater. "Now, will you please go!"

Ilse touched Slater's left hand for a second, opened the outside door and closed it behind her.

Slater felt trapped. He had the almost irresistible impulse to cut and run. Everything he had ever wanted had just gone out that door. But Dinar's safety and the information he possessed were more important to his country, possibly to the world, than either Ilse or himself. This, he thought bitterly, was the "big picture" viewed by the little man. And suddenly Slater knew a kind of hate he had never known before. It was a hate he could almost taste, except at that moment his mouth was dry and his hands were hot.

Slater stood his gound and let Wyman approach him.

"Hello, Slater," he said. "Didn't I see Ilse go outside just now?"

"Maybe." There was no point in denying the obvious. Wyman moved a little closer. Slater shifted his balance casually. He had to look up at Wyman.

"Looks like you're planning to do the same." Wyman looked pointedly at the parka in Slater's left hand.

"No," said Slater, "I just came in. I was about to check it."

"Don't try to kid me, Slater," said Wyman. "I saw her get your parka for you. Where did Ilse go?" Wyman looked as though he was about to take some action.

"I don't see that where she's gone should concern you," said Slater evenly. He stared at Wyman.

The look in Slater's eyes was so menacing that Wyman was visibly startled. The two men had reached an impasse. Any moment something would snap. One of them would have to give way or a fight would start. Slater did not want to be forced to shoot Wyman, especially in view of what he thought he had discovered in the bar. There just was not time to make absolutely certain.

Slater made a quick decision. It was a long shot; but if it worked, he would not have to kill an innocent man.

"I'm an American Intelligence officer." Slater's voice was pitched very low, and he spoke fast. "I was sent down here by Putnam to investigate you. You're under suspicion of espionage, Wyman!"

Wyman's face flushed and he tried to cut in, but Slater continued relentlessly. "You were observed photographing classified material in the Zurich Consulate."

"That's a lie!" Wyman blurted out. "You're just trying to twist things around. You're the one under suspicion of being a Communist. I didn't photograph those documents. Webber did, and I caught him."

That was what Slater had wanted to hear, but he still hesitated to believe it.

"It's your word against Webber's." Slater was scornful. "Webber reported you, Wyman, and Webber's dead."

"What do you mean?" For the first time Wyman appeared confused. "Webber's not dead." Wyman was suddenly angry again. "He's right here in this hotel, and I'm working for him on a special project. You and that Wieland woman are the Communists!"

Slater swore. He had been right. It was Webber he had seen talking with Anton. He should have known. At least, he should have been suspicious that Webber was alive. After all, it would be easy enough for Webber to remain under cover in Kitzbühel since he had a highly organized net at his disposal. Also, the note asking Slater to come to the farmhouse was in Webber's own handwriting, and yet Slater had not seen Webber's body. The whole business, all the evidence against Wyman, had been purely circumstantial and entirely too pat. Almost all of it had been contained in Webber's letter to Putnam! There was still a lot to explain, but, Slater clamped his jaw tight, if he lived, he would find some way to get an explanation—from Webber himself, if possible.

"Look, Wyman. Things look pretty bad for you. Webber's a spy—and a damn clever one. He's been using you, at the very least, both as a decoy and as a watchdog to keep an eye on me and Ilse. For your information, Wyman, Ilse is a member of German Intelligence."

Slater could see Hormsby, the Baron and Webber heading rapidly in his direction. "I haven't time to explain any more. Just think over what I've said. If you do, I think you can put the pieces together and come up with the right answer." Slater backed up to the door. "In the meantime, Wyman, don't try to stop me. My hand is less than four inches from my revolver. One move toward me, and I'll kill you!"

Wyman appeared honestly confused. He did not seem to know what to do.

"My guess," said Slater, "is that now your usefulness is over, your life will be in danger. I'm taking the Fleck. If you want to get out of here, I'll try to wait for you at the bottom, but I can't wait long. Good luck!"

Slater disappeared through the door just as Hormsby and Webber reached Wyman.

Chapter 30

Slater ran down the steps out onto the snow and grabbed his skis and poles on the run. He had to climb the elevation behind the hotel. He might have tried to ski around it, but it would have been slow going; and he estimated that, if he could make the top, he would get off to a much faster start. He kept his body as low as he could, but the skis and poles were awkward to handle, and the slope was fairly steep.

He hadn't gone fifty yards when he heard the flat reports of gunfire, and several bullets thudded into the snow below and above him. The sound made him go faster than he had thought possible. He was glad he had made Ilse go first.

He got to the top and scrambled over it to the far side before he tried to put on his skis. He knew it would not be long before his pursuers would get their equipment on and be after him. The Baron, or somebody, would telephone for assistance from below; that is, if there was anyone down there they could still rely on. There was always Rüdi, the headwaiter, Slater thought grimly. They could not be certain which trail he had taken so they would have to cover them all.

Slater stood up. His skis were on. He pushed off and went into a low crouch for maximum speed. The way was open for at least two miles. The first drop was terrifying to take at top speed, but the danger from behind was worse. Slater squinted his eyes against the wind and the cold. He went down the hard-packed, wind-blown slope like a cannon ball and took the wide turn at the bottom at a speed of over sixty miles an hour. He had never hit such a high speed in his life. It was an exhilarating, almost balanceless feeling. When he came out of the turn, his pants whipping and his skis chattering, he could not tell for a second whether he was going to stay up or fall. His feeling of balance had not yet caught up with his terrific speed. He raced out into the flat, and, still standing, swayed into a turn and plunged down again toward an enormous snowfield.

Slater thanked God for the moon. It had been his enemy before, but it was a blessing now. He raced on through the night, and his legs began to tighten up and tremble. He had to check his speed or fall. He was certain he was going to fall. He hit another flat and a slight rise. He check-turned on the tips of his skis, coming down sharply on his heels between times. It had an effect similar to that of pumping lightly on the brake pedal of a car. He topped the rise at half speed.

It was a good thing he had slowed down as the track suddenly dropped almost vertically away below him. None of the previous skiers had taken it straight, and the course was crisscrossed with the deep ruts made by those who had S-turned it to the bottom. Between the turns, all the way down, was deep, soft, powder snow which would trap his skis if he did not follow the S-shaped path. He had to make the split-second decision whether to take it straight and risk a broken leg or worse, or to follow the sensible path that others had made.

He tried to compromise. He pointed his skis straight down, hoping to be able to check himself when necessary by turning in the loops of the hard-packed snow. He raced through powder so deep he could not see his boots, but it didn't appear to slow him down. The slope was too steep and he went faster and faster. Spotting a hard-packed area ahead, he tried to swing into it. The strain on his leg muscles was terrific. He could feel them tighten up and grow rigid as he dug in with the downhill edges of his skis. The snow piled up against the bottoms of his skis, braking him suddenly. He had overdone it. It was like hitting a stone wall, and his body kited crazily down the mountain. All he could think of was his effort to keep his skis from tangling somehow, or he would snap his legs in two. He finally came to a stop far below.

Slater tried to get up, but he couldn't. He had lost his poles, and the snow was deep where he was lying. He tried to untangle himself, but every time he put out his arms to push himself up into a sitting position they would sink into a fluffy white nothingness which appeared to have no bottom. He cursed the last snowfall, but that didn't help, and he found himself becoming panicky. He couldn't just lie there! He had to get up! He was losing his time advantage. He tried to talk to himself calmly and consider his position. If he could just work his skis around and, somehow, get them under him. He tried that over and over again until he was forced to lie back exhausted.

It was then, as he lay there, that he heard above him the whipping noise that must be a skier coming down like seven devils. Slater wrenched his body around, fumbled for the heavy .38 in his parka and pointed it uphill, determined to pick them off one by one, if necessary. If he could get them and keep from freezing to death until morning, he would be all right.

He picked out the skier above him in the moonlight. He was moving fast all right, and he made a poor target. Slater got him in his sights, gauged the skier's speed, tracked him with his revolver, but he did not fire. He thought he had recognized the green and white sweater. He fired twice, but he fired straight up in the air and waited. He watched anxiously as the figure started to check and finally swung into a snow-spraying turn. There was no question about it, thought Slater with envy, that man Wyman could ski! Wyman fell into the snow.

"It's all right, Wyman," Slater yelled. "It's me, Slater. I've taken quite a spill. I don't think anything's broken, but I'm in snow up to my neck and I can't seem to get out."

Wyman stood up cautiously. "Use your poles!" he yelled.

"I lost them!"

Wyman located Slater's voice and skied over to him. He reached out his pole; Slater grabbed it and pulled himself up. His legs trembled, but he managed, still hanging on to Wyman's pole, to get himself out of the deep snow and back onto the track.

"Thanks, Wyman," said Slater. "I guess I'm not the skier I thought I was."

"Bad stretch back there," he said. "If you can travel, we'd better get moving. I'm afraid the boys are not far behind."

Slater nodded and handed Wyman the revolver.

"There are two shots gone, but you'd better take this."

"What about you?"

"I have another one," said Slater. "Let's go!"

The two men started down the long snowfield side by side.

"Pretty fair going," yelled Wyman, "from here on! We hit a patch of woods below here, but the trail isn't bad and then we hit an open stretch the rest of the way to the bottom."

Slater wished that the woods extended to the road. They would present too good a target should anyone be waiting for them at the bottom. Wyman's company reassured him and his legs felt better. The skiing was much easier, not nearly so steep. Going straight as they were, they could not have been going over forty miles an hour.

Suddenly, Slater heard some shots behind him, and his lack of speed was no longer at all attractive. Whoever was behind them must be taking that bad stretch wide open. If he didn't fall, he would be bound to catch up.

Slater crouched as low as he could and Wyman did the same. Wyman began to pull ahead. His extra weight made him go faster than Slater. The woods were still fifty yards below them.

Slater prayed that they would make them in time. The bullets were coming closer. It might have been his imagination, but he could have sworn he had felt the hot breath of a slug passing his right cheek. Wyman disappeared into the wood below, and Slater heard another volley of shots behind him. He felt a slug burn its way into the flesh of his shoulder just as he entered the woods.

The trail dipped suddenly and turned sharply at the same time. Slater picked up speed again, never so grateful for woods and a steep run in his life. He tore down through the woods like an Olympic downhill champion. Death was riding at his heels, and the speed meant nothing. He took every turn wide open. The wind tore at his clothes and burned his cheeks. The filtered moonlight gave the trail an eerie look as the trees on either side cast crazy deceptive shadows.

Slater flew out into the open. He could see the roadway below. Wyman wasn't twenty yards ahead of him. Slater felt exalted and very lightheaded. He was skiing with the best and going like hell. The two men sped down across the open field and christied to a full stop at the bottom by the road. They tore off their skis and scrambled up the embankment. More shots rang out, and this time they were really close.

Wyman and Slater threw themselves, face down, on the snow. Slater looked wildly around for the car. He couldn't see very much. The snow was in his eyes, but there was no car across the street. It looked as though he and Wyman would somehow have to stand and fight.

"Afraid I've gotten you into a worse mess than you were already in," Slater said to Wyman, who was lying in the snow beside him.

"Not on your life," said Wyman. "I tried to face Webber with the truth up there, and that scrawny little rat Hormsby tried to finish me off. I damn near never got out of that hotel."

Slater managed to get the revolver at his waist. He winced at the pain in his right shoulder. Wyman already had the gun out that Slater had given him. They inched their way around so that they would be facing anyone foolish enough to appear above the embankment.

Suddenly they heard the sound of shots. Slater thought for a moment that Webber and Hormsby were firing to keep him pinned down, while the two of them rushed up the embankment. Then he heard the car. He turned his head in time to see a Volkswagen coming toward them from the direction of Kitzbühel. The shots were coming from the car, and they were aimed over his head at the embankment. The back door opened as the car pulled up opposite them. The car was moving much more slowly, but it was still moving. Slater saw Ilse holding open the door.

"Come on, Wyman!" yelled Slater, getting to his feet. "Run like hell and fire behind you at the same time."

Wyman did not need to be told twice. The two men sprinted for the car on the other side of the road. Slater jumped in first, and Wyman followed right behind him.

"Gun it, Hollingsworth!" yelled Slater. "Let's get out of here!"

George put his foot all the way to the floor. Wyman fired out of the window, but no one appeared above the enbankment.

"Sorry I didn't meet you immediately," George was out of breath, "but after I picked up Miss Wieland and the Colonel, she told me to back the car up out of sight until she could make sure it was you."

"Can't you go any faster?" Ilse was looking out of the rear window.

"I've got the pedal down to the floor now."

"You have any trouble getting here?" asked Slater.

"Yes. Some tall thin fellow tried to stop me at the bottom about a hundred yards from the cable station."

"What did you do to him?" Slater remembered noticing that Anton had looked a little mussed.

"I knocked him out and left him lying in the snow." George sounded quite proud of himself. "I may have killed him! I never hit anyone that hard before!"

Slater smiled, but he decided not to disillusion him. Instead he said, "Thanks, George. You did a good job."

George was so startled by the praise he nearly drove off the road.

Chapter 31

Slater gave instructions to Hollingsworth to drive to Wörgl and told him to stop in front of the small garage where Slater had left his car only two days before. The owner lived in an apartment above and, encouraged by a generous number of schillings, offered the group some food and the warmth of his kitchen in the rear of his apartment.

Slater closed the kitchen door and went to the phone in the hallway. He asked for a number in Salzburg and waited patiently while the number rang and rang.

"Hello." The voice at the other end sounded overeager, as though its owner had been asleep and didn't want it to be obvious.

"Slater, here," he said. "Connect me with Kartovski."

"Give me your number, and I'll have him call you."

Slater looked at the dial and gave the number.

"Is it urgent?" said the voice. "Shall I have him call right away?"

"You're damn right it's urgent." Slater was disgusted. "Why in hell else would I call at this hour? Have him phone me immediately. And," Slater added, "you'd better stay awake next time."

"Yes, sir!"

Slater hung up. "Damn fool!" he muttered and went into the kitchen.

Dinar and Hollingsworth were seated at the table. Ilse was standing by the window, looking outside, and Wyman was helping the old man to prepare the food.

"Do you speak English?" Slater asked the old man.

"Nein."

Slater insulted him in English a few times, decided the answer was the truth and turned to Wyman.

"Do you have more than one bank account in Zurich?"

Wyman looked surprised and then grinned. "No," he said, "and the one I do have isn't exactly chock full."

"Do you know a girl named Trude Kupfer?"

Wyman frowned. "Only by reputation. She isn't exactly my dish of tea."

"Did you ever find any money in your room at the Winterhof?"

"Are you kidding?" Wyman was incredulous.

"Do I look like I'm kidding?" asked Slater.

"No." Wyman was immediately subdued.

George was listening with great interest. He decided that Slater was fast becoming his old self.

"Did you receive any American money while you were in Kitzbühel?"

"Well—yes. Webber gave me some ten-dollar bills."

"I knew it," said George. "Wyman's a spy after all."

"What are you talking about, Hollingsworth?" Wyman turned on George. "Hold your jaw, while you've still got one!"

"That's enough," said Slater. "Things still don't look too good for you, Wyman."

"Well," said Wyman, shaking his head, "I've obviously been mixed up with the wrong team, but I swear I didn't know it."

"That's all right, Wyman," said Slater. "I believe you, but," he added, "I have one or two more questions."

"Go ahead," said Wyman.

"Why did you buy a round-trip ticket to Munich the night you left Zurich, and then change trains?"

"How did you know that?"

"Answer my question," Slater said.

"Webber told me to," said Wyman, "as a precaution against being followed."

"Wise man, that Webber." Slater was bitter. Someday, maybe—"Webber told you a lot of things, didn't he?"

Wyman nodded.

"Webber also told us a lot of things—about you." Slater handed Wyman Webber's letter to Putnam. "Go ahead, read it!"

The phone rang and Slater went out into the hall.

"Hello."

"Hello, lover!"

Slater smiled. "Farouk?"

"That's I'm!" said Kartovski. "You want my big feet now?"

"Yes," said Slater. "I want your big feet. I need them, and a couple of other pairs about the same size. I've got the man you're looking for and a couple of tea drinkers who have turned out okay."

"I'll leave here in fifteen minutes. Give with the directions."

Slater gave detailed directions and hung up. Lazlo had promised to arrive in a couple of hours.

When Slater returned to the kitchen, George and Wyman were having an argument.

"I'm telling you, George," said Wyman, waving Webber's letter in his hand, "I caught Charlie Webber photographing classified material!"

"Then why didn't you report him?" said George.

"Because I'm as new to all this as you are, and Webber was the senior man." Wyman frowned. "He actually made me feel guilty for catching him."

"Man, were you fooled!" said George.

"So were all of us," said Slater ruefully. "Only, I should know better."

"Well," said Wyman, "after that night in the Consulate, I got to thinking it over, and I felt just uneasy enough to follow him to Kitzbühel. It was there," Wyman shook his head disgustedly, "that Webber really took me in. He told me he was on a special mission, that I had really blundered into the thing now. He had me worried. I was the one who had to convince him that I was okay."

"And then," said Slater, "he asked you to help him."

"Yes," said Wyman. "He told me to go back to Zurich so he wouldn't have to explain my absence to anyone, as no one in the Consulate, including Putnam, was in the know on this business."

"So, naturally," said Slater, "he told you to keep quiet about all this."

Wyman nodded. Hollingsworth was spellbound.

"He told me to come back the next weekend," Wyman continued. "You already know about the ticket."

"What about Mr. Schlessinger's skis?"

"Oh," Wyman shrugged, "they belonged to a friend of the Baron. He told me I could use them. That saved me money as I don't have a decent pair of my own."

"Did you know there was a message in a small drawer between the bindings and the bottom?" asked Slater.

Wyman looked so honestly amazed that no answer was required.

"Did Webber tell you to keep an eye on Ilse?" said Slater.

"Yes," said Wyman, and then he grinned. "That, Fräulein Wieland, was pure pleasure."

Ilse smiled. She had seated herself at the table and was taking all this in.

"I'm sorry, Ilse," said Slater. "I'm afraid all this business with Wyman is foreign to you. Give her Webber's letter."

Wyman handed it over.

"What about that routine with Rüdi?"

"Webber told me that the business with the Tuborg beer and signing the check was a routine that, if given at the evening meals, would produce some results. Rüdi seemed to understand it all right, but nothing ever happened. I hate beer!" said Wyman.

Slater laughed. It was his own private joke. He didn't think it wise to give them too much of the Communist setup.

Slater forced his mind back to the beginning, to his introduction to the case, only this time he was able to see Charles Webber's neatly placed roadblocks for what they were. He shook his head sadly. Webber had taken a long chance, but Slater closed his eyes—he had come too close for comfort.

Webber had been a top agent for the Communists. As assistant to the Political Attaché, he must have been funneling information to the Russian Embassy for no one knew how long. And then along came Wyman, an eager young vice-consul, who just happened to catch Webber in the act. Webber convinced Wyman that Webber was only doing his job and that Wyman was in the wrong place at the wrong time.

Just to make certain Wyman would not trip him in the future, Webber told Putnam, the Consul General, that he had caught Wyman photographing classified material.

And then along came the special assignment with Dinar, which required a prolonged absence from the Zurich Consulate. Webber went to Kitzbühel, and Wyman followed him because Wyman was still vaguely suspicious. And that, thought Slater, to put it in Wyman's words, was where Webber really took Wyman in. Webber not only made Wyman keep quiet about the whole affair, but made him serve as a decoy. Wyman was sent back to Zurich, and in the meantime Webber created the pile of evidence against Wyman.

Webber opened a bogus account, by postal money order, in the Zuricher Kantonalbank in the name of Martin Hazel. There was no connection between Hazel and Wyman, but nobody investigated that far. He instructed Trude Kupfer to pose as Wyman's mistress and display expensive presents. He sent the letter to Putnam foretelling his own disappearance, and probable murder. In the letter, Webber planted the suspicion that Schlessinger's skis were important and then planted an incriminating note inside.

Webber even partially exposed the Communist pay net so that Slater would believe Wyman was being paid with Red money. Webber supplied Wyman with ten-dollar bills for "expenses" as the clinching proof.

Webber deliberately exposed Krüpl, Stadler and, indirectly, Hauser. Webber had probably believed, however, that Carmichael, for it was as Carmichael that Slater had shown himself until near the end, would be taken care of. If it had not been for Carmichael, Slater might have been dead and Webber might have succeeded.

And in the end, if Webber had been successful, he would undoubtedly have murdered Wyman, burned his body and then disappeared behind the Iron Curtain. Wyman would have been considered a traitor to his country, and Webber a martyr to Wyman's treachery. Webber was a clever man.

And that, thought Slater, was the understatement of the year. The worst of it was, Webber was probably in the Russian Embassy in Vienna by now—free to cause more trouble in the future.

Slater turned to George. "I don't think I'll call you an amateur any more, George. I should have been suspicious when I didn't find Webber's body. No corpse, no positive proof. You should only believe what you see for yourself, and only half of what you hear. That," said Slater, "is a pretty safe maxim for most people, but it doesn't go nearly far enough for this business." He paused. "I also want to thank you again for being at the bottom with the car."

"I nearly didn't make it," said Hollingsworth. "Having failed you twice, I just couldn't do it the third time."

Slater then addressed the Colonel. "I wonder, sir, if you would be kind enough to step out into the corridor with me and Fräulein Wieland."

Dinar nodded and led the way. Slater stood aside for Ilse and then followed, closing the kitchen door behind him.

"Colonel Dinar," said Slater, "in a few hours, if all goes well—and I see no reason for further delay—you will be in contact with American and German Intelligence." He smiled at Ilse. "What your mission is," he continued, "is not my affair, unless my office chooses to make it so, but," Slater hesitated, "we are now faced with a problem of protocol—if there is such a thing in the Intelligence business."

Dinar raised his eyebrows.

"You will leave here with two members of the American Foreign Service and three members of American Intelligence. As this may not be entirely satisfactory to my German colleague," Slater smiled again, "I would like to ask you to give your word in front of Fräulein Wieland that you will refuse to disclose your information without the presence of a representative of her organization whom she will name."

"But, of course," said Dinar. "Whom shall I ask for, Fräulein?"

Ilse flushed. It was a touchy problem. Now that they were, for the moment at least, not in danger, they both had to consider the independent interests of their countries. She was angry, nevertheless, that Slater had approached the subject first.

"All right," she said. "You will please ask for Wilhelm Dietrich."

"Thank you, Fräulein," said Dinar. "I think I will return to kitchen now." He smiled. "Is too cold out here for an old man."

They both watched him until he had closed the door. Ilse's eyes were aflame when she turned on Slater.

"You have humiliated me for the last time!" she said fiercely. "Twice I have forgotten my duty to my country for you, and both times you have reminded me of it. Ever since we got in that car, you have taken command of everything, and now you have had the effrontery to remind me of my duty again. You are absolutely inhuman, and I hate you!"

Ilse turned away from him and started for the kitchen. Slater grabbed her and turned her around.

"Ilse, please," he said. "I only wanted to clear you with your office."

"I don't want to talk to you," she said, "not right now, anyway."

She turned toward the kitchen again, and Slater let her go.

Chapter 32

It was eleven o'clock when Slater and Ilse finally pulled into Kufstein. They had not said much to one another during the short drive. Ilse had not actually admitted that she was driving alone with Slater. She was only coming with him because there was "no room in Kartovski's automobile."

Slater had wanted to say something, but every time he tried to the words stuck in his throat; and when he looked at her, she was so beautiful and he wanted her so much he was afraid to say anything that might make things worse between them. When he couldn't stand the silence any longer, he said, "Ilse."

"Yes."

"You didn't care for Carmichael very much, did you?"

"No."

"I want you to know that Carmichael is really dead," he said.

"I'm glad to hear that," said Ilse, but her voice was noncommittal.

"Ilse, please, put me out of my misery one way or the other. I love you, Ilse. You know that."

"I love you, too," she said quietly.

"Please, Ilse," said Slater. Her reply had apparently not registered. "You said you loved me, once. Can't you try—What did you say?"

"I said I loved you." She looked at him and smiled. "I just wanted to make you pay for being so right all the time."

Slater would have stopped the car and taken her in his arms, but they were in the middle of Kufstein, and there was quite a bit of traffic. He decided to wait until they had crossed the border. Kiefersfelden was now only a few hundred yards away.

He pulled up in front of the striped gate. The passport officer approached the window and asked for their papers. Ilse handed her passport to Slater, and he relayed it to the official. The man looked at it for a moment, looked briefly at Ilse, back to the passport and finally smiled.

"Thank you, Fräulein Wieland. I hope that your vacation in Austria was very pleasant."

Ilse nodded and smiled, and Slater handed over his passport. The officer looked at it for a moment and then frowned.

"May I see your Triptych, please?"

"Yes, of course."

Slater got out the car's international travel papers and gave them to the official.

"Your name, please," the man asked. His tone was becoming more and more formal. The car's papers had disturbed him.

"Slater. William A. Slater." Slater was annoyed.

"This car," said the official, tapping the papers against his palm, "is registered in Munich to a man by the name of Carmichael."

"I know that," Slater replied quickly, suddenly realizing what he had done. "He is a friend of mine."

"Really?" The passport officer raised his eyebrows. "How do I know that?"

"Because I just said so," said Slater.

"In addition to having a car that is not yours," the official continued relentlessly, "you have no exit stamp from Germany or Austrian entry stamp in your passport. You are in Austria illegally!"

Slater was undone, and he knew it. Carmichael's passport and wig were locked in a suitcase in Kitzbühel, as was his forging equipment. To make matters worse, Ilse began to laugh. Slater turned on her, annoyed.

"What in hell are you laughing at?" His angry, defeated, ashamed expression made her laugh harder than before.

"Stop laughing!" he said desperately. "This isn't funny."

"Oh, yes, it is." Ilse looked at him. The tears were rolling down her cheeks. She was fast becoming hysterical. "The great," she gasped, "William Slater has been so busy being efficient, he forgot who he was."

Ilse's laughter filled the car.

"Please, Ilse," said Slater. "You've got to stop laughing and help me."

He turned to the official. "Look," he said, "I'm here in Austria, that's obvious. My passport is valid. The passport officer must have forgotten to stamp my passport when I came in. I'm taking this car back to Munich for my friend. You are free to alert the rental agency that I am returning this car."

Ilse's laughter had begun to have an effect on the official. He was, by now, convinced that there was at least nothing sinister about the affair and, besides, that redhead had a wonderful laugh. The corners of his mouth had begun to twitch.

"All right," he said, "I will let you through. Possibly Fräulein Wieland," he bowed to Ilse, "can help you with the German customs official."

The gate raised and Slater drove through toward the German customs house. He stopped the car halfway between.

"Will you help me, Ilse? I guess I'm just a damn fool after all."

Ilse stopped laughing and looked at Slater carefully. Her

cheeks were still tear-stained, but she was suddenly very serious.

"No, Liebchen," she said finally. "You are no fool. That's what was troubling me—you, your infallibility. You had forgotten to be human. You were so afraid to be wrong." Ilse took his face between her hands. "Of course, I will help you. I love you, Bill Slater."

The two agents kissed and confessed their love in the only suitable place that agents for different nations could—in a land that no one claimed, a land between two borders.

Reviews of Legacy of a Spy

"I would nominate Legacy of a Spy one of the finest espionage novels I have ever read. I venture to predict you will not put this book down until you have read it through. Then you will hunger for another novel by Henry S. Maxfield.

But the value of this novel is in its depth. First of all, Slater is a convincing character, a man torn between his desire to live a normal life and the constant tension and distortion of his life. Secondly, it details the continuing war beneath the surface of at least a nominal peace, a quiet, interminable conflict without publicity for its victories and defeats, but nevertheless as dangerous to the individuals and nations involved as great battles." Robert Kirsch, **Los Angeles Times.**

"Like the best of Graham Greene and Eric Ambler .... one of the best espionage novels ever written." **NY Times**

"Better than Ian Fleming." **Los Angeles Times**

"as far as I'm concerned Maxfield will be a major writer in these parts." Curt Casewit, **Denver Post**.

"Henry S. Maxfield's **Legacy of a Spy** is equipped with a fine set of very sharp hooks: Plausibility – it could have happened; Style: it is smooth, literate, easy; Convincing human beings . . . if they are cut, they bleed." Marsh Maslin, **San Francisco Call-Bulletin**

"I found **Legacy of a Spy** one of the most fascinating authentic, yet dramatically excellent books I have ever read on espionage and counterintelligence . . . . Mr. Maxfield has an unusual facility for creating plausible people and characters against a backgrounds that are completely convincing." **F. van Wyck Mason**